BLOOD IN THE SOIL, TERROR ON THE WIND

"Brilliant stories that drag you screaming into the rotten, turbulent heart of the Old West."

– Coy Hall, author of
The Hangman Feeds the Jackal
and *Grimoire of the Four Imposters.*

An Anthology Edited by
Kenneth W. Cain

BLOOD IN THE SOIL, TERROR ON THE WIND

Edited by Kenneth W. Cain.

Cover illustration and design by Chad Lutzke.
www.chadlutzke.com/cover-design.html

Formatted by Kenneth W. Cain

First Edition: August 2022

ISBN (paperback): 978-1-957537-33-7
ISBN (Kindle ebook): 978-1-957537-32-0
Library of Congress Control Number: 2022943494

BRIGIDS GATE PRESS
Bucyrus, Kansas
www.brigidsgatepress.com

Printed in the United States of America

Content warnings are provided at the end of this book.

TABLE OF CONTENTS

For everyone losing sleep right now, worrying about their future, their rights, the world, our planet… This one is for you. We see you. We hear you. We stand with you. May your candle shine brightly.

ACKNOWLEDGEMENTS

Thank you, first and foremost to my wife, Heather, who has been my rock, tethering me to reality and keeping me in this chair all these years, doing what I love most. And thank you to Brigids Gate Press, Heather and Steve and our slush readers, for making this project a reality, when it could have been left for dead on the side of this dusty trail. Thank you to everyone who submitted for bringing such high quality writing to my desk, and to those who were accepted for working so hard with me to make their stories the very best. A special thanks to Chad Lutzke for creating a wonderful cover that really puts an exclamation point on the excellence of this book. Also, thank you to each and every one of you who gave this project a like or a share and especially those who take the time to read the book, as without you, these projects wouldn't be possible.

INTRODUCTION

by Ronald Kelly

During one of her marathon storytelling sessions, my grandmother, Clara Spicer, once told me that my great-great grandfather, Andrew Nesbitt, was a Confederate spy. That, following the bloody Battle of Fort Donelson near Dover, Tennessee, he returned home, kissed his wife and son goodbye, and rode away, never to be seen again. Union soldiers tracked him to the banks of the Cumberland River where all traces of him and his horse vanished. Many thought that he had drowned while attempting to cross, but not his wife. She never lost hope. Following the War Between the States, she hired a private detective to find him. Over the next few years, she received unsubstantiated reports. That he had been seen in towns like Abilene and Tombstone. That he had once served as a lawman in Tucumcari in New Mexico. That he may have fallen on hard times around 1876 and turned renegade; that he'd taken part in robbing a stagecoach in Utah and been hanged from a tree near Provo. My great-great grandmother believed none of these stories. She could not wrap her mind around the fact that he might have abandoned the green hills and hollows of his native Tennessee—and his beloved family—to wander and drift aimlessly from one town to the next in the desolation of the Western territories.

On the Kelly side of my family, there were tales of how my great-great grandparents had often allowed Frank and Jesse James, and the Younger Brothers, to take shelter in their barn during their various escapades. According to Grandpa Kelly, his kin had considered the James Brothers and their followers to be 'desperate and put-upon men'; persecuted by the North for their part in the Civil War and forced to live on the sly, robbing banks and trains and such. They also considered them to be Reconstruction-era Robin Hoods in a sense, robbing from the rich and affluent to give to the poor and destitute. Many a time, stolen gold was laid beneath the milking bucket as payment for a night's rest and concealment.

Those tales, for the most part, were the reason I wanted to be a Western writer when I decided to pursue a life devoted to spinning yarns on the printed page. No, not a horror author as I am now, but a writer of 'oaters'; tales of lawmen, desperadoes, cattle drives, and gunfighters facing one another down in a deserted street. Believe it or not, in the early to mid-1980s, I had no desire whatsoever to be the next Stephen King. I wanted to be Louis L'amour, Charles Portis, or Larry McMurtry instead.

Even when I switched genres and began writing tales of Southern-fried horror, I would gravitate back to fiction based in the Old West. A character named Dead-Eye made the rounds among the mass market publishers, first as a traditional gunfighter, then later a zombie variation, but without success. I wrote a western novel about a lone wolf hunter titled *Timber Gray,* then lucked out during my years as a mass-market paperback writer with Zebra Books and ghost-wrote several novels for the Jake Logan series for Berkley Books. True, horror was my bread and butter, but western fiction was the tantalizing jar of gooseberry jam that I always had a secret hankering for.

Around 2020, during the outbreak of the Covid pandemic, something interesting took place on the independent publishing scene. My two favorite genres, horror and western, merged into what we now know as the Splatterwestern. Thanks to the newly-founded Death's Head Press, all manner of bizarre and grisly fiction was penned by folks such as Wile E. Young, Kristopher Triana, Kenzie Jennings, Patrick C. Harrison, Christine Morgan, Chris Miller, and others. In turn, I decided to resurrect my zombie gunfighter, Dead-Eye, and give him a sidekick…a sassy Louisiana mojo man by the name of Job. In partnership with Thunderstorm Books and Crossroad Press, *The Saga of Dead-Eye* will soon be releasing its second book of the series, with more on the way.

So, it was no surprise to me when the popularity of western-horror fiction spawned the collection of dark, rip-roaring tales you currently hold in your hands. Thanks to Brigids Gate and the editorial expertise of Kenneth W. Cain, this tome is precisely what you have been waiting for. *Blood in the Soil, Terror on the Wind*…a western splatterpunk anthology featuring a gathering of some of the most talented writers working in any genre today. As though conjured from the dust of a Nevada desert, the sweat of a Wyoming cattle drive, and the spilled blood of a drunken gunfight on the streets of Laredo, this volume explores the dark and deranged side of the Old West; a side that Roy Rogers and Gene Autry never sang about, or John Wayne and Gary Cooper never dared depict on the silver screen. Just gazing upon Chad Lutzke's disturbing and atmospheric cover sets the stage and conjures a mood that will guide you as page after disturbing page is turned.

Within these tales you'll find folks, both good and bad, isolated by miles of wilderness or the shadows of a dire past, encountering the most hellacious horrors imaginable. Across the Rocky Mountains, through the fiery deserts of New Mexico and Arizona, and into the vast territories of Wyoming, Montana, and the Dakotas, Death rides tall in the saddle, dealing darkness and desolation in the form of the wicked and otherworldly. Malevolent spirits, devourers of flesh and blood, shapeshifters, as well as those who crave murder and bloodshed the way others desire a shot of rotgut or the stroke of a whore's velvet hand at the end of a long journey. They are the stuff of nightmarish legend and an even more terrifying reality.

Look westward. The dark rider awaits you at the mouth of a shadowy pass, with an equally ebony horse, saddled and ready. If you choose to accompany him, ride at your own risk and peril…for Hell is prepared for those who seek it.

The question is…are you prepared to follow the hoof-trodden path that leads there?

Bloody trails to you, my friend. Until we meet again.

Ronald Kelly
July 5th, 2022

CRIMSON NOON

by Antonia Rachel Ward

The convoy of wagons crawled through the desert like an orderly line of ants. From his vantage point atop a rocky outcrop, with the midday sun beating down on his uncovered head, Boy reached for his canteen, unstoppered it, and took a swig of warm water, all without ever taking his eyes off the wagons. He hadn't seen newcomers arrive in Mirage for a long while. Not since most of the gold prospectors had headed elsewhere, in search of better mines and richer seams.

"Boy!"

Old Man Norris could holler louder than anyone else in Mirage, even above the noise of the miners talking and laughing as they ate their lunch. Boy leaped to his feet and scrambled down the dusty cliff-side, then sprinted toward the mine entrance as fast as his legs could carry him.

"Boy!"

By the time he reached the mine shaft, Boy was panting, and Old Man Norris was red-faced and furious. He thwacked Boy on the side of the head, leaving his left ear stinging.

"What do you think you're doing, boy, idling when there's work to be done?"

"I seen a convoy," Boy said, pointing.

"And I've seen a pile of ore needs washing, so get to it!" Norris shoved Boy hard in the direction of the river, and Boy lost his footing, muttering under his breath as he stumbled and almost fell.

"You got something to say, boy?" Norris snapped.

Boy's face burned. He looked back over his shoulder, but refused to meet Norris's eye. "No."

"No, *sir.*"

"No, sir."

"Better. Get that pile sorted by nightfall, or there'll be no supper for you."

Boy stared at a point somewhere to the left of Norris's head. "Yes, sir."

As evening fell, Boy walked back to the town, chewing on the hunk of bread Norris had given him for supper. The convoy of wagons was parked at the far end of Mirage's main street. The town's only street, in fact. With the new arrivals in their wagons, the population might as well have doubled. Main Street was almost as busy as Boy remembered it being when he was small—back when the mine was new and the seams still rich with gold. There were four wagons, several horses, and more people than Boy could count. He'd heard that there were other towns far bigger than Mirage—cities, even, with many streets and hundreds of people. Perhaps the convoy had come from one of those places.

He loitered in the shadow of the saloon where Miss Estrella worked and watched the strangers settle around their campfire, laughing and talking. Some of the younger men tied up their horses and swaggered into the saloon. Boy narrowed his eyes at them as they passed, and once their backs were turned, he cocked two fingers at them like a pistol and pretended to fire.

The women of the convoy set up a cooking pot above the fire, and before long the air filled with the scent of sizzling meat. Boy's stomach rumbled. Light poured out from the saloon windows, and sounds of laughter rang out from within. Some nights, Miss Estrella would try to sneak him extra food from the saloon's kitchen. But tonight, Boy doubted she'd have the time to take notice of him.

Instead, he drifted closer to the warmth of the fire and the smell of cooking—not hoping for anything, really, but drawn all the same. The women, busy with their tasks and the children scurrying around their feet, paid no attention to him. The older men—the ones who hadn't gone to the saloon—gave him a quick look up and down then turned back to their bowls of stew.

The only person whose eyes lingered on him was a small, pale girl with lank blonde hair and a gaunt face. Boy guessed she was probably around his age, or a little older, perhaps. As one of the women ladled stew into her bowl, the girl gazed at him across the fire—not with interest or curiosity, just a blank, distant stare. Once her bowl was full, she got up and walked around the fire, and, with a nod toward Boy, slipped behind one of the wagons.

Boy checked that no one else was watching and followed her. She was waiting, and she held the bowl out to him with both hands.

"Take it," she said. "You look like you need it." There was an unfamiliar lilt to her accent that Boy couldn't quite place. It reminded him of a Polish man who'd visited the town once.

"What about you?" he asked.

The girl shrugged. Her dress hung loosely off her bones. "I'm not hungry."

Boy hesitated. She sure *looked* hungry. Starving, in fact. She was so thin it made him wince. But her people had a big pot full of this stew. If she wanted more, she could get more. And the thought of trying to sleep with just a hunk of bread to fill his belly made him want to cry. He took the bowl and sat down behind the wagon to guzzle down the stew, savoring every chunk of meat. When he was done, he looked up for the girl, but she was gone.

At noon the next day, Boy was sifting ore by the river when he heard screaming. He dropped his sieve and ran to the mine entrance, clambering on top of a discarded cart to see over the heads of the gathered crowd. There amid the clamor stood Larry Ketch, shivering and convulsing in the bright sun, howling as though the light itself burned him. Ketch raised his hands to his face; they were covered in sores, blistering even as he stood there, breaking and splitting into bloody gashes that tore down his arms, up his chest, across his face—everywhere the light touched. He screamed and whirled around mindlessly, falling on the nearest miner, knocking the big man to the ground as though he were no more than a feather.

The big miner—Crawford, his name was—tried to fight off his attacker to no avail. Ketch was like a rabid animal, bleeding and screaming and now puking blood, all over Crawford's face. Crawford roared and threw him aside, but Ketch leaped onto him again and sank his teeth straight into Crawford's throat. There was a hideous *rip* of flesh, and Ketch drew back, blood and gristle hanging from between his teeth. He turned to look directly at Boy, who shrank back, too terrified to move or even breathe. Ketch's eyes were wild. Glazed. There was nothing human left in them at all. Just hunger. Crawford let out a strangled groan, blood bubbling from the gash in his throat.

For a moment, Boy was certain he would be next. Then shots rang out. Ketch shuddered and slumped forward, a dead weight on top of Crawford's chest.

The other miners rushed to help him, dragging Ketch's body away, surrounding Crawford as they tried to stem the bleeding from his throat. Their backs formed an impassible wall, and even from his cart, Boy couldn't see anything anymore. Quietly, unnoticed, he climbed down and ran all the way back to town.

That night, after Crawford had been taken home to recover from his wounds, Sheriff O'Connell called a town meeting in the saloon. None of the newcomers were invited. Neither was Boy. He loitered outside the bar's back door until Estrella came out, wiping her hands on her apron. People said Estrella's mother had been Spanish, which might've explained her golden-brown skin and dark eyes. For as long as he could remember, Boy had thought of her as the most beautiful woman he'd ever seen. If he'd had a mother, he thought, she might've looked like that.

"Don't you have a bed to go to?" she asked.

Boy shrugged. He usually slept in the loft above the stables, where it was warm and dry, and the stray dogs kept him company. Sometimes, if it was hot, he slept out under the stars and imagined he was a bounty hunter camping out as he tracked his prey.

He stared at Estrella until she sighed and let him into the kitchen.

"You saw what happened at the mineshaft?" She cut a hunk of bread and handed it to him.

Boy nodded. "Yes, ma'am."

"People are saying…" Estrella glanced over her shoulder to make sure there was nobody else in the kitchen and lowered her voice. "They're saying Ketch attacked Crawford. Like he was trying to…to eat him."

Boy looked down at his bread and nodded again. Truth be told, he'd been off his feed all day.

"You must've been so scared." Estrella put an arm around his shoulders and led him to a seat near the stove.

"No, ma'am." Boy lifted his chin. "Not scared."

Estrella smiled. She had a sweet smile. Boy liked the way her cheeks dimpled.

"No, of course not. A future gunslinger like yourself would never be scared. But me? I'm frightened. So if you wanted to sleep here in the kitchen tonight, you know, just so I know you're here to take care of me… I wouldn't tell anybody. You understand?"

"I can do that, ma'am," Boy said. "If it makes you feel better."

Estrella brushed the top of his head with her palm as she headed back out to the bar. "Thank you, kind sir. It does."

Boy followed her to the door and peered through the crack into the warm glow of the saloon. Sheriff O'Connell held court from his favorite table facing the door, while Mirage's townsfolk gathered in a semicircle around him. He told them that he was ordering a halt to activities at the mine until such time as the cause of Ketch's "sickness," as he called it, could be found out.

"It's got something to do with those new folk," one of the miners called out. "Weren't no problems in this town before they showed up here."

Several others nodded their agreement, but O'Connell shook his head. "We don't know that. None of them have even been near the mine, to my knowledge."

"To *your* knowledge," Norris parroted back. "And what do you think they're here for in the first place?"

"Pull in your horns," said O'Connell. "They're from New York City. On their way to one of the new mines on the West Coast."

"Sure, that's what they told you. Funny they should show up just a few weeks after we found a new untapped seam, though, ain't it? You oughta go down there and tell them to move on, see how they take it."

"Quit your whining, Norris," Estrella said. "They're good for business."

Norris snorted. "Good for *your* business, maybe. We can't all work on our backs."

Boy wasn't sure how Estrella made her money, but hearing Norris say that sent a rush of hot blood to his cheeks nonetheless. He turned back to the dark kitchen and lay down on the rug in front of the flickering embers of the fire.

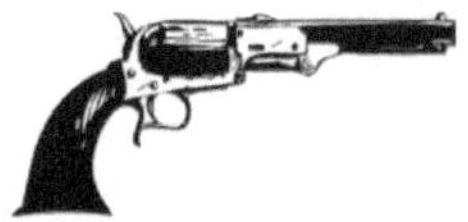

Boy slept badly. Ketch's face kept intruding into his dreams, and he woke in a cold sweat, thinking of the man's crazed, hungry eyes. With the mine closed, there was nothing for Boy to do to earn his bread that day, and he decided to head up to the strangers' encampment, hoping he could persuade the pale girl to give him a little more food. He circled the wagons a few times, but there was no sign of her anywhere, and eventually one of the gruff old men chased him off. Instead, Boy sauntered down Main Street, peering in the windows of the grocer's and the tobacconist's, to see what everybody was up to. When he reached the blacksmith's, he was amazed to see Crawford on his way out. He had a rag wrapped around his throat, but otherwise there was no hint of what Ketch had done to him the day before.

"What's the matter with you, boy? You look nervous as a cat in a room full o' rockers." He patted Boy on the shoulder, then stopped. Froze. Looked up at the sun blazing a hole in the cloudless blue sky. Boy had only a split second to realize something was wrong before Crawford's mouth opened in a silent scream. His skin began to boil and split, just as Ketch's had the day before.

Boy didn't wait around to see what happened next. He turned tail and fled to the stables, where he burst through the door, past the horses, and scrambled up the ladder to safety. From the tiny window in the loft, he peered out at Crawford, shrieking and howling and vomiting blood. The sheriff and some of the storekeepers ran out to see what the matter was, and one of them—Boy couldn't quite see which—put a bullet in Crawford's chest. Crawford hit the dirt, and Boy was sure he was dead, but then he flipped over and crawled toward the sheriff, dragging himself along with his fingers. His mouth opened wide. His eyes were... They were *bleeding*.

The sheriff aimed his gun, but before he could shoot, Crawford clamped his jaws around O'Connell's ankle. He fired wildly, and so did the others, letting off their pistols until Crawford finally went limp, face down in the dust.

Boy turned and flung himself back against the wall, chest rising and falling with his sharp breaths. He was shaking all over. Estrella was right; he *was* scared. Scared of where this sickness was coming from. Scared of who might be next. Of the thought that it might be *him*.

Boy stayed in the loft until nightfall, when he slipped out onto Main Street. The darkness covered him like a cloak, making him feel safer. He crept to the saloon, backing hurriedly away from the front door as a group of men from the wagon camp headed inside. Then, gathering his courage and hoping he would not be spotted, he sneaked in after them.

The saloon was filled with light and music, busier than Boy had ever seen it before. Sheriff O'Connell sat at the bar, knocking back a whiskey, his leg wrapped in bandages and propped on the stool next to him. The others were giving him a wide berth, but the sheriff seemed too preoccupied with his drink to care. Boy stared for a long moment, half expecting him to start bleeding and snarling right before his eyes, but nothing happened.

"It's them, I'm telling you," somebody snarled, glaring across at the newcomers who'd just entered the bar. "They've brought something evil with them. Weren't no problems in Mirage before *they* showed up."

"There were plenty o' problems in Mirage before they showed up," O'Connell replied. "I don't want no trouble tonight."

But Boy could tell from the look on the mens' faces that there was trouble brewing, anyhow. He hung around until Estrella came out to the bar and mouthed at him to get gone. Then he slipped back out into the dark night and headed for the camp. Perhaps the pale girl would have some food for him. Perhaps she might even *know* something. He didn't like the thought of Estrella in there, standing right by O'Connell as he drank. If the men were right and the sickness had something to do with the newcomers, perhaps the pale girl could tell him how they were spreading it. Maybe even how to stop it. Boy imagined himself rushing back to the saloon, being the one to save Estrella just in time. The thought made him puff out his chest a little as he reached the camp.

This time, the pale girl was there, sitting in front of the campfire, gazing into the flames. When she saw Boy, he put his finger to his lips and beckoned to her. Then he headed behind one of the wagons and waited.

For a moment, he thought she wouldn't come, but eventually he heard the soft pad of her feet, and she rounded the corner. She looked better than she had the last time he'd seen her. Her face was rounder, her lips redder. He thought she might even be approaching Estrella, in terms of prettiness.

"I don't have any stew tonight," she whispered. "You're too late."

"I don't need no stew," Boy replied. "You gotta tell me what's going on."

"What?"

"The blood sickness; your family brought it here. That's what everyone's saying."

"I don't know anything about that," the girl said. "Besides, they're not my family."

"They're not?"

She shook her head, biting her lip. "I don't have any family. They're just… I had to get out of New York, and they let me hitch a ride. That's all."

Boy shrugged. "Doesn't matter what they are. There's gonna be trouble if they don't get gone soon. And you with 'em."

"Why?"

"Why what?"

"Why'd you care? You don't know me."

"You were kind to me, is all."

The girl approached him. She placed a gentle hand on his arm, and all the hairs on Boy's skin stood up. "I can't make them leave. They won't listen to me."

Boy thought of Estrella. "Then you've gotta tell me how to stop the sickness."

"You can't stop it. Just…please, do me a favor?"

"What's that?"

The girl leaned in close, gripping his arm. "Promise me you won't come here during the day."

Shouts rang out across the camp. Boy ran to look out from behind the wagon. Men were fighting outside the saloon—the newcomers against the townsfolk, the women and children crowding around to watch, to goad them on or beg them to stop.

Then Sheriff O'Connell limped out and fired three shots into the sky. "Get back to your homes," he growled. "Or I'll be putting bullets in the lot of you."

The men grumbled, and some of them swore or spat at one another, but the people of Mirage respected O'Connell enough to let the argument go—for now.

Boy turned back to the girl, meaning to ask for her name, but she was gone.

Morning came, and Boy stirred in his bed of hay, thinking on the girl's words. *Promise me you won't come here during the day.* It seemed to Boy that the lesions on Ketch and Crawford's skin only appeared when they stepped into the midday sun. Did the girl know something after all? She'd said she didn't, but could he really trust a newcomer?

Boy crept out from his loft and watched the people of Mirage prepare for Ketch and Crawford's funeral. They were fearful enough of the sickness to want to burn the bodies and were building a pyre several feet high at the far end of Main Street, where the wind would blow the smoke away from the town. Boy sat on the steps of the General Store and counted the minutes as the sun crawled higher and higher in the sky. The back of his neck prickled with sweat. As noon approached, he realized he was holding his breath.

The townsfolk lit the pyre, the flames quickly flaring into a blaze.

Sheriff O'Connell limped down the center of Main Street at the head of the funeral procession. Behind him was Old Man Norris and the rest of the miners, along with Estrella and the other girls from the saloon, who were veiled in black. O'Connell stopped in front of the bonfire, turning his face to the sky.

Boy put his hands over his eyes, peeking out from between his fingers.

And then it happened.

Not just the sheriff, but some of the miners, too. Even some of the girls from the saloon. All of them clutched at their faces as the lesions took hold. They screamed, they howled, they shuddered and fell on each other, foaming at the mouths, bleeding at the eyes.

Boy took flight and ran, fast as he could, around the back of the General Store, behind the buildings on Main Street, until he reached the wagon camp.

He burst into the middle of the camp, disturbing women with their laundry hanging out by the fire, men cleaning their guns, children kicking around a stray clump of tumbleweed.

"Help!" he shouted. "Help, please! You've got to help us!"

The strangers didn't have to ask what the matter was; the shouting from Main Street was enough to alert them. The men called instructions to each other, loaded their guns up, mobilizing as though they'd dealt with something like this before. As they headed for town, Boy followed them, thinking of Estrella. He wished he had a gun. He wished he wasn't so scared.

When they reached Main Street, they found a bloodbath. The folk afflicted with the sickness had turned on the others, and now the whole town was feral. Bodies crawled over one another. Faces that had once been human leered with red, dripping teeth. Black blood soaked into the dust.

The strangers released shot after shot, and Boy, hiding behind their legs and shaking so hard he could barely stand, watched the townsfolk fall. Sheriff O'Connell. Old Man Norris. The miners and the grocer and the girls from the saloon. The only people he'd known in his short life. The air was sharp with the metallic scent of blood.

Boy didn't want to look, but he had to. He had to know if Estrella was still alive.

And then he saw her. Peering out from behind the saloon door. She spotted him and waved him over, and he ran as fast as he could, slamming into her, burying his face in her stomach. To his intense shame, he started to cry, and then he couldn't stop. The tears came in great, gulping waves that wracked his whole body. He didn't want Estrella to see him like this, but at the same time, he didn't care. He just wanted to escape. To be somewhere—anywhere—else.

"Come on." Estrella pulled him into the saloon, leading him through the bar and out of the door at the back of the kitchen. Together they sneaked into the stables, and Estrella freed one of the horses. It was spooked by the noise of the shooting, and it took a lot of coaxing to get it out the door, but soon they were riding bareback away from town. Boy sat between Estrella's legs, clinging desperately to the horse's mane while the saloon girl held him by the waist.

"Wait!" he cried, as they passed the wagon camp. "The girl!"

Estrella slowed the horse. "What girl?"

Boy was already wriggling his way out of her grip, slipping off the horse's back. "I can't go without her."

He dropped to the ground and ran over to the wagons, ignoring the stares of the women and children still huddled there.

"Girl!" he shouted. "Pale girl! Where are you?"

"Get out of here, you little fool," one of the women yelled. "They'll be back soon. Just go!"

Boy spun around and faced her. "Where is she? The pale girl?"

The woman's face hardened. She pointed to one of the wagons. "You want to take her, be our guest. Just don't say we didn't warn you."

Boy sped past her, clambered into the wagon. It was dark and musty, and filled with furniture. It took his eyes a moment to adjust. At first, he stumbled around blindly, so he went and pulled the curtain as far back as it would go, letting a shaft of sunlight pierce the darkness. Then he spotted the girl. She was crouched in the darkest corner. No, not just crouched—locked up in a cage.

Anger boiled in Boy's stomach. How could her people do this to her?

As Boy approached, she shook her head hurriedly, trying to wave him away. "Don't," she whispered. "Don't."

"Don't worry." Boy looked around hastily, trying to find something that would break the lock. "I'm going to get you out of here."

Her pale eyes followed him around the wagon. "Don't."

Boy opened the drawer of a cabinet and rooted around until he found something that felt heavy in his hand. A brass ornament of some sort. Approaching the cage, he slammed it against the lock as hard as he could, until it broke and the door swung open. Grabbing the girl's arm, he tugged at her, but she stayed stubbornly in place. The faint shaft of sunlight just grazed her face, and in the glow, she looked prettier than ever, her lips and cheeks now rosy-red.

"Come on!" he hissed. "Please."

"I can't." She was shaking. "I can't go out there."

"It's all right. We've got a horse. We can ride to the next town. We'll be safe there. Please."

The girl stared at him, her breath fast and shallow. There was a strange look in her eyes. She licked her lips.

"Come on," he tried again.

Slowly, her eyes never leaving his face, the girl crept out of her cage. The moment she was free, Boy pulled her out of the wagon and the two of them hopped down to the ground. The women and children watched as they ran across the camp to where Estrella waited with the horse, but nobody tried to stop them.

"Quickly, quickly!" Estrella looked over her shoulder at the town. The funeral pyre must have spread—smoke rose high into the air, almost blotting out the sun. Amidst it, shadowy figures approached the camp—the men returning with their guns.

Estrella pulled Boy and the girl up onto the horse in front of her, then spurred it on, picking up speed across the empty desert. The girl grasped the horse's mane, and Boy clung to her, burying his face in her hair. She smelled strange. Almost of…burning.

"Don't worry," he told her. "We'll be safe soon. Why were they keeping you in there?"

"I told you!" the girl said, her voice a choked sob. "I told you…not to come…in the daylight."

She twisted around, and suddenly her face filled Boy's vision, her eyes blazing red, her mouth open wide, displaying teeth sharp as nails. Hissing, she threw herself at him, pushing him off the horse. He hit the ground with a thud that jarred all the air from his lungs. And then she was on him, pinning him down with her hands on his shoulders, drooling blood onto his face. Boy kicked his heels against the ground, trying to push himself back, to get out from under her grip. It was impossible.

Where was Estrella? Had she fallen from the horse? Was she hurt?

He couldn't tell. There was nothing now—nothing but the girl's snarling face, looming in, aiming for his throat. It was her, had been all along. She had brought the sickness to Mirage. But somewhere in her eyes, behind the hunger and the animal fury, he saw something else—fear. The eyes of a girl who knew what she was, what she was doing. Who had tried to warn him. And then her teeth sank into his flesh, and all went dark.

It was almost midnight in the town of Red Creek when a local drunk emerged from the saloon and spotted a lone horse winding its way into town. He peered at it, trying to make sense of the dark shape through his blurred vision. The horse stopped, and someone dropped from its back. A woman, and two children with her.

One hand on his pistol, the drunk staggered over to meet the newcomer. Her face was gaunt and wan in the moonlight. Hungry. The children seemed drowsy, as though they'd been sleeping. One was a pale girl with hair almost as silver as the moon, the other a skinny little urchin boy.

"Spare a bed for the night, sir?" the woman asked. She was pretty—beautiful, even—and the drunk could hardly believe his luck. He glanced around to make sure that nobody else had noticed them, but the streets of Red Creek were silent.

"Y'all look like you could use a decent meal," he slurred, his eyes lingering on the boy, who was the most starved-looking of them all. But to his surprise, the boy shook his head.

"No thank you, sir," Boy said, his lips curling into a smile. "We can wait until morning."

THE GOOD DOCTOR

by Nick Kolakowski

There are few tasks in creation more difficult than yanking a bullet from the quivering, bleeding meat of a thigh. Especially when the thigh in question belongs to Bill Rivers, a lawbreaker ornery enough for the governors of three territories to have placed the princeliest of sums on his head. But the Good Doctor has steady hands and a sharp knife, and he only grunts agreeably as Rivers curses and spits and waves his Colt at the ceiling. Five minutes into the operation, a crumpled bullet plinks into the tin plate beside the bed, followed by the Good Doctor's bloody blade.

Rivers wheezes "Fuuuuuuu…" before passing out for the rest of the night.

The Good Doctor steps outside the mudbrick hut that serves as his operating room. Taking a knee, he sinks his skillful fingers into the warm sand beyond the covered porch. He twists his wrists clockwise, then counterclockwise, scraping off the dried blood and bits of muscle. A fresh feast for the scorpions and mice.

"Quite a thing," Maxwell says from the porch. The night is moonless, reducing him to a silhouette amidst deeper shadows. A rasp, and a flicker of orange flame illuminates the bony curve of his face. A cigar flares to life, puffing smoke. "Where'd you learn to chop meat like that, old man?"

"The University of Ingolstadt," the Good Doctor offers, squinting at the sky afire with stars. He takes a deep breath, holds it, and closes his eyes, imagining the snowy peaks and deep blue lakes of Switzerland. The air was so crisp and cold it made your lungs ache—a world away from this cracked, hellish desert.

"University of Ingo-what?" Maxwell chuckles. "That in America, old man?"

The Good Doctor exhales, picturing himself walking a stony path through the looming majesty of the Alps, the blessed rain pelting his face. "Europe."

"Well, la-de-da. That's fancy. They taught you to cut real good."

Before he opens his eyes, the Good Doctor treats himself to one last memory: the tiered amphitheater where he learned his art, and the lantern-circled table at its center. The lecturer sliced through the pale skin and yellow fat of a body before drawing out its treasures—heart, lungs, kidneys, stomach. The students' heads were bowed, brows furrowed, hunters in pursuit of pure knowledge. No lawbreaking occurred in that sacred space. No murder. No pain.

"How long can he rest?" the Good Doctor asks, turning to Maxwell.

The cigar bobs as Maxwell shrugs. "Don't rightly know. A day, maybe two. Law's smelling after us pretty hard. We got to meet up with our gang."

"The wound is a bad one. You should stay until he can walk."

Maxwell snorts. "Figure you'd like us to stick around 'til we're about broke, right? Three dollars a day right in your fancy pocket."

"If he moves too soon, it will only get worse."

"If we don't move smartly, we'll dangle from a rope."

The Good Doctor wants to tell Maxwell how all outlaws become fodder for the hangman's noose or another outlaw's bullets. How he's spent years in this dry nowhere, pulling arrows and bullets from any ruffian with the money, no questions asked. His patients' stories always end the same way. But Maxwell seems agitated now, shifting from foot to foot, and the Good Doctor decides it's best to take his leave.

Slapping his hands on his trousers, the Good Doctor crosses the small yard to the simple wooden shack where he sleeps.

"Old man," Maxwell calls after him.

"Yes?"

"If Bill dies," Maxwell says, pausing to puff his cigar. "It won't turn out well for you. Understand?"

"The patient will improve," the Good Doctor calls over his shoulder, never looking back.

Rivers—the scourge of the Western territories—fails to improve as the Good Doctor promised. Beneath the bandages, the wound in his thigh ejects clotted blood and pus. It smells of rotting meat, and the upper leg has swollen until the knee has almost disappeared. Rivers sweats and moans and babbles. He downs shot after shot of the cheap whiskey reserved for patients. Worst of all, he waves the big Colt around as the Good Doctor changes the bandages three times a day.

"Better make me better," the outlaw keeps telling him. "Better make me better."

After every bandage-change, the Good Doctor leaves the hut as quickly as he can, lest that slippery finger squeeze the Colt's trigger while he's in the way. Outside, Maxwell never moves from the porch, often sitting with his legs wrapped in a ratty blanket, a cigar always jammed in the corner of his mouth, and a bottle of whiskey in his left hand.

On the second day after the operation, as the Good Doctor kneels to clean his hands in the sand, Maxwell asks, "Will you take the limb?"

The Good Doctor has considered it. In Rivers' weakened state, such an operation might kill him. With another surgeon to tie off the vessels as the Good Doctor saws, the chance of survival would increase. But the nearest surgeon is Paul McCarry who lives in Red Junction—thirty miles distant across the salt flats.

"Not unless it becomes absolutely necessary," says the Good Doctor.

Maxwell nods, pulls the cork from the bottle with his teeth, and takes a deep slug. "We'll stick around," he says. "Until he improves. Because he will improve, hear me?"

The Good Doctor retreats to his shack, its door secured with a massive padlock. Inside, he opens the battered cabinet beside his humble cot. The cabinet is lined with tools of all shapes and sizes, from scalpels and tweezers to larger, stranger things—devices built from iron coils and delicately spun glass, filled with strange liquids that glimmer iridescent in the light filtering through the dusty windows. He retrieves the bone saw tucked into a leather sheath and places it on the desk, just in case.

The Good Doctor naps. He dreams of black waters, the infinite coolness of ice, but soon awakens to a fist pounding on his door.

Maxwell stands outside, panicked, hissing. "Something's wrong."

That turns out to be an understatement. Soaked in hot sweat, his injured leg thick and tight and red as a cooked sausage, Rivers screeches at the hut's low ceiling, the dreaded Colt swinging wildly. The Good Doctor has seen men in this condition before and knows death lurks in the doorway, ready to pounce.

"I'll… I'll…kill you," Rivers wheezes, his arm muscles twitching as the heavy Colt veers toward the Good Doctor's head. At the edge of his vision, the Good Doctor catches a flicker of movement as Maxwell draws either a blade or a gun, ready to back his dying partner's play.

And then something miraculous happens.

Rivers' finger squeezes the trigger. The Colt's roar in the constricted space is deafening, but the outlaw's shaky aim sends the bullet past the Good Doctor's head and through Maxwell's neck, exiting with a spray of hot blood across the mudbrick wall. Maxwell thumps to his knees, his pistol dropping from loose fingers, and manages a final bubbly squawk before slamming face-first onto the dirt floor.

The recoil knocks frail Rivers against the wall behind the bed, the Colt loose in his hand as he slaps its hammer, which knocks the barrel tight against his chest as his finger spasms on the trigger.

Another explosion.

This time the bullet plows through Rivers' guts, most of which end up on the sheets.

The Good Doctor closes his eyes, trying to imagine cool lakes and snowy mountains and gentle rain. Nothing comes. Fate, it seems, has spared his life. But is that a gift or a curse?

He opens his eyes again and regards the most vicious outlaws in the territory, reduced to dead and leaking meat.

A fresh feast for the scorpions and mice. After he performs a few experiments, of course.

The Good Doctor maintains a small burial ground on the arid plain behind his miserable compound. After he plants what's left of Rivers and Maxwell under a few feet of sand, marking the spot with twin piles of small rocks, he pauses to lean on his shovel and rest his aching muscles. He observes the sad cairns stretching toward the horizon, the last earthly sign of two-dozen men and women who died despite his best efforts to save their miserable lives.

It rarely rains here. Those stacks of rocks may stand for an eternity, long after the Good Doctor is dust. Yet another monument to his life's many failures. No, that is far too harsh an assessment. He has succeeded in ways that few men could ever hope to achieve. His lack of sleep is fueling this foul mood.

He returns home to find four horses tethered to the porch railing. Four men wait for him inside the mudbrick hut. They have sun-blasted faces, hard gazes, strong hands, and waists heavy with guns and knives. One of them has a black patch over his left eye. He tilts his head like an anxious dog as he examines the bed with its fresh sheets.

"Can I help you gentlemen?" asks the Good Doctor. Despite the fear pulsing through his guts, his face remains impassive. If there's been a single benefit to living in these desperate circumstances, it's his ability to meet such situations with outward calm.

"We're here for Bill," responds Eyepatch, turning away from the bed. Around him, the other three men spread out, their hands on their weapons.

The Good Doctor debates whether to feign ignorance. No, these men are too tense, too willing to fill him with lead if they think he's toying with them. "He departed. Along with the other one."

"Where did they go?" Eyepatch steps so close the Good Doctor can smell the endless desert miles on him, the tang of dust and blood and shit.

"May I ask who you are?"

"Friends of Bill's." Eyepatch leans forward until they're almost nose to nose. "And I swear to Christ, we'll beat you dead if you steer us wrong."

The Good Doctor points at the wall behind them. "They journeyed west. Started off yesterday."

"Just kill him," murmurs the man to Eyepatch's left, a hulking gentleman with an equally epic moustache.

Eyepatch raises a hand for silence. "Not yet. How bad was Bill hurt?"

"Shot in the leg," the Good Doctor replies. "A bad wound. Very bad. But he could climb onto a horse." He's grateful for his decision to bury the bloody sheet with the remaining bits of Maxwell and Rivers, and to wipe down the walls splashed with the outlaws' blood. Any evidence of last night's carnage would have sparked too many questions, even among cretins like these.

"We shoulda never let him rob that bank," the one with the moustache mutters. "I told you that was a bad idea, what with the Pinkertons and all…"

"One more word outta ya," Eyepatch tells him, "and I'll twist off your neck."

"They were moving slowly," the Good Doctor says. "If you leave now, you may catch up with them by tomorrow. Perhaps even sooner."

Eyepatch steps back, tilting his chin so he can peer down the barrel of his nose at the Good Doctor. His hand is on his pistol, thumb tight on the hammer, ready to draw.

The Good Doctor stares into the outlaw's good eye and sees Death waiting in there. He struggles to draw breath. The air feels electric.

"They leave any money for ya?" Eyepatch asks. "I figure you ain't a sawbones out of Christian charity."

"If I give it to you—the money, I mean, because yes, there is a little money—you will ride away and let me live, *ja?*" The Good Doctor tries to keep his tone even, but his heart is a bucking horse.

"Of course," Eyepatch says brightly.

The Good Doctor knows he's lying. "Then let us step outside. The money is in my humble abode across the way."

Eyepatch nods to the two men standing to his right, a pair of ruffians nearly identical in appearance. The twins nod back, and one of them steps to the doorway, gesturing with his drawn pistol for the Good Doctor to follow him outside.

As the Good Doctor steps off the porch and into the brutal midday heat, one of the twins ahead and the other behind, he considers what to do next. His survival rests on one thing. Nothing is ready, of course. But what choice does he have?

Sometimes the world rushes science, at the former's peril.

Standing on the porch of the mudbrick hut, Craig adjusts his eyepatch as he watches as the twins escort this pissant doctor to the shack. Beside him, Doolin smooths his ridiculous moustache, draws a cigar from his pocket, and lights it with a match, the white flare of phosphorous bright even against the day.

"How much you think ol' Bill left the doc?" Doolin asks. "Couldn't have been much, considering Bill's exalted state of miserliness."

"A few dollars, I reckon." Craig squints at the shack.

The doctor pulls the enormous padlock from the shack door's hasp, nudges the door open with the side of his foot. With a theatrical bow, he bids the twins to enter. But the twins haven't survived a decade of robbery and murder by being fools. One of them jams his pistol into the doctor's ribs, prodding him into the shack ahead of them.

"A few dollars?" Doolin chuckles, blasting smoke out the edges of his mouth.

"It's a line of work," Craig says. "Nobody said it was a good line of work."

A faint click comes from inside the shack. Next, there's a humming sound that reminds Craig of insects in the night, low and rhythmic.

And then the screaming starts.

It sounds less like a man and more like a rabbit with its leg snarled in a trap, an eardrum-splitting screech that rises and rises without pausing for breath…until it cuts off, abruptly, and all they can hear is the faint rasp of wind on sand.

"The fuck?" Doolin yaps.

"Go." Craig gestures for Doolin to advance on the shack.

Doolin takes a step off the porch, his pistol drawn, cigar still billowing smoke—and stops. Under ordinary circumstances, Craig might have cussed him out, even drawn his own weapon and forced the coward to march forward, except any words he might have die in his throat.

What emerges from the doctor's shack has two arms, two legs—and two heads. Its bulging, misshapen stomach is slashed with deep, dark wounds stitched with leather strips—tight, but not tight enough to prevent reddish fluids from seeping out. The being stumbles forward, its knees barely able to support the massive weight of the torso and heads. Its arms rise, fingers hooked into claws.

Craig finds his voice, which rises to a quivering shriek. "*What in the name of motherfucking Hell and creation is that—?*"

One of the two heads rotates on its stitched, oozing neck, tracking Craig. It blinks in the strong light, and its lopsided jaw opens. "It won't turn out well for you," it warbles, almost comically high-pitched.

Doolin's pistol wavers. "Maxwell?"

Yes, it's Maxwell. The head is misshapen, covered in slices and bruises, its hair hacked away, but it's unmistakably him.

"Won't turn out well," it says again, and air whistles from a gash in its neck.

The other head tilts in the same direction as the first, revealing the bruised, cracked face of Bill Rivers. "Kill you," Rivers' head tells them. "Kill you, kill you, kill you."

Whatever this hell spawn is, Craig has no intention of letting it live. He raises his Smith & Wesson in a two-handed grip, tensing the muscles in his forearms to stop the shivering, and pulls the trigger six times. At least three of his bullets find their mark. The flesh on the thing's enormous chest puckers and explodes, spraying clotted blood and bits of meat onto the sand. But it keeps coming, so close now that he can see how the legs stitched at the hips are different, one more muscular and darker than the other, and he wonders, *How is that…*

Doolin recovers from his fear long enough to raise his pistol and aim, but the creature is upon him, one large hand gripping the barrel and tearing it away. The other one finds Doolin's jaw and twists. With a wet crack, the jaw comes off as easily as an overcooked chicken drumstick, Doolin's freed tongue flopping wildly as he unleashes a bubbling screech.

Craig breaks open his Smith & Wesson and dumps the hot shells on the sand and tries to reload, bullets slipping through his numb fingers. He needs to fire again, to kill this damned thing, but he's too slow…

The creature tosses the jaw aside and its red-wet arm pistons forward, disappearing down Doolin's wide-open throat. Doolin trembles, his eyes rolling back in his head, hopefully dead before suffering the final indignity. The creature's arm reappears with a black orb in its hand, pulsing, squirting, trembling. It's Doolin's heart—or at least part of it.

As Doolin crumples to the sand, the creature turns to Craig, who has only managed to slip one fresh bullet into his revolver. Its four milky eyes seem to recognize him. Something shifts in those weird, bloodless faces.

"Boss?" Maxwell's head wheezes.

"It's me!" Craig yelps, suddenly elated beyond all reason.

Rivers—or the head that once belonged to him—either groans or laughs, its lips peeling back to reveal yellowed teeth like fangs. With this monstrosity looming over him, Craig surrenders for the first time in his wayward life, tossing his pistol into the sand and raising his hands. From three feet away, the creature smells like a field of skinned buffalo left to rot in the sun for days.

"I'm your amigo," Craig whispers into the dripping wall of flesh.

The creature grips his shoulders, as if about to embrace him. Craig tenses, telling himself not to turn coward. If it senses fear, it might kill him.

The creature's hands tighten. Craig's shoulder bones grind together, exploding in pain—

Before he realizes what's happening, Craig is in flight, moving at such speed that for an absurd moment he wonders if the fucking thing has thrown him with enough force to send him into the sun, where he'll burn in blazing Hell for all eternity. But no—his body arcs, the desert rising to meet him. He impacts beside the doctor's shack, and he hears his bones break. The pain is so intense, he's helpless to do anything except scream.

The Good Doctor appears above him, blotting out the sky. Craig tries to scramble away, but he can't feel anything below his shoulders.

"If only I had more time, I could have perfected it in the image of man," says the Good Doctor, who holds a small blade in his left hand. "But your appearance forced me to awaken it early. Far too early."

Craig tries to curse and spits bloody foam.

"Do not be concerned," the Good Doctor says, kneeling on cracking knees. "This is not the first time I have created such a thing. I think I have learned to control them now. They recognize me as *vater*."

Craig grunts. His head feels like a cauldron of boiling blood. At the edge of his blurring vision, he sees the creature lurching into the desert, its form shimmering in the heat—like a dream of something that should never exist.

"Oh, I have lived in these territories for far too long. It is a place for no civilized man," the Good Doctor says, as if responding to a question. "But a place for no civilized man is perhaps the only place left for me to conduct my work."

His lungs crackling with pain, Craig manages to take a sip of air. He has time for last words. "You're a damn fucking devil."

"No, I am Victor," replies the Good Doctor, pressing the small blade against Craig's scalp. "Victor Frankenstein, at your service."

SUNDOWN SHOWDOWN

by Villimey Mist & Damascus Mincemeyer

The blood trail led from the saloon's swinging doors out to the stagecoach. As she neared it, the smell from the dead coachman's recently-rent carcass turned Emilía's stomach.

The blistering heat in Texas would make sure to rapidly speed up the decomposition of his corpse. She shook her head. Such a feat would be near impossible back in Iceland. How she managed to stay afloat in this business was a mystery to her. The arid, flat, endless desert vista surrounding her was as alien as the glaciers and fjords of that faraway volcanic isle she'd once called home would be to the inhabitants of the blighted West Texas town she was in now.

"Where did Grady go?" Emilía asked the man on the wooden boardwalk. He was slumped near the horse trough, his derby cap fallen from his head, clenching the opened wound in his gut with one scarlet-slicked hand. The man, Ambrose—that's what the saloon keeper had called him before the brawl broke out—grimaced and gestured down the dusty lane that served as Blackwell's road.

"T-That way," he groaned. "I saw him go up past the bank, on the other side of the post office, toward the…towards the church." Ambrose coughed red spittle. "I'm gonna fuckin' die from this, ain't I? Goddamn me, I survived Shiloh only to get my innards sliced open in some shit-nothin' saloon."

Emilía knelt and put a hand on Ambrose's quivering shoulder. The wound did look bad, but she was honest when she said, "I've seen men survive worse injuries than that. Once I cast the spirit out of Grady, we'll get you to a doctor."

Ambrose laughed. "Doctor Vargas is a goddamn thievin' drunk. I'd sooner take my chances with the Grim Reaper than go under that shaky bastard's bone saw." He gave Emilía a serious glare. *"Go.* Go get that son of a bitch before he does any more damage. And save Bobby if you can. He's a good kid."

Emilía withdrew her hand and got to her feet. A part of her was reluctant to leave the suffering man's side, but a scream from deeper in the town snatched her immediate attention. She placed a palm on the whip coiled at her waist and ran, passing the disemboweled body of the stagecoach's driver lying face down in the dirt.

Emilía couldn't believe it was happening again. Couldn't believe they had followed her when she'd thought she had gotten away.

It was only supposed to be a routine stopover for her in Blackwell, but she drew some satisfaction from Ambrose's words nonetheless: *Reaper* was often slang for a bounty hunter among those in the trade. The odds of someone outside the guild knowing that were rarer, though. Just like it was unlikely that a twenty-year-old girl from above the Arctic Circle hunted down criminals for money on the untamed American frontier.

She gave a quick glance back to the saloon she'd just exited. The sun was low in the sky, and the survivors of the destruction within cast long, dagger-like shadows as they stumbled out to the street—Walter, the bartender; Joaquin, the town's farrier; a couple of the saloon's dazed patrons. All of them were cut and bleeding, wearing torn clothes and shock on their faces at the grisly sights outside. Though the interior of the saloon, when Emilía fled, had been equally horrifying even if she'd scarcely noticed.

Despite her revulsion, she knew that she was getting too used to it.

Another scream, louder, closer, forced Emilía to stop. This time the cry held the anguish of freshly inflicted pain, so shrill it chilled her spine despite the overbearing heat. Looking around, she spotted the town's bank just where Ambrose said it would be, beside the post office and two-hundred meters from the source of the shrieks—Blackwell's church.

The building was a crumbling mission, erected during the days when Texas still owed loyalty to the King of Spain. The church was by far the oldest in Blackwell. As she ran, Emilía idly wondered about what strife the structure endured over the unstable centuries: Spain, then Mexico, then the short-lived Republic of Texas, the ill-fated Confederacy, and now the United States; each had laid claim to the land at one point or other. How much bloodshed had that place seen? Not enough to dissuade the creature stalking across its threshold. That much Emilía knew.

She caught sight of the shape just before it disappeared within the church's front entrance. There was another body laid out in the old mission's sandy courtyard, yet unlike Ambrose, there wasn't even the slightest hope for recovery. The town's reverend was on his back, but he'd never preach again. His eyes were wide and frozen—a fly had already landed on one unblinking lid—his chest exposed from sternum to waist with the quick slice of a thick blade. A purplish length of large intestine peeked from the slash.

"Djöfullinn," Emilía cursed in Icelandic, and advanced to the church's granite steps.

How in the world did the day end up like this? She'd started out by finding and apprehending that thief in the saloon, only to witness his possession from *Hinir Fölu,* The Pale Ones, so horrific a sight Emilía doubted restful sleep would come again. How did those malicious spirits find her? She'd been so careful wearing the runic talisman her grandmother had given her back in Iceland, the one that would make her invisible to their relentless search for revenge.

She ground her teeth. All that slaughter for pushing a boulder down a cliff. Ridiculous. Her grandmother had warned her about the *Huldufólk's* penchant for holding grudges. But to send their most vicious spirits after her?

That was a bit too much. Especially when the atrocities affected those around her.

"This is all my fault. I'm sorry," she whispered, bent down, and gently closed the reverend's eyes. "Don't worry. I'll make things right."

Pushing open the heavy wooden doors, she slowly stepped inside. The interior was darker, cooler, but musty and thick with the coppery scent of blood. Emilía could hear the sounds of scuffling feet ahead of her along the central nave, echoed by a chorus of soft whimpers.

Gripping the whip tighter, she took a deep breath and moved forward.

"I'd stop right there if I were you, Reaper girl," a voice said, gnarled and gravelly, too low to be human. "Any closer and the boy will regret it."

A form moved in front of the altar. In the gloom, Emilía couldn't see much more than an outline. But enough light remained to discern two shapes, one clenching tight to the other.

"The kid has nothing to do with this, Grady. Let him go," Emilía called as she crouched behind one of the pews.

She mentally counted the steps from where she was to the altar, calculating the reach for her whip. If Grady was going to flail around with the Bowie knife he held anywhere near Bobby, she'd have to aim correctly to knock it from his hand.

Maniacal laughter bounced from the church's stone walls. "He's got *everything* to do with this!"

Choked sobs from Bobby urged Emilía to peek from her hideout just in time for the sun's setting rays to illuminate Grady O'Toole's hard-bitten expression. Emilía blanched at the mere sight of him. O'Toole's wanted poster portrayed him as a sulking, unshaven bastard. And the description, once she'd come eye to eye with him in the saloon, wasn't too far off, either. But the possession of The Pale Ones brought forth something else in the man altogether—a monstrous visage that distorted his features to an almost demonic fervency. Black tar leaked from his sunken eyes, and the reversed rune of *Othala* branded his forehead, glowing so ember-red the symbol appeared to be aflame. Blood from the citizens of Blackwell stained his already dirty clothes. Drops of crimson hit the floor from the spattered Bowie knife hovering too damn near Bobby's carotid artery.

Emilía stifled a snort. Being spirits from her homeland, it was typical of The Pale Ones to use the rune to secure their victims. She rummaged in her pouch for the correct runic counter-stone. Nestled between the runes for strength and luck laid *Uruz*, the one of healing. She'd used it plenty of times to expel unwanted spirits from people's homes. Was that how they knew to find her? Through spiritual communication? Emilía had no time to ponder it. A boy's life was at stake.

"Cut the bullshit, Grady. I know it's me you want. *I'm addressing you, Hinir Fölu,*" Emilía spoke the last part in clear Icelandic.

Grady's face split into a hideous rictus grin. "So, we found you at last." The otherworldly voice vibrated in different tunes, like an insidious phantom choir congregated within the church. Now she saw it; strands of tall grass from the prairie surrounding Blackwell clung to his blood-soaked shirt.

Emilía's chest tingled seeing the tall grass. The *Huldufólk* and The Pale Ones usually sought out places where nature was plentiful. The prairie was their home. Grady must have stumbled upon the grass there by some unlucky chance, unsuspecting to what horrors would consume him.

A cold bead of sweat trickled down Emilía's back. She swallowed her fear and uncoiled her whip. It was now or never. She stood up and faced the eidolon responsible for all the bad things in her life, whip hidden behind her back. "Yes, you've found me. Took you long enough."

Grady dragged Bobby forward by the scruff of his neck. It was exactly what Emilía needed. The whip slithered on the floor. She twisted her body, gave her arm a yank, and thrust it forward. The whip went flying, and the snap that followed pierced the air. Grady screamed, raised his hands to protect his ears, and the Bowie knife clattered on the floor.

Without hesitation, Emilía lunged at the horse thief and tackled him. They both slammed into the altar, cracking the wooden pedestal.

Ignoring the throbbing pain in her arm, Emilía raised the rune of *Uruz* and pressed it squarely upon Grady's forehead. "With this rune, I cast you out!"

She expected the usual bodily jerks, the stream of curses spewing from the mouth and the sigh of relief afterwards. She received none of those. Emilía blinked rapidly. Rocks lined her stomach. Why wasn't the exorcism working?

Grady laughed. "You think petty runes work on *us?*"

Before Emilía could try a second time, Grady's fist connected with her jaw. Blood burst from her split lip. Stars winked before her eyes, blurring her vision. Disoriented but determined, Emilía tried again with the rune, but Grady slapped the stone from her hand. It bounced under one of the pews where Bobby sat hunched in a ball, shielding his head with his arms.

"We have lived for eons in this realm. No simple magic of *yours* can cast us out," The Pales One said through Grady's mouth.

Confusion rattled Emilía's mind. The runes were supposed to work against any spirits. Then, why were none of them working? Her talisman, her strongest protection, somehow had failed in preventing any harm done to her.

Her hand fumbled for the obsidian hanging around her neck. Her finger felt a miniscule crack on the carved rune. She held back a scream. Her grandmother's protection had been broken after the collision with the altar.

Another strike pummeled Emilía in the stomach, knocking the air out of her lungs. She stumbled backward, coughing. Her eyes met the ceiling when she tripped on something long and wooden. Emilía fell to the floor, her head already blazing with pain before Grady straddled her abdomen and began throttling her.

Emilía's eyes bulged. Panic squeezed her heart. She scratched at her attacker's arms, punched them, anything to relinquish his hold.

He merely laughed.

"I'm going to take my sweet time with you. That's something you didn't do when you pushed my family to their deaths," Grady whispered hoarsely, the vindication dripping from the multitude of voices inside him.

Emilía couldn't believe this was how she was going to die. She often imagined her own demise—pursuing bounties was a dangerous occupation for anyone, let alone a woman—but she'd visualized a final act for herself more dignified than being strangled by a simple horse thief. And what of her family? If she *did* die, she couldn't send money to her grandparents. They would surely starve back in Iceland. She couldn't let that happen. They were the only connection to her old life. Helping them was the one thing she could do to amend her own wrongdoings in the past.

Death was not an option.

Emilía grunted, abandoned her assault on Grady's arms, and groped along the floor. She had tripped on something. If only she could reach it now. Dark spots obscured parts of her vision. Her head pounded. Breath came in short bursts.

"Almost done." Grady wheezed, the smirk of triumph cutting into Emilía. "I've heard your type of Hell is a brutal one. Too bad I won't get to see you suffering there."

Emilía's fingers touched wood, long and slender. What was it? A toppled candlestick? The reverend's dropped cane? In the dark, she couldn't know. But with what strength still pumped through her veins, Emilía grabbed it and swung as hard as she could at Grady. The end of the stick landed with a sickening *crunch*. Blood trickled onto her chin.

She blinked, realizing she held onto an axe, its blade lobbed in Grady's skull. His mouth's movement was sluggish, his remaining words coming out garbled, unintelligible and faint. Coughing and wheezing, Emilía shoved his weight aside and scrambled to her feet, still clutching the axe. She wasn't sure if the initial blow had been enough. When it came to The Pale Ones, a person had to make sure.

She unwedged the blade from Grady's cranium, raised her trembling arms, and swung down more forcefully, decapitating him in a single clean swipe. Grady's body twitched like a broken marionette on the floor. His newly-severed head rolled underneath the nearby pew, leaving a winding stream of blood in its wake.

It was over. Emilía wanted to cry. Adder-like shivers crawled all over her body.

"It's okay to come out, Bobby. You're—" Her voice transformed into a pained yowl as searing, stinging fire bolted down her left arm. Glancing over, she was startled to see Grady's fallen Bowie knife protruding from deep in her shoulder and the sadistically gleeful smirk on Bobby's face.

"You think you can be rid of us that easily?" The Pale Ones gloated while pointing to a cluster of tall grass stuck to Bobby's piss-stained pants. "As long as nature binds us to humankind, we will *always* come back."

Dizziness swam in Emilía's head as blood poured from the knife's wound. Her limbs trembled. The need to sit, to sleep, to pass out, nearly overwhelmed her. Teetering on the verge of tears, she shook her head violently. "No, no, *no.* Please, don't make me do this."

Bobby cackled like a madman. "*What* are you going to do, Reaper girl?"

A storm of emotions raged within Emilía. If she left Bobby alive, The Pale Ones would torment his mind, use his body as an instrument to enact their heinous bidding. If she killed him, his parents would be without a child and Emilía would be left with yet another scar in her soul that would never heal.

She wanted to scream.

She tipped her head heavenward, for guidance, for some sort of sign. In the end, she asked only for forgiveness for what was about to happen. Her damaged shoulder slumped as she sighed dejectedly. She banished all of her emotions, allowing only numbness to encase her.

She turned her hardened eyes to the possessed boy and gripped the axe tightly. "I'm going to finish what I started."

THE WERECHRIST

by Jonathan Kemmerer-Scovner

"*Sins?*" Silas Spillman asked dubiously. "I don't know about all that."

Riding beside him, the Reverend Timothy Stevenson gaped. "Clearly it's against the natural order! It's a perversion!"

"I suppose rattlesnakes are sinful, too? And sandstorms? Anything that makes life harder?"

"At New Hope, we saw it for what it is, though I'm sure to a man with your…experiences, it's just one more terror in a world of terrors."

Silas chuckled. Time was, he would've made this trip in one long day, but now his bones wouldn't hear of it.

The reverend gazed across the desolate landscape. "How was Fort Mason containing the curse—or whatever you want to call it?"

"Better than some, worse than some. I've seen places completely destroyed, and not just by the demons. It's not just killing your enemy; it's knowing how to live."

The reverend nodded. "I think I would've enjoyed meeting you under different circumstances, Mr. Spillman."

"I get that a lot. Whoa now, Archie." He tugged on the reins.

The reverend glanced about nervously. "What is it?"

"Sun's about to set."

"But it's still light! There's a good hour left!"

Silas touched the top of his shotgun lightly. "Let's do this the easy way, Reverend."

"Fine!" Reverend Timothy got down and marched toward the empty cage which Silas' horse, Archduke, dragged behind by a length of rattling chain, secured firmly on a platform with ill-formed wheels. "I know you must think this is some delicious irony for a man of the cloth!"

"Back away from the bars." Silas latched the cage door. "They've been blessed, and they'll burn your flesh."

"I still have my dignity!" Silas draped a large blanket over the cage so that the reverend was completely enclosed. "I'll suffocate!"

"It'll cool off."

Cool off it did, as the sun set over one mountain range and darkness filled the sky.

"Is the moon out?" asked the voice from beneath the blanket.

"We'll be underway before sunrise." Silas got a small fire going—canteen to his right, shotgun to his left.

"Mr. Spillman? I want to thank you. I know my congregation is paying you, but I do appreciate it."

"Just doing my job."

"There are easier ways of making a living."

"Such as preaching?"

It was the first time he'd heard the reverend laugh since they'd been underway. It was a good note to end the day on.

Moonlight lengthened shadows across the dunes.

Silas dreamt he was back at Picacho Pass, thunderous stampedes of oncoming calvary, confederates not old enough to shave screaming for mercy. When his eyes snapped opened, he knew it for what it was: riders. Three of them.

In a moment, Silas had his shotgun in hand. He could just make them out and could maybe pick off one or two. The moon had its uses after all.

He squeezed the trigger and the Stetson belonging to the closest flew from a balding head. The horse whinnied and bucked. Two other guns cocked in the darkness.

"Put the gun down, gramps!" one of the unknown men yelled.

Silas grunted as the horsemen encircled him. "What can I do for you boys?"

"You're a long way out." A hatless man approached. "Joey! Jim! Search his gear!"

Two boys climbed down from their horses and did as they were told. One called out, "Pa, there's something big under this blanket!"

"You don't want to go looking under there," said Silas.

No sooner had he ripped off the blanket than he tripped over himself as he backed away. *What in the hell…?"*

Within the cage, Reverend Timothy shivered. "You idiot! Put the blanket back on!"

"The hell is this?" The man shoved his sons aside, inspected the cowering reverend. "You a damned slaver?"

"Far from it."

He turned on Silas. "Bounty hunter?"

"Marginally closer."

"Please!" Reverend Timothy broke out now in a cold sweat, face distorted in desperation. "I'm sure Mr. Spillman will respond to all of your fascinating suppositions, but for right now will you *please for the love of Christ cover me back up!"*

"Boys," said their father, voice gone quiet. "I reckon I know what this is…"

The reverend buried his head between his knees, ran fingers through thinning hair as though his scalp were on fire. "Please…!" he plead one last time. Then, in one violent moment, he transformed into a red-eyed demon which grabbed at the smoking bars.

Archduke whinnied and bucked, jolting the cage as the demon tried to break free.

"We've got to get…"

Silas snatched that Winchester from the stupefied man, walloped him good, then took aim at the two boys. "I'm Silas Spillman, and I've been charged with taking this beast to the Demon Monastery! Grab your daddy and *get!*"

"You okay under there, Reverend? Sun's almost up."

Some time had passed. Silas had draped the thick blanket back over the cage, waiting for the snarling to subside, which it eventually did. There was no sign of the riders, nor of anyone else. The desert sky took on a lighter hue.

Finally, the irritated voice issued from beneath the blanket. "I *do* hope you brought a change of clothes."

"Always." Silas grabbed a shirt and a pair of pants, shoved them under.

"I thought you were going to kill them."

"They'll tell their friends about the old man with the demon in a cage, crossing the desert. That's how I stay safe, people knowing my name. Now c'mon, coffee's hot."

The reverend stepped uncertainly from the cage, knees shaking. He grabbed for the steaming tin, then glanced at the palms of his hands. Each had burn marks. "You say those bars were blessed by the monks?"

"They inscribed it along the top."

Indeed, the reverend could see the symbols of some desert language set into the cold steel. "I'm anxious to meet these monks."

"That was only the second time you've changed?"

The reverend nodded. "The first time I hardly knew what was happening, it came upon me so fast. *This* time…" He sipped at the coffee. "I *felt* it happening. I was *aware*."

"Let's hope there isn't a third time."

There came footsteps from behind. In an instant, Silas had pistol unholstered, aimed at their interloper.

"Don't shoot!"

Silas narrowed his eyes. It was Jimmy, the younger of the two boys from the previous night. "Where's your daddy?"

"At the saloon in Rockford." Jimmy looked to the reverend. "He's really taking you to the Demon Monastery?"

"That's right."

"My sister, Lilian, she was taken there five years ago. She'd been bitten by one of those…*things*. Pa killed the demon that did it, then grabbed my sister and locked her in our barn. Thing is, with all the holes in the roof, the moonlight shone through no problem. If she got out, we were to just shoot her." Jimmy breathed heavy. "Next morning, she was asleep on the hay, skin all cut up. Pa wanted to kill her anyway, but mom had heard about the Demon Monastery, that the monks there could heal you. No one's seen her since. They won't even admit that she ever lived."

"There's no cure," said Silas. "All the monks do is allow you to live with dignity."

"Let me come with you, I want to see if she's okay!"

Silas sighed, holstered his pistol. "What do you say, Reverend? Fancy some company?"

Jimmy clung to the back of the reverend, not wincing at the squeal of the steel cage rolling behind.

"How did it happen for you?" the boy asked.

"I'd been praying with a parishioner who'd been afflicted. When the moon came out, he changed and attacked me. A mob gunned him down, and I was told to leave town immediately before the…" He looked to see if Silas was listening. "The *sin* wrought its effect on me. But I *am* looking forward to my new life at the monastery. God hasn't finished with me yet."

"There it is," Silas announced, the sandy walls of the monastery cresting the horizon. "Remember, it's not *the Demon Monastery*, it's the Monastery of St. Arsenius, and that's how you'll refer to it. Back in the cage, Reverend."

"It's the middle of the day!"

"It's just to pass through the gate."

The wooden gates loomed before them, inscribed with the same symbols on the cage itself.

"*Desert magic*," the reverend muttered nervously, getting in.

Silas drew up Archduke, rapped loudly. High above, a kettle of black vultures circled. "Something's not right."

"Perhaps they're napping?"

Jimmy, meanwhile, had climbed on top of the cage, standing precariously. He leapt and grabbed onto the edge of the wall. Grunting, he hoisted himself up and over and was gone.

When the gates opened from the inside a minute later, Jimmy had his shirt pulled up around his nose and mouth.

"*Damn* it!" Silas ran in, both pistols out.

The stench was overpowering, thick with flies. The bodies in the courtyard were half-covered in fur, limbs disjointed. He'd never seen any in half-transformed states before, hadn't known such was possible.

"Lilian? Lilian Mayfield?" Jimmy called out, anxiously looking through the bodies.

"What happened?" exclaimed the reverend, stepping out of the cage now that it had passed through the gate. "You said it was safe here!"

Silas kicked over a body, its face distorted in a half-snout, maggots squirming from empty sockets. "Killed by a gunshot. And they're all facing the same direction, as though they were after someone…" He glanced up.

A large enclosed storeroom lay in the center of the courtyard.

Carefully, the three of them stepped toward it. Silas rapped on the metal doors.

"Who is it…?" came a weak voice from within.

"Silas Spillman!"

There was movement from within, something heavy scraping against metal. An assortment of fearful eyes peered out. "Silas? Thank Jesus!"

It was too small of a space to be crammed with as many men and woman as there were, each thin and scared.

"I knew if anyone came, it would be you!" said one old woman.

"You're all that's left?" asked Silas.

Jimmy shoved his way in. "Is there a Lilian Mayfield in here?"

A voice near the back muttered, "Th-that's me…"

"Lily!" Jimmy rushed toward the malnourished woman against the far wall, propped up by an old rifle.

"Jimmy? My God!"

"What happened here, Lily?"

"There was a monk, Brother Jeremiah. He— He tried to cure us…"

The reverend's eyes grew wide at that statement. "So, there *is* a cure!"

"He performed exorcisms, spoke words. Not Christian words. There was a burning in his eyes…" Lilian turned away. "Some were successful, others remained in an in-between state. We barricaded ourselves in here and fought them off, even though they'd been our friends."

"Where's this Brother Jeremiah now?" asked Silas.

"Haven't seen him since then, and we've been in here for…" She looked to the others for confirmation. "Three days? Four?"

Silas drew himself up. "I'll find him."

He left them, stepping slowly through the courtyard. Mangled corpses thinned out the further from the storeroom he stepped. "Anyone still alive?"

There were no takers.

A tiled walkway outlined by flowering cacti led the way to the main sanctuary. Above, the bell tower loomed over the cloistered, outer walls.

Silas was not familiar with this Brother Jeremiah by name, but he did know that the nature of the Monastery of St. Arsenius tended to attract those with an interest in the darker arts. He swung the door open and entered.

The interior was blanketed in red light, cast through stained glass along the western wall. Wooden pews had been shoved aside violently, though it was the piles of old books which unnerved him most. First, one book, then a pile of three or four, then another dozen, yellowed and torn. These were volumes from Brother Artemis' private library, printed and bound within the bookbinding halls that were practically their own monastic sect, written attempts at sussing out secrets of creation, the exact mechanism by which a supernatural deity could take upon itself the sins of humanity.

When Silas' cage had been constructed, years ago, adorned with a blessing which would keep any demon enclosed, it was these texts that had been consulted.

A breeze took a torn page, blew it toward the pulpit. Behind the pulpit stood a cloaked monk, as though in prayerful meditation. A skeletal hand snatched that page, dipping a quill into an inkwell with its other hand, transcribed the text of that page onto its own exposed arm which, Silas now saw, was covered in such transcriptions, flesh black with ink.

When the monk had finished, it replaced the quill and spoke. "Silas Spillman."

"Present."

"I am indebted to you. All the demons scattered across the desert, you brought them here, brought them to me!"

"I brought them to the care of the monks of St. Arsenius."

"But there's another name for this place, isn't there?" The monk glanced up now, and Silas saw red eyes glowing in the darkness of the hood, flames burning through dry parchment.

"Where are the other monks? Where is Brothers Artemis?"

"Christ was not born the son of God. Did you know that, Silas Spillman? He became godlike only in his death and resurrection." The monk returned its attention to the dusty volume laid out on the pulpit. "He did not take on the sins of humanity out of piety, but from a lust for power."

"I'm not one for theology."

"By ingesting all of their sins, I claim my godhood as well. And you've brought me more, I can feel it! You've brought me…a minister of the faith? Delicious! Leave him and you can take the rest with you!"

"I— I can't do that…" But he wanted to. The fear had now fully wormed its way into him, just as the sweat freely flowed down his forehead. "He's under my protection," Silas stammered. "They all are. I'm Silas Spillman, and I…"

It seemed to Silas that the monk had grown larger, arching over the pulpit as the ends of its long robes narrowed as the end of a tail. Where fabric ended and flesh began could not be discerned. *"And you have fulfilled your charge!"*

The monk-like creature floated into the upper shadows of the belfry where the thunderous toll of the bell rattled the whole of the sanctuary. The sound compelled Silas' legs—finally—to rush out the front doors, tripping over the flowering cacti.

"Reverend!" he shouted. "Get everyone out of here!"

But Reverend Timothy was bringing water to the chapped lips of a nearly unconscious man, making no move to abscond.

Again, the bell rang out, shook the walls of the monastery itself.

"It always tolls before an exorcism!" Lilian looked about in sudden terror. "We've got to—"

At the final toll, a shadow swooped from above. Silas fired, but the bullets did no good against the monk-like creature, long hands now reaching out from the folds of its flesh-cloak, grabbing the startled reverend. "I shall forgive thee of thy sins!" it seethed, lifting him into the sky.

Silas tracked it, not willing to take the shot. "Damn it!"

"What's happening?" Jimmy yelled, running from the storeroom.

They all watched as the creature and the reverend vanished behind the tower.

"It performs the exorcisms in the catacombs," said Lilian. "I know the way down there."

"Wait!" yelled Jimmy.

They both looked to the boy expectantly.

"You got any spare shotguns in that wagon?"

"Explain the exorcism to me," said Silas. "What happens, exactly?"

"It's like a nightmare." The three of them stepped through the subterranean passages of the monastery. "It involved death and resurrection; I remember that much."

They came to a dormitory, cots arranged equidistant beside small tables with oil lamps.

"Everyone sleeps underground?" Jimmy looked around with wide eyes.

"We only came up during the daytime," Lilian explained. "So there was no chance of any moonlight touching us."

Rats scurried in the shadows. Jimmy took aim at each fearfully. "Doesn't sound like much of a life."

"It beat being locked in a barn. Brother Jeremiah wasn't the first to try to cure us. There were others, coming from all over, professing to have some power from God—praying in tongues, laying of hands, jumping up and down like lunatics."

Wood scraped in the shadows.

Silas took out his six-shooters slowly. "Both of you, backs against mine."

The were-demon bore down on them. Jimmy shot it through the throat in a panic. It fell, choking on its blood.

Lilian then blasted its skull with her shotgun.

"I... I thought they only came out in the moonlight!" Jimmy gasped.

"These were the hybrids, for whom the exorcism did not fully take. They—" She looked down. "They were my friends."

Silas grabbed a burning torch from the wall, lit the fur of the dead demon. Several enormous were-demons then materialized in the light. He fired at the thing between the eyes, then at another which had leapt from above. "Don't let them bite you!"

Lilian wasted no shots either, with three bullets she'd killed one and mortally injured two more, splintering the old furniture beneath their mass.

"Are you okay?" Silas asked, looking to his two partners, covered in blood that wasn't their own and breathing heavy, which he took as a *yes*.

The air grew cooler as they continued their descent, stepping carefully over a skeleton still in its monk's attire, while other bodies in various states of decomposition lined the edges of the cold stone.

"Still confident you know the way?" Silas asked Lilian once they'd made it to the bottom, three identical torch-laden passageways branching out before them.

"Down there…" she indicated with the barrel of the gun.

"You okay, Mr. Spillman?" Jimmy whispered

"Just one more terror in a world of terrors," he answered.

In this vault beneath the desert, where blood had dried in the cracks of old stone, where walls had been covered in the markings of other worlds, the Reverend Timothy Stevenson of New Hope Baptist stood chained to a wall, face filled with tears.

"Don't do this!" he screeched. "It's sacrilege! Blasphemy!"

Brother Jeremiah floated before him as an apparition. "Blood atonement is the oldest story there is, Reverend!" It reached into its cloak. "As a man of the cloth, I'm sure you understand."

Language filled the acrid air, and the reverend winced at every alien syllable which had originated from a place no living person had seen. The monster *cloaked* itself in such language and the inked words on its flesh glowed vibrantly.

Silas, Lilian, and Jimmy had all come to the edge of the walkway above, could see down into the vault, this tableau playing out before them.

"This is the exorcism?" Silas whispered.

"We can't interfere, not yet," said Lilian.

The drama below continued as a blade appeared in the grasp of the monk, silver and sharp and ancient. "I am the perfect sacrifice for your sinful nature, Reverend! Willingly, I take your sins as my own! Let the cup be passed to mine own lips!"

"Please!" screamed the reverend.

Then, at the moment of that sinful man's greatest suffering, it was the monster itself which let out the final wail of anguish, having buried the blade within its own body, collapsed in a heap of rancid flesh. Black liquid issued forth from its wounds, like tendrils, forming a circle around the two of them.

"Is it dead?" asked Silas, inching closer, gun at the ready.

"This is all a part of the ceremony," whispered Lilian. *"It's all a part of the story."*

For the third time, the Reverend Timothy Stevenson transformed.

What had been a cursed human chained to a wall grew larger, more beastly, flesh breaking out in thick fur. In another moment, the reverend was gone, replaced by a demon which easily broke those chains and howled in wretched agony, falling to all fours.

The lifeless body of the monk, meanwhile, had begun to twitch. The black liquid had ceased flowing. *"I am the way,"* it groaned, *"and the truth."* It hobbled upright. "And the LIFE!" At that final declaration, it rose again to its full height, as though sovereign to the demonic creature before it. Its tattered hood fell away, revealing a face in which the flesh had long since rotted away.

The were-demon reverend howled, clutched at its palpitating body with retracting claws, oscillating painfully from one form to the other. From the mass of fur and leather skin, the reverend's own anguished face reemerged, swallowed by demon snout and jaws, then back again.

"What…what are you doing to me?" he yelled, then growled, clutching at awareness, then retreating from it.

"I have sacrificed myself on your behalf!" answered the monk plainly, advancing on the retreating half-demon, jaw dislocated, sharp teeth extending. "I have eaten your sin, and you have been born ag—"

"Evening," said Silas.

An explosion, a burst of black blood, stone foundations shuddering with sudden violence.

Silas breathed deep, stood over the crumpled form of Brother Jeremiah, smoke rising from both the corpse and his gun barrels.

"Did you kill it?" Jimmy yelled from above.

Silas looked to the former were-demon. "Reverend? Can you understand me?"

The reverend sought out Silas with inhuman yet imploring eyes.

"I am an agent of endless resurrection." A shadow loomed over Silas from behind. *"And with each resurrection, I grow more godlike.* Your *sins are quite tasty, war hero!"*

The horrors of Picacho Pass leapt at Silas unbidden and at full force, the young men he'd killed, lifting to the fore of his consciousness. "Get out of my head!" He stumbled backward, again firing at the demon-monk. "I like my sins where they are!"

In response, the demon-monk only coughed up black blood. "I told you, I can be resurrected endlessly."

From above came another volley of gun fire. The foundations shook again with the reverberations, bits of stone falling from the ceiling.

"Grab the reverend and get out of there!" Lilian shouted, as a chunk of rock landed beside Silas.

"Fools," the demon-monk muttered, black liquid pouring from its mouth. *"No one gets to the Father…except by…by…"*

Silas could hear Jimmy and Lilian frantically reloading. More ceiling had become dislodged, so much having fallen away that there was now a glimmer of moonlight. They had spent so long navigating the underground passageways of the monastery that night had returned in force, and the small space where the monk now struggled became illuminated in a glowing circle.

"Run!" Silas screamed.

He lifted the reverend and ran from the vault, through the dark, shuddering catacombs, and up a set of stairs which met with a frantic Jimmy and Lilian.

"What's happening?" Jimmy yelled as they ran across the dormitory. In the shadows, were-demons ran for their lives as well, and it was the fear on their mangled faces which cemented Silas' own.

There was an explosion of stone and masonry as they bolted into the courtyard, now no longer filled with moonlight, but blackened as the shadow covered them.

"BEHOLD, MY ULTIMATE FORM!" The voice was deep and ghastly, filled the desert for miles around.

Silas fell over backwards, gazing up at the creature that was now fully a demon with vast, unfurled wings. The cracks between its scales widened, black liquid cascading down its body.

"Get out of here!" Silas shouted to the remaining survivors, transfixed with horror.

Some of the wreckage had caught fire, and flames danced about the perimeter. Everyone ran for the front gates as the demon's laughter thundered behind them.

Once beyond the monastery walls, Silas scanned the desert, seeking out any kind of shelter, but there was nothing but endless horizon.

"He really *did* remove my sin," said a woman. "I'd never have been able to leave the city walls if I'd had any of the curse left in me!"

"Just keep moving…" Silas turned to consider the high walls of the monastery housing the thrashing demon from within. His eyes again scanned the symbols and desert language which had been long ago inscribed upon its gates. "Of course," he muttered.

"What is it?"

"See that star up there?" he said to Lilian, pointing up at the night sky. "Gather everyone and head in that direction. You should reach *Moencopi* by morning."

"But what are *you* going to do?"

Flames now reached all about the monastery, black plumes obscuring the moon.

The demon-god gazed down at him as he sauntered back, undaunted by the surrounding flames.

"You've returned."

"I'd expected you to give chase," Silas responded. "But that's not going to happen, is it?"

The demon-god glowered, and Silas knew he was right.

"It was a safeguard that Brother Artemis had put in place," Silas continued. "Just like the safeguard on my cage. No were-demon can escape, just as no were-demon can pass through the gates. I'm sure Brother Artemis could have explained this to you, if you hadn't killed him."

"I have all of his texts," seethed the demon-god. "It's only a matter of time before I can reverse his blessings."

"There's only one way for you to leave these walls." Silas indicated his cage, still upon its wheels, laying abandoned in the courtyard.

The demon-god laughed. "You want me to willingly enter your tiny prison?"

"The cage was imbued with the same blessing, so that one can pass through the other. Every infected person I've ever brought here over the years has come through that cage, and that's the only way any of them could have ever left."

"Then why not just leave me here?"

"It seemed the Christian thing to do."

The demon-god laughed, returning to its original form, the hood of its cloak covering its mangled face.

"So you can *reduce* your size at will, yet you're still clearly at the mercy of the moon when it comes to transforming back."

"*Silence!*" The monk angrily raised its hand and a surge of power threw Silas through the air.

He landed on the ground hard and something snapped. Pain coursed across his body. Struggling through the agony, he shakily pulled out his remaining six-shooter, one bullet remaining in the chamber, and took aim at the grinning monk.

"What a pathetic old man you've lived long enough to become, cowboy. Born in sin, and in sin you perish." The monk's eyes blazed from within its cowl, and in response, Silas's gun likewise glowed in intense heat.

Silas dropped it in pain, flesh smoking from where he'd held it. Around him, the blurry forms of four-legged demons crawled about the walls of the monastery, firelight gleaming from their hides.

He shut his eyes at the horror of it.

The steel of the cage ran cold. Brother Jeremiah felt the corresponding spiritual energy and knew that Silas had spoken truthfully. *One can pass through the other.* He should have worked it out on his own, two identical blessings canceling each other out, allowing safe passage to the world beyond...

How long *had* he been in the monastery? He'd spent so long poring over ancient texts that the sun and moon had careened across the empty desert with impunity. But no longer would such banalities as *the passage of time* be of concern. Now he would be instituting new religions to replace the old. Fresh symbols to replace the tired.

This do in remembrance of me? Not bloody likely.

He stole one last gloating glance at the unconscious form of Silas Spillman, then hoisted himself inside the cage. The remaining demons had received his call and came to their master, surrounding the cage, and pushed it forward.

As his demon porters grew closer to the front gate, their flesh burned, one fell as another shuddered with smoldering fur.

"Push!" Brother Jeremiah commanded, the gates just before him, the demons bursting into flame, urging them onward. "Keep moving!"

As the last demon was wiped from agonizing existence, as postmortem momentum had carried Brother Jeremiah just beyond the border and into a darkened world filled with delicious sinners needing salvation, he reached to open wide the cage in triumph.

A gunshot rang out.

The metal bars clanged, sparked, the cage shook, the latch now securely in place.

Hobbled, blood dripping from his forehead, Silas Spillman dropped his gun and the torn fabric of his shirt he'd held it in. He limped past the burning storeroom, through the plumes of smoke which covered the moon, beyond the gates.

"Open this at once! Let me out!"

"Afraid I can't do that, Brother."

"You can't trap me in here! You've seen my powers!"

Silas scanned the horizon, looking to see how far the caravan had gotten. Sure enough, they were making good time by the looks of it. Taking a deep breath, he limped after them.

"I am everywhere!" the monk yelled. "All-knowing and all-seeing!"

The wind shifted, as did the rising smoke.

"I am the living embodiment of myth and story!" The moon shone and Brother Jeremiah's arms bristled. His bones elongated and cracked, flesh stretched. "I LIVE IN YOUR HEARTS!"

Silas did not slow, not for the scream or the dull, pulpy reverberations from behind, nor for the chunks of rancid flesh raining down. He was an old fart who had once fought in a war and for whom now each step was agony.

I like my sins where they are, he'd said, and that memory made him chuckle.

At some point he must have blacked out, for he found himself laying prone, one with the cosmos.

"Need a hand?" someone said.

"Just leave me be."

"Let's do this the easy way, Mr. Spillman." Using all of his strength, Reverend Timothy helped the old man to his feet, then brought the canteen to Silas' lips.

"You're healed? No more curse?"

"Thanks to you. It would seem my sins have been forgiven!"

Silas smiled, returned the reverend's warm embrace, muttering softly, "That makes one of us."

BALLAD OF THE OVEREAGER GUN

by Sean Eads & Joshua Viola

"Chiriohwah," I said, spitting the word into General Thorndike's face.

"Never heard of them, Blake."

"Doubt you know much about tribes."

"I know which ones exist and which ones don't," Thorndike said. In retrospect, he had five minutes before he'd quit existing too, though neither of us knew it. The dumb bastard began counting on his fingers as he spoke. "Tonkawa, Blackfoot, Apache, Cheyenne, Crow, Kiowa, Lakota, Arapaho, Lipan, Ojibwe." He went thumb to pinkie, pinkie to thumb to prove his encyclopedic knowledge.

"*And* Chiriohwah. I always called them Cheerio. Sometimes it fits them, sometimes not. They're moody."

"And when did this non-existent tribe abduct you?"

"Eight years ago, when I was just thirteen."

"How long ago did you escape?"

"I didn't. They cast me out. Look, it's complicated."

Thorndike smiled. "What isn't these days? Here's what I think. You took part in the massacre."

"How did little old me massacre thirty soldiers?"

"Little old you had help. I think you belong to the Crazy Men who holed up in that canyon. Cowardly ambushes are just the sort of thing they'd do. Now you lot are desecrating bodies and dragging a few off. To do what, I wonder? Nothing tighter than a dead man's ass, is that it?"

"I imagine a general's ass is tighter. But I'm partial to beaver."

My gaze drifted to the sloped right wall of Thorndike's buff-colored command tent. I wasn't thinking about the flimsiness of the materials, the inadequacy of its protection. That came thirty seconds later, when the flickering silhouettes of soldiers cast onto the wall by adjacent campfires began to flinch, double-over, crumple—each noiseless pantomime a clue as to how they were being executed.

A massive gush of red soaked the wall and threatened to collapse the tent. Startled, Thorndike was still sitting when a bloody machete made a beaver slit in the canvas. Death's head crowned there a moment later.

"Cheerio," I said.

I recognized the six warriors who'd slaughtered Thorndike and his scout force of twenty men, but they pretended not to know me. Obwamat loyalists, no doubt. As they dragged me outside and made me kneel among the hacked bodies, it seemed obvious they meant to kill me, too. So, I made the Chiriohwah *sign of defiance*. The Cheerio language consisted of neologic constructions from words found in all those other tribes Thorndike enumerated on his fingertips. In this way, they weeded out unwanted concepts like peace and harmony, and therefore lacked any corresponding nonverbal cues. The signal I made consisted of several complex hand gestures that looked like fevered acts of self-gratification. The precise meaning of the signal was, *Fuck with me now, and I'll fuck with you from beyond the grave,* or in Cheerio shorthand: *Bitches beware.*

The warriors laughed.

"Thanks for the rescue, boys. That general was going to string me up by the balls for a crime I didn't commit. But that's typical for a Chiriohwah, isn't it?"

Their laughter died.

"Sha-Chani-Luko sent us."

I stiffened. "Is Father okay? Does he still live?"

They told me not to call the Chiriohwah chief *Father.*

"Why shouldn't I? Wasn't I brought up as Obwamat's brother? Obwamat, who taught me to seduce and fuck beaver. Do the ancient French mountain men still call him Obwamat the Fur Trapper?"

They howled laughter at this, and I was put onto one of several horses. We rode into the dusk. Being on the move again felt good after spending a full day being interrogated by a corporal, a captain, and then Thorndike himself. Despite my expulsion, I clung to old Chiriohwah habits, chief among them never staying any place too long.

We chased a bloody gash of sunset and after an hour of hard riding we came to ten cabins surrounded by the decimated remains of a split-rail fence. About a hundred Cheerio encamped in and around the buildings, but it was tough to be sure. The Chiriohwah never used campfires at night when on the warpath, so I had to make determinations by moonlight.

I was taken into the nearest cabin where I found Father stretched out on a crude mattress.

"Skinned Little White Stick," he said, sitting up. So unfair to be named after your adolescent erection, but I had them all the time in the weeks following my abduction. The Cheerio loincloth forced upon me had its delicious friction, it's maddening freedom.

I bowed.

"You look well," he said.

"How could I not? You taught me to survive."

"We are fortunate you weren't many hundreds of miles away."

"I've tried, but I just can't make myself stray too far from my true people and my Father. I suppose I shadow the Chiriohwah as best I can."

"You again prove yourself a credit to me."

Sha-Chani-Luko said the same when I was fourteen and my initiation became official. As the only white man ever taken into the Chiriohwah, I'd felt like quite the pick of the litter.

He got up, took his oil lamp, and walked past me. I fell into step and followed him outside, headed toward another cabin.

"Do you need an interpreter again, Father?"

"I do."

"You never should have let Obwamat show me the flaps of the tipi. I'm too useful."

I envisioned talking to a few bound people, some family scared out of their wits by *the savages*. Maybe I could save lives, do my good deed for the year.

There seemed to be the remains of four or five people inside, but figuring that out would require a serious reckoning. Butchered arms and legs were scattered about like disturbed stacks of lumber. Rigid hands clawed out from the heaps of body parts as if to clutch at their departing spirits. The room was painted with gallons of blood, the floor slippery with entrails. Flies buzzed around the congealed remains in a hungry fever. Deep gouges scored the wooden walls. It was like a blindman had been given both an axe and a good reason to start swinging. The air was stagnant and heavy, almost humid from the blood. The gore was too fresh to stink yet, but there was an unmistakable reek of rage here. And piss and defecation.

"This settlement was known to us," Father said. "Fifty people lived here. Now no one does."

He led me back to the first cabin. The Cheerio who camped outside watched us go. The peoples of the plains say they can predict who among them will go and join the Chiriohwah. It's not just certain identifiable mannerisms or perspectives. They claim there's such a thing as *Cheerio Face*. Looking at them now, even by moonlight, I knew it to be true. My complexion aside, I saw *Cheerio Face* whenever I looked in the mirror, so obvious it may have saved my life.

"Each cabin is the same. Slaughter and more slaughter of the invaders."

The note of despair in his voice astonished me. Where had it been when he cut my real father's throat with a sliver of buffalo bone as I pleaded for his life? Nor was I the only one to notice. The Chiriohwah language has several words for *bitch*, and I heard every one of them in the space of twenty seconds. It was hard for me to imagine Father allowing his authority to be mocked, but he ignored the jeering and we hurried back inside. He sat down on the edge of the mattress and bowed his head.

"What the hell is wrong with you? Where is the strength of Sha-Chani-Luko? Who is this fraud posing as my father?"

"Enough!"

Seeing a glimpse of his old venom satisfied me. I softened and said, "Who's responsible for this butchery? Even the Comanche wouldn't piss and shit on a corpse. And you don't need an interpreter to talk to the mangled."

Father called out to a subordinate, who came to the door. "Bring the box."

The subordinate bowed and hurried away.

"Tell me, Skinned Little White Stick. Do you remember Delsin Sakishet?"

As if I could forget the great Cheerio shaman and soothsayer, and source of all my troubles. "Is he still shucking corn and ruining lives?"

"He deserves more respect. Men who don't get respect go out of their way to avenge mockery."

Father's subordinate returned with a long wooden box. He placed it on the floor and withdrew fast, leaving Father and I to stare at it.

"Oh-en es awking bux n noint e et eh ety ace!" The sound came from inside the box, and I jumped back.

"What the *WhiteMan* is this?" I said, using the Cheerio word for hell.

"Not long after your expulsion, Delsin Sakishet told me a great spirit came in a vision and taught him all things have a mind and voice. Not just the works of nature, but of our own hands as well. Every creation has an intelligence waiting to be unlocked, as ours was unlocked at birth. The Chiriohwah do not run from a fight, but we do not believe in a noble death. There are no rules in warfare. *Any advantage is a fair advantage*, that has been the credo of our people from the time of the first Chiriohwah chief."

"This you taught me long ago, and I embrace it to this day."

"The pioneers keep coming, pushing the peoples of the plains harder than ever before. When Delsin told me what he'd learned, I asked him to bring forth intelligence into weapons, to make them killers as well as counselors. The shamans of other tribes content themselves with rituals and dances. Delsin Sakishet came to us because his heart was different—like any true Chiriohwah. I encouraged him. Pushed him. It seems I did both things too much."

Another urgent cry came from the box. The words, even muffled, had a distinct English feel, and I said so.

"You alone speak Chiriohwah and the settlers' vile tongue. Open the box," Father said.

"What will I find?"

"A weapon the usurpers call Horse Child 45."

"Colt 45," I said.

My throat was tight as I lifted the box lid. There was a collection of lead bullets laying loose like marbles next to a six-shooter, a true thing of beauty with its white bone grip, 5.5-inch barrel, and low luster military blue finish. I experienced all the awe some medieval knight must have felt upon seeing a fresh-forged sword.

"You're just perfection," I said.

"And you're just the finger I've been needing."

I was dumbfounded. The human voice came from no identifiable place on the gun, which lay there inert. I expected it to rattle or something, but its life seemed confined to the verbal.

"Who are we going to kill?"

"Who says we're killing anyone?"

Father stood over my shoulder and said, "You understand it?"

"Let me put a hole in someone, and then hold me against the wound and let the blood flow over me."

I closed the lid. "The gun is obnoxious, Father."

"We've known it to screech for hours like an unfed baby. We felt it was berating us and decided to bury it deep in the earth. Then Obwamat found the bow."

"What bow?"

Obwamat's distinct voice sounded from the open door behind us. "This one, Usurper."

I turned and saw Obwamat standing there, tall and proud and lean, a nocked arrow drawn back to maximum tension. He drew a bead on my head.

"Our aim is true. The arrow will kill him. But I urge reconsideration."

I side-eyed Father. "The bow talks, too?"

"Augh ed omen es awking bux n noint e et eh ety ace!"

I raised the lid again. "What did you say?"

"I said open this fucking box and point me at a pretty face."

"Vulgarian," the bow said.

"Did that wooden bitch just call me something?"

Sha-Chani-Luko looked between the gun and the bow. "They are arguing?"

"To an extent. But they don't understand each other, either," I said.

Father shook his head. "Like brothers who've lost their brotherhood."

Obwamat's arm was starting to shake. "A true brother does not seek to usurp another." He had great strength, but he'd been holding the bow drawn and steady for a few minutes now.

"That bow is an absolute bitch, and the man holding him sounds like an asshole. I specialize in assholes. Just aim and give my trigger a little goose. It doesn't take much to get me off. I'll remove this problem from your life. I have no issue being the guilty party."

I closed the lid, and the gun cussed me out as a coward and beaver.

Obwamat lowered the bow. The bow in turn celebrated his wisdom. It spoke fluent Cheerio with a refinement no Chiriohwah would ever possess. It should have been wrapped in a cushioned dressing-gown and propped on a divan.

Slinging the bow across his left shoulder, Obwamat spared a single contemptuous glance at me, then addressed Father. "Our party found no trace of Delsin except more carnage. We encountered the remains of a small Arapaho hunting party, twenty in total. Delsin slaughtered sixteen outright. The other four he left behind for the same evil purpose."

Father leaned forward. "Were you in time?"

"Yes," Obwamat said. "We beheaded and burned their bodies."

"What in the *WhiteMan* are you both saying? That Delsin Sakishet is responsible for what I saw in that cabin? That he can decimate an Arapaho hunting party by himself? He was a frail old man even from the time I knew him. This is—"

I noticed Obwamat's head was inclined to the left. A low murmur came from the bow.

"Does my brother want to share with the rest of the family?"

"If you had a brother, he might."

Sha-Chani-Luko raised his hands. "I'll hear no more of this. Skinned Little White Stick, I've sought your help to communicate with the gun and see if it will ally with us. Delsin Sakishet brought intelligence to the weapons to help the Chiriohwah. And they *shall* help us—by killing him."

Father struggled with the last three words. Obwamat and I both reached out as Sha-Chani-Luko's body shook from a sob. Our hands braced his shoulders at the same time. Father crossed his arms, reaching up to pat the tops of our hands. "You are both Chiriohwah—"

"He *isn't*," Obwamat said.

"And both my sons, equal in my eyes. Go together. Obwamat with the bow, White Stick with the gun. Find our shaman and kill him."

"I don't need him, Father," Obwamat said. "I can use both the gun and the bow."

"You cannot use a weapon you don't understand."

"There is great wisdom in your father's words," the bow said.

Obwamat unhooked the bow from his shoulder and shook it. The bow said nothing, but I could almost taste its hurt feelings.

"I *understand* how to aim and pull the trigger, Father. What else is there to know?"

"The language of the gun. It does not speak Chiriohwah. I think this means it was destined for the hands of White Stick as much as the bow was meant for you."

"Perhaps this is all a trick to put the gun in the usurper's hand so he can shoot me and make Delsin's prophecy come true."

Sha-Chani-Luko gave us a pitiable look. "The quarrel between you is tied to Delsin Sakishet's crimes. Ride together and do not return until both are put to an end."

Father turned his back, a gesture that made me feel like I was a teenager again—except back then Obwamat and I would struggle not to laugh because we'd done something outrageous together to earn his disappointment. He and I were a tribe unto ourselves in those days.

I took the box, and we left the cabin. The Cheerio watched us mount our horses. A woman gave us some provisions wrapped in a burlap sack. I slipped mine into the saddlebag, along with the box. The gun continued its silent sulk.

"Where are we headed?" I asked.

Obwamat pointed into the darkness.

"Care to be more specific?"

He spurred his horse. I sighed and gave chase. We rode like that for over an hour before the bonfires came into clear view—the aftermath of the Arapaho hunting party. We approached the flames at a trot with Obwamat looking to his left and right.

"How many people has the old man killed?" I said.

"Your mocking tone offends me."

"I'm just trying to figure out how a frail medicine man can rip people from limb from limb."

"Can you doubt his magic after experiencing the gun and the bow?"

"The only thing I ever doubted was the prophecy. But I guess you didn't, considering all the efforts you made to force me out. It bothers you, doesn't it? If Delsin Sakishet can give inanimate objects a voice, it must mean his other powers were real, and therefore the prophecy."

"Shut up."

We stopped at the edge of the fire. The odor of burning flesh remained in the air, but not as overwhelming as it must have been from the start. The flames licked at the blackened ends of wood and bones.

Obwamat stared hard into the flames. "What do you call yourself— out there?"

"Blake. That was my first birth name."

"Your only birth name. Never refer to yourself as Chiriohwah again, Blake."

"I am, regardless of—"

He pivoted so swift and fluid, I couldn't so much as flinch before he had the bow drawn, the arrow inches from my forehead.

"Obwamat, I urge you to let go of your hate."

"I must agree with the bow," I said, swallowing hard. "But if you can't let go of the hate, then at least don't let go of the arrow until it's aimed away from my face."

Obwamat held the arrow on me a moment longer. After he eased tension off the bow, he said, "I want you to leave."

"Did you know that I can't stand to even look at corn?"

Obwamat dismounted, and I followed. He took a stick and poked at a charred skull, causing its jaw to collapse. *"Please* depart."

"You can't expect me to continue without knowing what's happening. If nothing else, I want to protect myself when I'm out there on my own."

"I will tell him," the bow said.

Obwamat scowled and shoved the bow into my hands.

"Everyone and everything betrays me." He stalked off to the opposite side of the fire.

I sat down and placed the bow on my lap.

"Father Shaman had brought forward our consciousness one month prior to his great turn toward darkness. Brother Gun could not be comprehended, but it never stopped badgering him. Father Shaman begged him for silence to no avail. Then he said, 'It is all meaningless. Two weapons or a hundred or even a thousand will not help us. The invaders are animals, and only animals can fight animals.' Father Shaman then set about crafting dentures for himself comprised of wolves' teeth.

"After the dental plate was complete, he sat on the floor, in the middle of a circle formed by the decapitated heads of several wolves. All of them had given a portion of their teeth to the dentures. Father Shaman placed a bowl in his lap and hunched forward. The bowl soon filled with blood as he pried and ripped each of his teeth free and let them drop into the basin. How he howled with each extraction, but a greater howling remained. When the last of his teeth were gone and his mouth was a wet oval smear fronting sunken cheeks, he began a thick, hoarse chant that continued even as his

shaking, blood-slick hands worked the dentures past his palsied lips and settled them against the raw, inflamed gums. He bit down and screamed. I marked his transformation, his writhing, the growth of hair followed by the splitting of his skin and the creature that clawed its way from the ripped seams. A gray man became a gray beast, muscled beyond all comprehension. It sat back on its haunches and gave a full-throated cry, and this howl awakened the decapitated heads, which likewise opened their mouths to make an impossible chorus."

Obwamat must have been listening, because he ran back and snatched the bow away. "That's enough. The rest is carnage and murder. Delsin Sakishet has become a beast. There are those among us now who were once Navajo, and they call Delsin a *skin-walker.*"

"The white people—"

"*Your* people, Blake," Obwamat said, interrupting me.

I wanted to correct him, but I knew it wouldn't matter. To Obwamat, I'd always be an outsider. I pushed the comment aside and continued. "*Werewolves.* That's what *they* call them. I remember hearing about them when I was very young. They transform at the full moon, and only silver can kill them."

"If only this threat slept between full moons. You describe a monster of order and structure. Delsin Sakishet is the beast both day and night. He attacks at will. Perhaps he does not even need sleep."

"That makes one of us," I said.

"I too am fatigued. But we must press on."

"We'll get ourselves killed out there if we're too tired to see straight. Better to wait until morning."

"Every moment we delay, we risk his evil spreading."

He motioned me toward the fire, took a stick and sifted some of the ashes to reveal the rounded top of a human skull. But as more ashes were removed, however, the skull developed a protruding muzzle and jaw. "The change starts soon on those left alive. Even in fire, the change continues. A battle of wills ensues between the flesh and the flame. Had our party arrived here even a few minutes too late, we could not have stopped them from running off to join Delsin."

I imagined a gigantic wolf loping across the plains with a pack trailing behind. The Cheerio were a tribe of outcasts and castaways. Delsin

Sakishet was making his own version of the Chiriohwah as seen through a dark glass.

"How many people has he turned?"

"Who can say? But if it's greater than twenty-four, our purpose may be too late."

"That's…specific. Why?"

Obwamat told me to stay by the fire. He went and retrieved the box from my saddlebag. I heard the gun blathering from within. He put the box on the ground between us and removed the lid.

"Well thank fucking God."

I knelt. "That's exactly what I am, as far as you're concerned."

"Want to hear me say a prayer to you, O' Lord? Just put my mouth right up against your ear. I want to make sure I'm heard."

I glanced at Obwamat. "I think the gun's growing on me. Maybe a little too high for its nut, but not lacking confidence."

"I will take your word for it," Obwamat said.

I took the Colt from the box and cradled it in both palms. "Do you have a name?"

"Papi. And you're Blake. Now that we're on a first name basis, let's shoot someone."

"Looks like we need to kill your creator."

"That just strokes my barrel straight up and down."

"You don't have a problem with it?"

"Name me a son who wouldn't blow his father away?"

"Jesus," I said, not meaning it as an answer, though the gun took it as one. Papi questioned whether the act would be patricide or suicide if the son and the father are the same person. Then the gun told me to load its chambers.

Obwamat took up the bow when he saw me reach for the bullets.

"I'd shoot myself before I shot you," I said. "Can't you believe that?"

"No," he said. "But load the gun. Feel the bullets."

They were lighter than I expected. Not that I had great familiarity with munitions, as Father had raised me to use a bow like any Cheerio. I slipped the first one into place.

"Oh, that's tasty. You might even call it toothsome. Give me another."

I paused, and Obwamat asked me what was wrong.

"The gun is making cryptic remarks about the bullets. And they have a strange weight."

"The bow counseled Father on how Delsin might be destroyed. By exchanging his teeth for a wolf's, he traded his humanity for the beast. But the teeth remain powerful and potent. They can be used to break the dark magic that compels him if they can be returned to his body."

"Good luck finding a dentist with that much courage!"

"No, Blake," Obwamat said. "If Bow is correct—"

"I am."

"Then it does not matter how the tooth is delivered, or where."

"Are the three of you still yapping away like bitch coyotes? Fill my belly, Blake. I smell werewolf piss in the air. Territory is getting marked nearby."

I considered the second bullet before loading it. "This isn't solid."

"No," Obwamat said.

"Delsin Sakishet's teeth are inside?"

"We found twenty-four of them in the bloody bowl. Twelve bullets were forged with teeth in their center, and twelve arrowheads were crafted with teeth wedged into their sockets."

"How does firing the teeth into someone Delsin transformed help us?"

"The transformation stems from his animal bite. If we bite back with his human teeth, the effect should be the same."

"I wasn't bullshitting you about that werewolf piss, Blake. The reek is getting very strong."

The bow also sounded the alert.

Obwamat got up, arrow ready, as I thumbed five more bullets into Papi.

"I've actually never used one of you," I said.

"Just aim. I do most of the work."

A howl rang out, followed by a bellowing answer from what must have been several throats. I took the remaining bullets and shoved them into my right pocket.

"Can you make your arm quit shaking like that? I'm starting to see double."

The howls sounded again. Very close.

"You don't happen to speak werewolf, do you, Papi?"

"They smell your fear. I, on the other hand, smell tremendous opportunity. Let's murder some pooch."

We got our chance half a minute later. Our horses were already whinnying in panic and pulling on their tethers. Then they let loose with a scream of bloody terror. Two ashen beasts charged them from behind and bit their right legs off with the ease of men snapping twigs. The horses toppled onto their sides and the wolves clawed their underbellies open and draped themselves in entrails.

I fired and missed.

Papi shouted at me to keep my hand steady. *"Damn you, Blake! Sack up and let's kennel these bitches in Hell."*

Obwamat stepped ahead of me. He and the bow looked like minuet dancers moving in unison. He fired and strung, fired and strung, strumming his fatal cord. The arrows hit their marks, striking each wolf in the neck. They writhed, clutching at geysers of crimson that glistened in the moonlight.

"Blake, if you let that wooden fucker take all the glory, I swear I'm going to blow up in your hand."

Another wolf leapt out of the darkness, right over the fire, snarling. I shot without thinking, too numb to be nervous. Papi knew it was good as soon I pulled the trigger, and the bullet released like some overdue cock-teased ejaculation. The slug punched through the wolf's snout, spraying brain and bone out the back of its skull. Blood spattered my face, and I tasted copper as the stricken wolf crashed down next to me, twitching. Papi's pleasure made me feel like some whore who's just been tipped a nickel for a decent handjob.

The wolves developed a little more respect for us now. I took a moment to refill the empty chambers, then aimed Papi straight ahead. Eight pairs of yellow eyes glittered in the darkness, low to the ground, almost floating as if the rest of their bodies were invisible.

"Any of them Delsin?"

The bow answered. *"He is here. I sense confusion."*

"Because of the teeth?"

"No. Because of your presence."

Obwamat grimaced. It was impossible not to notice or guess at his thoughts, and I said, "You're my brother. You always have been. You always will be. I stand with you, prophecy be damned."

He spared a second to squeeze my shoulder, and I remembered many things then from the closest days of our brotherhood. I recalled the time he and I peeled away from Father and the Cheerio convoy under the pretense of scouting the northern plains for enemies. In reality, we wanted to return to a pretty Lakota we'd shared the day before. She was as glad and welcoming as ever, and said it was more exciting because we were Chiriohwah. She claimed she could be Chiriohwah too, but we told her she lacked *Cheerio Face*. This saddened her, and we consoled her…three times each before returning to our people. We found Father waiting for us in his tipi with Delsin Sakishet, who had two ears of maize with him.

I remembered how he began to shuck them—

"Blake, they're moving toward us. Blake!" Obwamat yelled.

Too many voices, too many sounds battered me. Obwamat shouting, Papi screaming, wolves howling. Somehow, for all that, the subtler noises undid me. The bonfire's smolder, the soft *thwip* of the arrows striking into the chests of the charging beasts.

"White Stick, fire now!"

I unleashed Papi. *One, two, three* beasts fell *just like that,* the stench of blood and gunpowder and wet fur mingling in the fresh kills.

"Goddamn, you're the real animal, Blake. I love your finger. I need your finger, Blake. Finger me, Blake, keep fingering that hard trigger."

Obwamat's quiver was down to four arrows. I had three bullets in the gun and four left in my pocket. There were more wolves than that and still no evidence of Delsin Sakishet.

The bow said, *"We're being maneuvered too far away from the fire. Keeping close to it is an advantage."*

Obwamat fired another arrow, catching the nearest werewolf through the neck. It fell back on the flames, sending up a *poomf* of glowing embers. Another werewolf sprang at me. I ducked down to let it go past me, then spun and Papi put a tooth right through its spine with a shattering of bone.

"I'm almost out. Hurry, Blake, fill me up. Fill the beast to kill the beast; that's my motto."

Obwamat nocked another arrow. His target took the arrowhead straight into the breastbone but powered forward. I was trying to load Papi and couldn't help. Obwamat gave ground, reaching for his next-to-last arrow when the wolf fell upon him. In his panic, Obwamat used the bow itself to fend the jaws off his throat. One swipe of a claw knocked the bow from his grip. The wolf opened its slavering jaws wide and prepared to feast. As it did, Obwamat made a desperate play for the arrow lodged in the beast's chest, gripping the shaft and driving it up fast and hard. You could hear the exact moment the arrowhead cracked through the werewolf's sternum and pierced its heart. It let out a whimper like a scared puppy and collapsed in a heap, trapping Obwamat beneath.

I fired three more shots and three more wolves dropped. This cleared some space and I risked trying to pry Obwamat free of the dead wolf. Papi was screaming at me to pay attention, and I had to give up and turn back to the fight. I noticed the bow on the ground, broken and dead silent.

As I loaded the remaining bullets, a wolf taller than all the others by at least a foot loomed out of the darkness. It came forward on muscled hind legs, an enormous sack dangling between them with nuts the size of poultice balls. Enraged, gold-flecked eyes stared in hunger at Obwamat before I put myself between the beast and my brother.

"Delsin," I said. "Delsin Sakishet!"

"I got four bullets left, Blake. The good news is they contain his wisdom teeth. Let's raise this bitch's intelligence a little."

I pointed Papi at the ground.

"What the fuck is this, Blake? Don't quit on me now!"

"I remember the maize, Delsin. One for Obwamat, one for me. You shucked the heavy green husks until there were two naked, yellow ears in your hands. You pointed one ear at Obwamat. Then you closed your eyes and bit into its raw cob. You twisted the ear and bit at random, over and over, scraping your gums. Blood flowed through the crevices of the kernels. 'As the blood chooses its path, destiny is revealed.' Then you inspected the pattern and scorned it."

The great wolf bared its savage fangs but cocked its head to the right, listening.

"You turned to Father and said, 'Chiriohwah is not a birthright. Chiriohwah is not a lineage. We do not father new Chiriohwah. We do not have heirs.' Then you drew your lips back to reveal a menstrual smile and bit into my maize. I thought you ate more from mine that Obwamat's. There were so many bloody gaps in the kernels when you finished, so much diminishment. Yet you pointed out the path of the blood with great contentment. 'The maize has spoken. This is the pattern of a true Chiriohwah. It matches your own, Sha-Chani-Luko. *He* must be our future chieftain.'

I clenched my teeth. "You destroyed my life. Ended my brotherhood with Obwamat. Ended my life as a Chiriohwah. Made me an outcast. It seemed your prophecy was thwarted. Then the weapons you made did not turn out like you wanted. Did these failures drive you mad? Make you feel ignored, unappreciated? Push you to take matters into your own hands? Well, here I am, standing tall with Obwamat crippled on the ground. Here I am, holding the gun you brought to life. Won't the prophecy be fulfilled now? Your victory at last?"

Obwamat moaned and cursed me. Delsin Sakishet drew himself up taller than ever before, lifted his head to the moon, and gave a full-throated howl. I let Delsin savor his moment. Then I raised Papi and fired a shot into his stomach.

The beast staggered back, fixing me with a murderous, betrayed stare as blood began flowing.

"I couldn't say anything to you then. I hadn't the words. But I do now."

The second shot tore through his chest in a red mist. *"Fuck."*

The third shot into his neck, gushing spurts. *"Your."*

The final shot into his ball sack, bursting it like some over-ripe melon, hurling greasy clots of flesh onto the ground. *"Teeth."*

Papi was orgasming in my hand. *"Keep pulling. Keep pulling. I don't care if I'm empty, just keep pulling. Pull, goddamnit!"* I indulged him with several dry clicks and then went to Obwamat, freeing him from the beast. He gasped for air and put one hand on my shoulders as I helped him stand. He picked up the pieces of the bow and closed his eyes. Chiriowah aren't often the praying sort, but Obwamat offered a prayer of thanks.

"How about showing me a little gratitude? I did most of the work."

I hushed Papi and waited on Obwamat. He placed the bow's pieces atop the remains of the fire.

"It is over," he said.

"With Delsin Saksishet and his wolves? I think so."

"And our quarrel." Obwamat offered me his hand. I took it. "Let us get cleaned up and go tell Father."

"Cheerio," I said, and we walked toward the sunrise.

THE OWL WITCH
OF THE COMANCHERIA

by Craig E. Sawyer

A half dozen Comanche warriors materialized out of the thick dust that lofted over the basin from a recent black blizzard. Two wounded men were being dragged behind the group on makeshift sleds. One of their hostages had been described as the toughest Texas Ranger in the Great Plains, but he had recently changed his profession to that of a bounty hunter. He was dressed in wool trousers, covered halfway with leather chaps, a healed over scalped head, and a pair of "Prince of Wales" military-issued spurs.

Captain Sidacious Tomlinson should be dead right now, but he was as hard as hickory and stubborn as a gallon of heady shine. One of his ex-wives said that he couldn't be killed because the Devil was too jealous to have someone viler in Hell.

It only took him one glance around the dead and desolate landscape to know he was in the heart of the harshest region in the country—the Comancheria. The name means Comanche Earth, and it was their domain—a vast region that stretched across much of the Great Plains from Colorado in the North to the great state of Texas and eastern New Mexico.

The procession stopped.

One of the Comanche got down from his horse and untied the terrified man next to the captain. He grabbed him by his blood-matted hair and tossed him into the dirt bedside a flat rock. The warrior then instructed him to start digging a hole, while the others took time to eat and water their horses. After a few hours, the man had dug a fairly deep hole.

They pushed him in it and moved the dirt over his body, leaving only his head exposed. A blue faced warrior causally walked over to the man and pulled out his knife.

"Please…d-don't!"

The warrior ignored his pleas, as he proceeded to cut off the man's eyelids and nose.

A weakened captain was forced to look at the event, even though he attempted to jerk his head away. This wasn't the first time he had been captured by Comanches, and he knew if he didn't escape, he would be skinned alive, or have his heel tendons cut and left in the middle of nowhere to be eaten by coyotes. This was how they amused themselves on long rides.

Captain Tomlinson was known among them, and the Comancheros of the region, as la mano derecha del diablo—the *Devil's Right Hand*, due to his deadly precision with a Colt revolver, and the many souls he had banished from the living world. He looked over at the blue-faced warrior beside him. The man was wearing the captain's beaten bolero hat and a wolf skin hide. "My skull umbrella looks good on you. How 'bout I trade it for some goddamn water?"

The intense-looking native smiled, before walking over and kicking him in the face.

"We are called Numinu, white dog! That name was given to us by our enemies."

Captain Tomlinsonn shook his head. "You speak any English, 'cause I only know a little Comanche?"

"It is not hard to do so. It is a simple and stupid language."

The buried man with no eyelids moaned and yelled.

"Why don't you just put that poor bastard out of his misery?" A stony-faced captain said.

The warrior nodded his head to the east. "He took one of our women, then raped and killed her. Now the sun will bake his eyes, and the coyotes will eat his face."

"I don't know that asshole," the captain growled.

"You would already be begging for death, if you did. We found you lying in a field, half dead."

"Eh, what do they call you?"

"I am Blue Wolf—great killer of taibo sarii."

"Sarii?"

"It's what we call white men and useless dogs."

"What are you waiting for? Just get on with it and kill me!" the captain said, spitting out a glob of blood onto the hot earth. His body was racked with hellish pain.

"Our spirit talker said you may be helpful to us or I would have fed your guts to the crows by now. He says your soul walks between this world and the next, and that you may be helpful."

"And if I'm not helpful?"

"Then we will sacrifice The Devil's Right Hand to our Gods."

"I would give your Gods the shits."

They rode for what seemed like forever through the sage brush-filled desolation. Even the vultures looked like they were dying of dehydration. The captain's thirst had only been quenched by the scant drippings from cactus given to him by his captors, and the blood from biting into his tongue.

He could hear the howls of "murder dogs" at night. They were survivors, like the captain, and he respected survivors. The reckoning of things out here in the plains—two opposing forces fighting it out and letting pure grit decide who was *right*, and who was *dead*. He felt that mortals' natural state was killing others and taking what they needed, and the only one that provided equality was Sam Colt. He came down to earth and bestowed upon mortals his sacred revolver, and he made demigods of those willing to master the iron. When the captain prayed, he didn't pray to a god hung with nails; he prayed to the one who provided the nails.

The captain could see in the distance a grouping of Buffalo hide tipis that filled a large area beside a fast-flowing river. This was a large tribe with over three hundred Comanche. The natives looked him over as they dragged their latest capture into the nomadic camp.

They passed a frowning old lady with sun-weathered skin. She wore a deerskin dress embroidered with a hundred colorful beads that were designed to look like a snake eating its tail. A red-hot sun was in the background.

"Howdy, ma'am," the captain said as he passed.

She slapped him.

Blue Wolf nearly fell off of his horse, laughing.

"The Comanche handshake hasn't changed much since the last time I came across one," the captain said.

"I think she likes you."

The sled he was being pulled on came to a rough stop.

A large group of women and men surrounded him, some whooping and hollering. More spat at him.

He craned his neck and saw he was at the entrance to a massive tipi— the biggest in the lot. It could easily hold thirty or forty people.

Blue Wolf untied the leather straps that held him. Once finished, he abruptly flipped the sled over causing the captain to tumble into the dirt. A scrappy-looking dog hiked his leg and pissed all over the captain's chest and face.

"That feels better, thanks!" Captain Tomlinson said, sitting up and flapping his hands over and over to get the blood flowing back to his trigger finger. What he wouldn't give for a revolver.

"Get up, ugly, and come with me," Blue Wolf said.

The beaten and sunburnt ex-ranger pulled himself up and dusted off before he followed the warrior.

The interior was lit by a fire, and its tanned hide walls smelled like sweetgrass and tobacco from years of gatherings. It took a moment for his vision to adjust to the flickering room. There were a dozen important and intense-looking tribe members sitting cross-legged around the fire pit. A strange character was circling the men holding a rattlesnake in each hand. He was their medicine man, Rukwooru.

All in attendance raised their hands as the ominous chanting stopped, and the shaman turned to face their white visitor. The medicine man said something in Comanche and tossed the rattler at the captain, who easily caught it and bit its head off. He started to lap up the gushing blood.

"Thanks for the drink!" he said, and tossed the snake into the fire.

The shaman yelled something and instructed him to sit.

"Okay, calm yourself down. I'm 'a sitting."

The room was sweltering.

Rukwooru reached into his pocket, came out with a handful of green dust, and flung it into the fire, which caused it to shoot up wildly toward the top of the tent.

Captain Tomlinson looked at each face to get a bead on their intentions, but they were impossible to read. The one directly across from him must have been Chief Reptile Man, because of his age and the fact his left eye looked like a snake.

He said something and waved his hand.

Everything melted into a dusty barn hall. The captain recognized this place from his childhood. The drums and the pounding of his heart became the same clang of a cross pein hammer striking iron held by his father, Simon Tomlinson, who was his childhood town's farrier. Sidacious Tomlinson was from the little town of Helsfount, Tennessee, near the Appalachian Mountains. When he was twelve, bandits rode in one day and killed damn near everyone

The small community fought bravely, but were shot down like dogs in the muddy streets. That's when the captain took his first human life with his daddy's ivory-handled Colt. And even though he had fought as bravely as any grown man that day, he was shot in the shoulder. He had managed to make it to the front of the local Baptist church before collapsing on its front steps.

A mountain woman found him there and fought away two giant vultures that had been trying to pick at his flesh. She had used herbs and hill-folk hoodoo to thresh him from myriad dead spirits ripped from their mortal coils on that blood drenched day, and it took all of her power to keep little Sidacious among the living.

She would tell him later that angels and devils had been clawing for his soul, just like those damn birds, and she had to forge a deal with the darker forces just to keep him alive. She was adept in the hoodoo, or "granny magic," which came from the Scots-Irish that immigrated to Western North Carolina and comingled with the indigenous Cherokee. She was called everything from a "cove druid" to a "granny witch" and used hard-to-find herbs, or "yarbs," for the healing and deep cave incantations that called upon ancient spirits from deep within the earth. The conjuring she'd done that day put a blood pact on the boy, his fate soaked in blood because, in order to save his life, she had to damn his soul. He was to live by the gun, and as long as he kept up his part of the bargain, he would keep riding the narrow trail between this world and the next. His "pact" would last until he killed the murderous wretches that killed his parents. Then, and only then, could his soul enter the pearly gates.

Captain Tomlinson suddenly came back from the vision and was standing outside. It was night and the stars were tossed across the sky like gold flakes in a miner's cradle.

"What happened?"

Blue Wolf was standing beside him eating from a hunk of freshly cooked deer meat. "You passed out and pissed your pants."

"I went somewhere. I was back in the town I grew up. What was that powder that owl fella threw in the air? It got me high as a hawk on a windy day."

"It was just colored dust from the river bed mixed with plants. You had a vision."

"What does your chief want from me?"

"Our people are under attack by an owl witch."

"What the Sam Hill is that?" He eyed the aromatic meat.

"An evil creature who feeds on children."

"I'm a gunslinger without a gun…what the hell good am I?"

"Our shaman says that only one who walks between worlds can harm it. It is not a living thing like us. Here, eat… You look like shit." The warrior handed him the meat.

The captain took it and ate liberally. "What if I'm of no help?" He wiped his greasy beard on his sleeve.

"Then we will smear your body with honey and bury you up to your chin. The sun will cook you, as the animals above and below slowly eat you."

"That's quite the choice you've given me. When do we start this bird hunt?"

"It will come to us, tonight. It always does."

"What about a gun? I can't fight with no bow and arrow."

"Your pistol and gun belt are there." Blue Wolf pointed toward a small tipi not far from where they stood. "Hey, where did you find me?"

"You were half dead, lying behind a burnt cabin. You must have crawled out just before it collapsed. You were still holding your gun. I was about to slit your throat when our shaman stopped me. He said you have a part to play in this."

"Thanks?" Captain Tomlinson said with a scowl.

Inside the tipi was more food and his Colt revolver. The five-shot Paterson had served the Texas Rangers well. He picked it up and grinned like a possum with a sweet potato. "Hello, *Darling*. I hate to wake you up from your nap, but we got some killing to do."

It was well after midnight, and all of the fires had been extinguished. The moon was just a sliver, but the stars gave decent enough light to see across the landscape. Blue Wolf and the captain were crouched down just on the outskirts of camp behind some pampas grass.

A coyote howled in the distance.

"How does one of these owl witches come to exist?" The captain kept his eyes on the dark field.

"A person makes a pact with darkness to return after death."

"So, this thing isn't alive?"

"It can also shapeshift to appear as a normal human during the day. But, at night, it becomes a giant owl with razor-sharp teeth and eyes that burn like hot coals. I hit it with an arrow in the heart, but that did nothing. It kills our horses and takes our children. We find only bloody clothes…or pieces of them."

An hour passed uneventful, then they heard a loud screech from behind.

"It's coming from the camp," Blue Wolf whispered.

They ran back toward the tents and there it was, a giant owl creature flapping over the camp with a wingspan of at least eight feet and a human-like head, as it swooped down over a screaming mother trying to take her child.

"I'll be bloody damned" the captain mumbled under his breath.

Blue Wolf and several other warriors let out a battle cry.

"Sam Colt, guide my iron!" The captain blasted away at the creature with his revolver, hitting it several times. To his surprise, the wounds closed up as fast as they materialized.

"It's eaten them bullets and spitting 'em out!" the captain said.

The creature screeched again, then flew upward and circled over a mother holding her child. It was the same woman that had spit on him when he first arrived. He broke open the chamber of his gun.

Blue Wolf landed on one knee and shot a series of arrows at the creature. "You should learn the bow!" he yelled, before landing on one knee and shooting a series of arrows at it. The Comanche were deadly masters of the bow and could shoot up to ten arrows in the time it took a man to reload most guns. The captain snapped his gun shut and started shooting again. "No thanks." His second shot hit the winged demon right between the eyes, causing it to fall to the ground near the woman and child.

Other warriors came out and started hurling spears and firing arrows at the downed owl witch. It appeared to be dead as they crept upon its limp body. But when one of the warriors got close enough to stab it again, the creature reached up with its claws and beheaded the man in one quick movement.

The beast leaped to its feet and seized the child from the terrified woman, hissed curses in what sounded like a native tongue, and took off into the sky.

"It's flying toward the river!" The captain took aim but was afraid to shoot for fear of hitting the child.

Blue Wolf whistled for his horse, a Spanish Mustang.

He slung his bow over his shoulder and mounted the magnificent animal, digging his heels into its side and bolting off in a dead gallop toward the escaping owl witch, and as he approached the creature, he rearmed himself and launched more arrows at it, two of them striking its back. The creature faltered, almost lost its grasp on the screaming child, but managed to hold on. The captain made his way to the riverbank and aimed at the owl witch's talons. He took one shot that took the end of its claw, and the child fell into the fast-moving waters.

Blue Wolf rode fast down the bank, trying to get ahead of the child drifting swiftly in the rapids.

A second later, the owl witch vanished into the night sky.

The captain collapsed, out of breath. "Dammit!"

Blue Wolf dove into the river with his horse and caught the child, hoisting him up into the saddle, and then steered his steed back to dry land. Galloping up to camp, Blue Wolf handed off the child to his mother before returning to the captain's side.

"That thing is stuck in my craw, now," the captain growled. "I don't like something that hurts children."

"It flew west. And it spoke in the Apache tongue."

"Then, what the hell are we waiting for?"

"We will have to pass through Apache land. Last I heard, they don't care much for Whites or Comanche."

Blue Wolf nodded. "We will dance before we go. Ask the gods to give us strength."

"That blue paint is affecting your head. We can dance after we kill it."

"My father, the chief, will demand we dance."

"I'll be damned, your Chief Reptile Man's son?"

"What is…damned?"

"It's something that happens to a man's soul when he pisses his gods off." He reached up and grabbed his bolero hat from Blue Wolf's head, adjusted it a bit, then placed it on his head. "My hat will suffice as payment for me helping to kill this thing."

"Have your gods damned you?"

Captain Tomlinson patted the ivory handle of his Colt revolver. "I only have one god, and his name is Sam Colt."

"I hope Sam Colt is with us on our journey," the sharp-featured Comanche said. "Oh, he's with us, all right, and his six little friends, too."

Blue Wolf led a war dance that night around a huge bonfire. The shaman and chief asked the sun, the earth, and the moon to bless their weapons. And they asked for mother wolf and brother fox to imbue them with their prowess. Other Comanche tribes—the Penateka "Honey Eaters" and the Kotsoteka "Buffalo Eaters"—came to give offerings and good words, for they had both been plagued by the great evil, as well.

The next morning was quiet when the captain exited his tipi. His body was racked with bruises and cuts from the recent battle with the witch.

He eyed Blue Wolf with his wife and children, saying his goodbyes, because they might not return.

Shaman Rukwooru was marking up Blue Wolf's chest and arms with magical symbols, taking paint from a small clay jar. He stopped working on Blue Wolf and walked over to the captain. Dipping his fingers in the pot, and went to paint the captain's face.

"Whoa there, Rukwooru. I don't mean no disrespect, but I'm good."

The shaman said something in his language and tried again.

The captain slapped his hand back. "I said, no!"

Blue Wolf chuckled at the exchange between the two. "He says it will protect you from the witch. So, her magic will not fool you."

"Tell him I have my magic. They're called bullets."

Blue Wolf waved off an angry Rukwooru. "Come with me, Captain. I have a horse waiting, and he's as stubborn as you are."

When the captain turned around, he saw his smoky colored "bulldog" quarter horse. "I'll be damned…" He grabbed the muscled steed's muzzle. "You found Hellfire!"

"I thought it was a good surprise. Your saddle and tack are all still there, too. He was grazing not far from where we found you. He is as stubborn as a donkey, just like his owner."

"Thank you for saving my friend." The captain climbed into the saddle.

They had been riding for most of the day when they entered a canyon area. Four other Comanche warriors made the trip with them. Besides Blue Wolf, they were the bravest and most capable in the camp. The captain would often catch glimpses of shadowy figures watching them from the cliffside. Hellfire snorted and pulled his head to the side.

"Easy, boy… I seen 'em, too."

Blue Wolf cocked his head. "Apaches."

An arrow struck one of the four Comanche warriors with them through his right eye socket and out the back of his head causing his body to tremble for a brief moment, and fall to the ground. The horses stepped backwards and reared up.

Galloping over the horizon was at least a dozen Apache warriors.

"We got no choice, but to run!"

Blue Wolf snarled and slapped his reins.

The five of them rode through the narrowing ravine. They were sitting ducks in this arroyo, but death was certain out in the open.

Another arrow struck a Comanche rider. He tumbled off the back of his horse and into the giant tail of dust, and only a few seconds had passed, before the oncoming Apache trampled him.

"I thought you said Sam Colt was with us!" Blue Wolf said, as he turned and let loose two arrows. One found its mark, but the other missed.

The Apache war party attempted to flank them, but they managed to stay just ahead of them in the ravine.

They rounded a sharp turn but were greeted by a line of Apache warriors blocking their escape.

Captain Tomlinson pulled hard on his reins, which caused Hellfire to rear up on his hind legs and paw the sky.

Blue Wolf and the other two warriors spun their horses around, just as the war party that had been chasing them walled them in.

The fierce-looking lead Apache trotted out from the rest. He appeared fearless, and his deep-set eyes glinted like precious stones. He had a rifle in his hands with eagle feathers dangling from its barrel. "I am Eagle Runner, chief of my tribe. You are Blue Wolf, son of Reptile Man, and you know better than to travel in my lands," he said in fairly good Comanche, which the captain could make out a few bits here and there.

"I travel here because my people are being attacked by a powerful owl witch," Blue Wolf said. "My companion and I plan to find it and kill it. It speaks your language."

The Apache chief's eyes flared at the mention of this great evil. "I know what plagues your people."

"How?"

Many of the warriors began to grumble, and even though the captain could not understand everything they said, he could tell how frightened they were. That concerned him, because the Apache weren't scared of much.

"This person has given themselves to darkness for revenge, and in return can become an animal and cheat death."

"How we kill it?" the captain butted in, in broken Apache.

"Is this white man your slave? He speaks our tongue?"

"Never mind him…shut up!" Blue Wolf said. "He speaks even worse Comanche."

Eagle Runner trotted past Blue Wolf and up to the captain, then circled him.

"You ain't getting my horse if that's what you're thinking?"

"It is a fine horse, but I wasn't looking at it. I was looking at what is inside," he spoke in broken English, as he pointed at his stomach.

"What do my guts have to do with this?" he answered back, not truly understanding what he meant.

The man was amused. "Your guts are not your spirit, white man," the Apache chief said and placed his hand to his heart "That's the part of you that will decide if you will survive this fight. And that part of you is severed."

"As long as my trigger finger ain't broke," he said, with a smug grin. "I'll get on just fine."

Eagle Runner leaned into him. "You are brave, white man, but you need something else to destroy it. You need its human name given to them at birth. Say that before you try to kill it and it can be defeated."

"How the hell do we get that?"

"She was my wife." A look of sadness crept into the Apache chief's eyes. "Our two children were killed by Comanche raiders many moons ago. She blamed them, and me, for not saving them and fell into great despair. She turned to the dark owl god for vengeance. We rode here to find and kill her, but I couldn't bring myself to do it. I still love her, but she not only kills your people's children but also ours. Her soul will find no peace until she is freed from this curse. You do this for me, and I will let you live. Her name is Muna Nascha."

"I am sorry for your loss, Chief," Captain Tomlinson said. "Where do we find her?"

He reached into a pouch and produced a child's blood-stained shirt and handed it to him. "This belonged to my son. She will be drawn to it."

The captain took it and stuck it in his saddlebag.

"Go now, before I change my mind and kill you all." Eagle Runner whistled for the others to follow before he turned his horse and galloped away.

The sun was sinking behind the back of the craggy mountainous terrain, as the captain, Blue Wolf, and the two Comanche warriors—Laughing Horse and Tall Feather—exited the maze-like canyon into a field of trees and cacti. One of the trees was bent down oddly as if made to grow that way. Captain Tomlinson knew it to be a "marker tree," bent that way as a sapling by Comanche and Apache of the area so that it would grow crooked. He knew that Blue Wolf understood this as well.

"We should camp here and when this witch shows up, we crawfish back into the canyon, and hopefully it will follow us. That's where we kill it," the captain said.

"I agree." Blue Wolf was about to dismount when they heard a female screaming not far from them.

They rode out to find a young Comanche woman, half dead and trying to bleed a cactus for a little bit of moisture.

"Na'ura?" Tall Feather said.

"You know her?"

"She went missing with her children weeks ago. We thought she was dead," Laughing Horse said.

Blue Wolf dismounted and went to her, gave her water. She collapsed into his arms.

He picked her up and took her back to the marker tree and made camp.

The night was cold, so they built a fire. Blue Wolf sat and worked on arrows in preparation for the witch.

The young Comanche woman opened her eyes a few hours later and began screaming for her children.

The captain went over to her and stroked her hair. "You're safe now, but you gotta calm down."

"Where are my babies? Did you find them?" "I'm sorry ma'am, but I don't understand what you're asking me."

Blue Wolf stood up. "She's asking if we found her children."

Captain Tomlinson lowered his head. "No, ma'am, we did not."

"You need to eat something," Blue Wolf told the grieving woman.

She shook her head. Tears poured down her face.

"I know you've been through a lot, but have you seen the owl witch?"

The woman just pointed to a nearby mesa.

"What's over there?" the Captain said.

"It took me to a cave. I woke up and she wasn't there, and neither were my children. I escaped and climbed down, and that's when you found me. I understood that it took her to a cave. So, you can take us to this cave?" the captain asked.

She nodded.

Blue Wolf gathered his gear and mounted his horse. "We go now." He lifted Na'ura up to his saddle, where she sat behind him.

"It will be nightfall by the time we get up there."

"Then we will fight it at night," Blue Wolf said, before letting out a whoop.

Tall Feather and Laughing Horse yelled a battle cry with him.

A rocky trail narrowed as they neared the top of the mesa. The sun had already ducked behind the horizon, and a half-moon moon surrounded by vibrant stars helped guide the way.

The captain glanced over the edge of the path, which was a sheer drop some one-hundred feet to the ground. Hellfire was as sure-footed as any horse, and his low and muscular build was perfect for this type of riding, but the ole bounty hunter wondered how they would fair if the owl witch attacked them here.

"Look!" Na'ura pointed to a small crack in the rock. "That is the entrance to its lair."

The captain slid off his Hellfire and tied him to the branch of a honey mesquite tree.

Blue Wolf did the same.

"You stay here and watch the horses and the girl," Blue Wolf told Tall Feather.

Captain Tomlinson pulled out a tinderbox and lit a small travel lantern he had with his belongings.

"I will protect her with my life," Tall Feather said.

The others entered the dark opening and followed a long tunnel that led to a large space. The inside of the cave was warm and strange images were painted on its walls. The floor was littered with bones and fragments of clothes.

Laughing Horse bent over and inspected the debris. "Children's dresses and shirts."

"This place is bad medicine," Blue Wolf said.

"Let's just kill this damn thing and get out of here. It gives me the willies."

They arrived at a larger room, which contained even more human remains, along with clay pots and a bed of animal furs. There were makeshift stone altars stained with blood. Piles of tiny moccasins surrounded it, but there was no sign of the owl witch.

"Listen… What's that noise?" The captain went over to the pile of animal furs and lifted them to discover a hole in the ground. Several Comanche and Apache children were inside. "Well, would you looky hear. You're going to be okay. Just stay quiet for Uncle Sidacious."

All the little ones nodded.

"Dammit, I forgot the bloody shirt," Captain Tomlinson said.

A female screamed outside.

"Na'ura?" Blue Wolf said.

They all hurried back through toward the entrance.

Once outside, they saw the dismembered body of Tall Feather. Na'ura was on her knees, facing away from them. She was holding something in her hands and still screaming.

Blue Wolf started to run to her, but the captain stopped him. "Don't, something isn't right."

"Na'ura!" Blue Wolf broke away from him.

"Where did you get this!" She held up the bloody shirt.

Blue Wolf stopped and nocked an arrow. When she stood and raised her hands, they no longer looked human. No, now they looked more like bloody talons.

"You can take the shape of anybody? That's a pretty neat trick," the captain said.

She cackled. Dark feathery wings sprouted from her shoulder blades. Her bones cracked and moved into new shapes. "I'm going to eat your hearts and rip your limbs off one by one."

"Well, like my ole friend John Coffee Hays used to say, 'don't let nothing but fear stop you.'" The captain pulled his revolver and started shooting.

She rose up in the air and whirled around. Her eyes glowing red, and she dove at the ex-Texas Ranger. Smoke and gun blasts filled the air.

Laughing Horse shot arrows, but he was brushed off the cliffside by one of the creature's wings.

The owl witch tackled the captain, knocking him to the ground. With one quick swipe, her claws cut the side of his face.

Blue Wolf let out a battle cry, and let loose a succession of arrows at the witch, hitting her in the wing and thigh.

Captain Tomlinson got to his feet. "This is over. We know that your name is Muna Nascha! Your children wouldn't want this."

She let out a terrible screech as if the very mention of her name was a knife stabbing her in the heart. "Do not speak of my children! They were taken from me, and now I will take others. I will soak the ground of this land in blood!"

"Muna Nascha!" he said again. And again, she screamed in pain.

"She's weakened! Fire!" The captain glanced at Blue Wolf, then they both attacked.

Their arrows and bullets wounded her, and she fell from the sky, writhing in pain.

The captain walked up to the owl witch, ready to finish it, but he didn't need to. She was already dead, having reverted to her human form right before his eyes. "It's over," Blue Wolf said, and took her body, along with the bloody shirt, and set them on fire.

Captain Tomlinson removed his hat and lowered his head.

The children emerged from the cave as the smoke from her burning body rose up and over the canyon. Her spirit was purified from the spell of hate and revenge.

The captain climbed into the saddle atop Hellfire.

"Where will you ride to?" Blue Wolf asked

"First, I'm going to head to Santa Fe for a drink of whiskey and a soft bed for a few days, and to see if I can get some work."

"You are a good warrior, the one they call The Devil's Right Hand, but maybe I'll kill you next time I see you and take your horse," he said, as he stroked Hellfire on the muzzle.

"Don't make any promises you can't keep." And with that, the captain rode off into the rising sun.

ADA

by Lana Elizabeth Gabris

When I was thirteen, my step-brother—three years older—started to take me hunting. After his pa died, this was common, and ma appreciated anything we could bring to the table. Merle was already filling his pa's shoes, and in Mama's eyes, he could do no wrong. I knew better than to speak of the late nights.

We'd go on foot to where our creek came out from under the mountain and to where Merle hid his "treasures". Things like necklaces, knives and even an engraved wedding band he'd scavenged from deserted goods discarded throughout the woods as earlier settlers tried to beat the snows, or gave up their hope to find fortune.

Our family was one of the few who had stayed after the Indians, disease, and misery swept through the scattered settlement. Now with the nearby gold rush, new blood was settling in, though it was still a good day's ride to Mama's closest friends. Merle always swore he'd never leave 'cept draped over the back of a horse, and sometimes late at night, *I'd wish for it*.

"Someone's been here." He was on his knees, staring into the moss, his pa's army revolver tucked into the back of his pants. His hair, wild and tangled, straggled out from under the bowler he insisted on wearing.

I sighed and cringed at the glare he shot over his shoulder. His light eyes narrowed, and I shook my head. "I didn't tell no one!" I was always defending something I'd never done. "'Sides, who'd I tell?"

Beyond Mama's friends, it was another day's ride to Fayville. Merle snorted and smiled, gently reaching a hand out, motioning me forward. When I hesitated, he grabbed my wrist and twisted it, still smiling. "Remember that," he whispered.

I nodded, gasping as his fingers dug harder before letting go and hunching back down over the rock pile. Behind it, hidden, was the short tunnel into a low cave I hadn't dared enter for fear of Merle's warnings.

Merle stood, scratching himself and stretched, pausing, his arms high in the air at the sound of a faint whistle. He cocked his head, then stuck two dirty fingers in his mouth and blew. A moment later, two sharp whistles answered, and he grinned.

"All right! Myers is back!" He laughed to himself and hurried ahead of me back to the deer trail following the creek.

Myers was Merle's uncle, and three or four times a year, he brought us chickens or a pig. Once, he brought us a cow from the ranch he ramrodded nearby. She'd had a festering leg wound that Mama poulticed for nigh on a week before it healed enough for the cow to walk again. She still limped around the yard, her brown cow eyes always watching.

I followed slowly, not really caring for the all-night visit that was sure to come and was met by Linc, a one-eyed cur who had refused to be chased away and had become part of our "stock." He hobbled toward me, dragging his game leg, and grunting. Petting him, I pushed his nose away and was almost home before I remembered the fish trap.

Ambling back to the pool, my eyes were on Mama's worn boots until I had to crawl under thick branches to reach the line, peering into the water, hoping I wouldn't have to haul out another fish. I had broken my knife a week back and was tired of the jagged blade slipping on the flesh. Seeing nothing trapped, I relaxed, then jumped at the sound of rocks rolling across the water. I looked over, ready to flee and froze.

Across the ten feet or so of creek knelt a man, drinking beside his horse. I shifted back quickly under the heavy brush and was lucky; the man's head was bent, and he hadn't seen or heard me. Crouched under the junipers, I watched, marveling for I had never seen such a man in my life.

He was clean-shaven; even under the layer of trail dust. Years later, I would learn he was a *vaquero*—the true cowboy. A wide-brimmed dark hat lay on the ground beside him. His pants, black, now dusted—gray, flared over worn boots and matched his chaqueta—or jacket—folded neatly under his sombrero. He rolled up his sleeves and unbuttoned his vest, splashing water over his face, and tipped his head back, eyes closed.

The horse nuzzled him gently on his shoulder. It was a creature like I had never seen before, a deep-chested buckskin with a broad forehead over a narrow nose, tail long and flowing over its striped hocks. I'd never seen a horse with markings like that—though Mama had a heavy book with hard-to-believe animals, and in it was a horse-like creature in a foreign country that was white with black stripes. Or maybe it was black with white stripes.

I got a good look at the man's deep brown eyes, neatly trimmed dark hair, and a smile lined with weariness, puzzled as he touched each shoulder and kissed his fist before shrugging into his jacket. Briefly, his fingers rolled over a gold cross around his neck, then slapped his hat against his leg before standing to check the girth. The worn saddle had been beautifully tooled and rested over a brightly colored blanket, the bridle braided with black leather. He swung gracefully into the saddle without using the stirrups, the horse whickering. For a heartbeat, they paused, and I held my breath as he glanced to where I was hiding.

I blinked and he was gone.

Later, walking alone on the path, I repeated his motions wondering and hoping I'd see him just once more.

Myers' horse was wandering the yard when I dragged my feet past the woodpile. I could hear his gravelly laugh from inside and peeked through the narrow window by the stove. He was standing behind Mama, his arm over her waist. She was laughing silently, her head thrown back against his shoulder. I turned away, and Merle came out from the barn, a sack half full of grain dangling from his shoulder.

"Mama's been waiting on you, Ada." He smirked and smacked his lips at the horse. After a moment of glaring at him, I went into the cabin.

"Ada honey, where've yah been?" Myers let go of Mama long enough to squeeze me against his gun belt and look me over. I squirmed out of his grasp.

"Lord a'mighty, Gracie, it's about time you find her husband." He chuckled, and I rolled my eyes.

Mama gave me gentle smile, running her hand over my hair. I leaned into to it. It had been so long since she smiled like that. Why couldn't I make her smile like that?

"Why Myers? So's she'll end up like me?" Just like that Mama left me. "Waiting for meals to come on the backs of favors?" She laughed her empty cold breath.

I began to set the table, my stomach starting to roll.

Myers snorted and slumped into a chair, snagging Mama's waist as she passed by. "Don't get started," he murmured. "I ain't got no fight in me for that tonight…"

She pushed his arm away. "We eat first." She snatched the still boiling coffee from the woodstove. "Go get Merle, Ada."

That night I crept from our room, leaving Merle snoring on his side. I tramped across the yard to the barn, climbed up into the loft, and sat alone on a lumpy blanket to stare up into the starry sky. I held my breath when the door of the cabin opened. Hearing heavy footsteps approach the far side of the wall, I let out a deep breath as Myers belched and relieved himself on the wood, muttering to himself.

After he returned to the house, I let my legs dangle through the dark manger, wondering if I fell, would I die? Or would I disappear into nothingness? Maybe, if I stretched my arms out wide, I'd fly…

I swallowed and crawled to the corner of the barn, retrieving the ring I had stolen from Merle's stash in his room, turning it over my fingers, tipping it into the moonlight. *FR from TW always'* had been perfectly inscribed on the inside of the band. It was too big even for my thumb, but I slipped it onto my finger fancying I was the mysterious *FR*.

The next morning Myers got us up even earlier than Mama usually did. He took *his* place at the head of the table, choking down the bacon he'd brought us and regaling Merle with tales of wild adventures. He even had Mama laughing, when his name was shouted from outside. Myers hand dropped to his holster before he laughed, hand relaxing.

"It's my newest puncher. You should see this *greaser*, Gracie. He's got a rig like you wouldn't believe, but a'mighty the Mex' can ride."

Merle snorted, but we trooped faithfully outside to meet Benigno Alvaro, *my* riverside stranger. He bowed to Mama and me, and shook Merle's hand before telling Myers that some of the miners had requested to see him. "They say they want to make a deal and have the cattle brought right into town." He spoke with the soft rolls of foreign language, and I drank it in.

Myers found the news amusing, laughing and asking Merle to get his horse.

Benigno remounted as smoothly as yesterday, tipping his hat to me and Mama before turning his horse, then sidestepped the animal to where Merle and Myers were standing.

Myers mounted and rode back before Mama. "I guess I'll be back tonight, Gracie." He turned in the saddle, looking to Merle. "You comin', boy, or what?"

Merle glanced at Mama, not really asking for her say-so. She shrugged, and he raced to bridle the ol' knock-kneed gray, following the two men bareback. Mama watched until they were gone, then stood staring after where'd they'd disappeared.

"Mama?" She turned the third time I called her and smiled sadly.

"Ada." She cupped my cheeks, and I felt tears welling up. "Ada…" she whispered my name and sighed. "It's been a while since it was just us." She hugged me, then shuffled back into the cabin.

I blinked back the loneliness, knowing she had it worse, then went to the barn. The chickens didn't care either.

Later, I walked to the creek to pick mushrooms and again found myself wondering what was beyond the trees. Before Mama met Merle's pa, we'd lived with her sister and Mama had taught school. But it was so long ago, I could only fancy I remembered. We could read because of her, but what good did that do? There was nothing out here to read but the Bible and Mama's animal book. I wondered if my aunt thought of us. We'd sent letters but it took so long for mail to go back and forth, I'd given up on finding out if anyone was still out there. Maybe the world had been swallowed up and we were all that was left.

Poking at rotten leaves, hoping for the bright orange mushrooms Mama favored and halfheartedly looked around. Fighting a yawn, I sat under a tree and let my eyes close.

I shifted onto a tree root and woke with a start. Wrapped around me was a brightly colored poncho. I stared at it for a moment before lifting my eyes. A small fire was being fed by *my* stranger.

He looked over, his eyes shining. "It is cold sometimes, on the ground." He stepped toward me, knelt, and held out a cup. In it, blueberries and leaves had been boiled into a thick broth.

I held it, grateful for something to do with my hands.

"You should not be here alone," he scolded, but he was smiling with his eyes. They were lighter up close, almost golden.

"I come all the time." Sipping at the tea, I drew my knees up under the poncho.

He shook his head. "It is not safe. I heard stories of…" he hesitated. "Of people losing their way around here."

I shook my head, "They're just stories. Lots of people leave over the horizon and never come back." Pa. *My* pa, not Merle's pa, had done just that. He'd left one day and was gone, gulped down by whatever was over the distant range.

Benigno frowned. "You are too young for such thoughts." He looked around. "You should not be around without a chaperone." At *my* frown, he smiled. "You are a young lady. Young ladies alone, is not good…"

I shrugged and handed him back the now empty mug. "Thank you."

His eyes fell on my wrist, and I thrust it under the poncho, hiding the ugly bruise. Benigno looked into the fire and rested on his heels. He touched his shoulders again and curious, I ventured to ask. "Why?"

Benigno echoed my question, then looked quizzically at his hand, watching me repeat his motions. "That is my way of showing God I ask for his love, guidance," He winked. "And occasionally for forgiveness."

I rubbed at my wrist, hidden under the wool. "Do you think he really listens?" *I had pleaded so many times for Mama and me.*

He gazed into the fire for so long, I'd thought he'd forgotten me and the forest around us. I jumped when he finally answered.

"I believe he listens, but we set his words, his teachings into motion." He looked back at me, his eyes deep. "He knows."

I looked away. After a moment, Benigno began to put the fire out.

"Can I go with you?" I blurted the words before I knew I had them on my tongue.

Benigno's hands froze, and he shook his head.

"I could…do things for you…" I couldn't say the words.

He gave me a long hard look. "Don't!" He almost snapped the words. "Don't ever feel that way, and never say that to any man." He nodded slowly. "You will leave here—I know you will—but I can't..." He shook his head.

I couldn't stop the steady stream of tears, so I let them fall.

Beningo sat for a moment then reached a steady hand out, resting it on my hair.

"I thought..." I stammered. "I thought maybe He sent you to help me..." I wasn't sure if I meant Pa or Him, up above.

Benigno laughed, tugging gently on my hair. He whispered, "Oh, *querida*, my dear, I cannot even help myself."

I sniffled and looked up at him. He handed me a kerchief, and I wiped my eyes.

"You must have faith," he dropped his hand, looking away. "I still believe..."

"Did you leave home?"

Benigno shook his head and shrugged one shoulder. "I had no home to leave."

"Maybe it's there now." I rested my cheek against the wet cloth.

"No...after the war there was nothing." He took a deep breath. "But that is not for your pain." He gave a short nod. "I still have faith, as should you. But I am not the one. Not now."

Benigno stood. "I must leave. I was searching for a lost *becerro* and instead of the calf, I found you, *paloma*." He tucked the mug back into his saddlebags, searching for the word, "Dove, a little dove."

I handed him his poncho with thanks.

He mounted his horse and stood quietly for a moment, looking into the trees. I stood beside them wanting to beg, but just looked up at him.

"*Querida*..." he murmured, and reached for the cross he wore. "Here, I want you have this."

I gaped at him, and he leaned over, dropping it over my shoulders.

"*Recuerde, usted nunca están solo.*" At my twisted face he chuckled. "Remember, you are never alone."

He started to turn his horse, and I grabbed his ankle. "Wait!" I fumbled in my skirts and found the one thing I had of Pa's—part of a leather engraved watch fob I had sewn to a strip of longer, soft deer hide and made into a bracelet.

Benigo caressed it and looped it over his high saddle horn. He looked back down at me. "One day…algún día!"

I clutched the cross all the way home, surprised to find no one there, tucked the chain inside my boot, not minding it pressing against my ankle, and hurried about the cabin, opening a jar of venison and mixing it into a thick stew. It was bubbling nicely when Mama came home. She thanked me and gave me a small hug; more than she had offered in months. I squeezed her back.

"Ada, my little girl…" she whispered, and released me, disappearing into her room and leaving me with the stew.

Myers came shortly after Mama, with Merle and another man, a gaunt-faced miner named Cowley. They gobbled the stew, not asking where Mama was and left me to clean around them as Cowley dealt the first of many cards.

I knocked on Mama's door and was delighted when she beckoned from within. She was sitting on the edge of the bed reading a letter, the covers thrown back and the coal oil lamp turned as high as possible. She folded it neatly and slipped into the Bible before turning to me.

"Can I sleep with you?" I asked.

Mama blinked, and I regretted being so foolish and began to turn around. Her answer was soft, I almost missed it. "That'd be nice."

The men played cards until the moon ruled the morning, and Mama slept through it all. I laid awake most of the night. And when they began to tell stories, I perked my ears.

Myers talked the loudest. When he started to talk about the rumors, I rolled my eyes to myself, not really listening.

"Ty's beside himself. Say's there ain't no way his woman woulda' run off. You watch out, boy… You never know what kind of bastards are out there."

Ty Wylstra. I rolled onto my side, a hazy image of Mr. Wylstra and his mute wife, Freida, rolling around in my dreams. I started to drift off when my breath caught.

My eyes flew open, and I stared over at the split-log door. I didn't know Freida's mama's name, but Ty and Frieda matched the initials in my ring.

"I heard they found part of a skull near the flats—smashed to bits." Cowley shifted, his chair squeaking.

"Goddamn injuns'll murder us all…" Myers slurred.

Cowley and Merle swore with him.

Myers and Cowley were long gone the next morning. I hurriedly fed the chickens, my heart racing. Merle was chopping wood, and for a moment—when the axe split a block with a snap—my breath caught, imagining a blood-splattered skull.

We ate breakfast in silence. Mama didn't leave her chair, just stared into her coffee.

Merle declared he was tired of the slop we were forcing down his gullet. "I'm after bigger game." He loaded the black powder and stormed out on foot, leaving me with the rest of the chores.

When I started to get what was left of the last batch of soap, Mama stopped me. "Take a day, Ada. Take today for yourself." She waved me away, still sitting at the table with a cold cup of coffee.

I fled the yard with glee, running along the creek until, without thinking of it, I ended up at the cave, ducking back into the bushes, trying to catch my breath. Needing to see for myself after a moment, I shimmied into the hole, stumbling and falling onto my knees. Forcing myself to move forward, I gagged at the foul air, pressing my back along the rocks until I was able to stand, my breathing rasping in my ears.

It was so dark. Darker than I had remembered. But the smell—there was nothing so dank as the smell. I tripped and fell, sending something clattering, and held my knees, too afraid to move. After I calmed down, I started to make out dark outlines of objects. After a few minutes of groping air and rock, I found the lantern and lit the wick.

I turned around and nearly dropped it, the metal digging into my palm. There were clothes everywhere: dresses, petticoats, shirts, pants, and hats, all stained with dark splatters and in haphazard piles. Pressing my hand against my mouth, I recognized Frieda's Sunday best—her only best. Backing away I stumbled, swinging the lantern around, I screamed at a bloodied hand reaching out from nothing.

"Find what you're looking for?" Behind me, Merle was waiting. In the lantern's light, his eyes were gleaming and his crooked teeth shone. "I'd hoped…" He sniffed, dropping the rabbit he was carrying and stepped across the cave, holding the army pistol in a loose grip. "I'd hoped we'd always be together…" He was talking through me, his gaze on something only he could see. His boot hit a stone, and he blinked, suddenly focusing on me. "Do you know what they did to my pa?" His voice was soft.

I shook my head. *His* pa been gone for too long.

"They cut his hand off. On the word of a whore, they cut his hand off before they hung 'em." He stared down at his own hand, clenching his fist.

"He was a thief," I whispered, always having known the truth.

Merle shook his head, "They let him bleed…let him suffer." He tipped his head up, "Well, I made them suffer too…" He stepped closer to me, his face changing into something unrecognizable, and he raised the gun. "I did this for us; you can't leave me. I know what Ma's up to…" He reached a hand out.

I screamed, dropping the lantern, and he the revolver. The latter blasted throughout the darkness.

I don't know how I found my way out of the cave. Kicking and screaming, somehow I made it out of the stench running the five miles home without stopping, feeling Merle close behind. I ran past the carriage in front of the barn and nearly knocked Mama over with the door.

"Ada…" She caught my shoulders and turned me around to an older version of herself and a tall, gaunt man. "Do you remember your Aunt Arnette?"

And just like that I was gone—past the trees and beyond the dying settlement. Turned out Mama had been waiting nigh on four months for Aunt Arnette to come take me. The letter the night before had told Mama when to expect her.

Mama told me before I left that she was afraid to tell me for fear I might want to stay. When I'd looked at her, not understanding, she only smiled and squeezed my arms.

I never told her about Merle—about anything. I didn't have to. Merle didn't follow me, he couldn't. When Myers and Cowley found him, he was dying from a gunshot wound to his face. Having followed me from the cave, he'd been found in the creek. He couldn't speak and passed before Mama or I could even want to try to get to him.

For her…for Mama, I hid the secret of the cave.

The last word I had from Mama was a year back. It was a simple note in her perfect pen.

A month later, Myers found her in the barn, gone by her own hand, the animal book and Bible wrapped in my quilt with Mama's wedding ring. Myers had a neighbor send her belongings to me. Everything she had fit into a small drawer at my aunt's.

As for me, Aunt Arnette fancies me marrying the blacksmith's son. I could settle for worse, I suppose. But as I stood on the boardwalk, waiting for Uncle to meet us for a real restaurant lunch, still a wonder to me after these years, my eyes were drawn to a buckskin with black rigging tied four horses away, its dark stripes dusty. My hand reached to finger at the cross I wore faithfully against my heart, a smile passing my lips as I thought back to the drawings in Mama's book.

The horse shifted, shaking its head, sending a smooth band of leather looped around the saddle horn swinging. My breath caught as its rider swung smoothly into the saddle and turned.

Hoy.

HANDS

by Joel McKay

John Hawes didn't know what they were, but he knew he had to kill them. It was the only thing on his mind as he thumbed the .44 calibre cartridges into his Winchester repeater. His grandpa used to say that life was real simple, and most men screwed it up when they made things too complicated. There are only two times in life, he would say, time for thinking and time for doing. Well, if Grandpa were still alive, he would be saying to John the clock had run out on the former and taken with it every ounce of give-a-shit he had left in him. And that only left one thing.

He levered a cartridge into the chamber and sucked in a breath, suppressing a hacking cough as the chill late winter breeze reached deep into his lungs. It was a painful reminder of the black work he'd carried out when he torched the farmhouse and barn. But he had to do it. It was the only way he could be sure that he'd killed them all, and even then, he'd known that at least one had gotten away. They were fast. Quiet too, like an arachnid slipping through the grass toward its prey. And dangerous. He had to seize the advantage wherever he could.

The greasy black smoke from the burning homestead had singed his lungs, but he knew he had to ignore the pain and supress the cough—any sound might give away his location. The element of surprise was his only advantage, and he did not intend to give it up. He muffled the noise with his hand, and when it was safe to breathe again, exhaled slowly and leaned his head against the overturned birch log behind him to gain a moment's respite. Rifle cradled in his lap, legs outstretched, he listened.

A delicate snap of a branch to his left drew his eyes. The sharp crack of his rifle answered it a moment later. There was a heavy thud. He climbed to his feet, ignoring the screaming pain in his legs, stifled a cough and ambled through the maze of naked trees toward his victim.

She lay in a small hollow beneath a copse of gnarled scrub oak, her body splayed across a horn of rock that jutted through the carpet of brown leaves and dead branches that littered the forest floor. The round had taken her in the chest. She made a sucking gurgling noise each time she drew a ragged breath. Her face lolled toward him as he stepped close.

"Dad…daddy… How could you?" she pleaded, as a cold tear streamed from the corner of her eye.

His knees buckled, and he dropped the rifle beside her. Panic swept through him, and for a moment, it felt as if all the blood had drained from his body, leaving only a weathered old statue as papery and still as the lonely birch trees he knelt between as he looked over the dying body of his daughter. She opened her mouth, but there was only the wet sound of fluid pumping out of her.

No, he screamed inwardly, it cannot be. Not again.

"Marlee, Marlee." New tears streamed down his face. He scooped her into his arms, the pine needles beneath her pricking his skin. "It can't be… I can't keep doing…"

The gurgling stopped, and her body went limp.

He held her, sobbing, burying his oily, matted hair in her chest. The forest grew silent except for his quiet whimper as John Hawes' heart shattered again. A frigid wind scraped over his neck and rattled the naked branches of the oak above him as his daughter—the one he'd seen die thrice over—grew rigid in his arms.

Not again. No. Please not again.

Marlee's pale face twisted toward him, and her eyes opened. She seemed to smile for a moment before her pale blue irises sucked into her head, leaving two black holes from which a pair of dirty hands leapt forward and scratched at his face. The fingers were thick and strong, and carried the fetid smell of old mushrooms.

He let go of her body with a yell, but the hands kept hold of his face, fingertips gouging into his eyes, nostrils, and mouth. He tore himself away and fell into the bed of pine needles, frantically searching for the rifle. His fist closed around a rock instead. When the hands from his daughter's skull reached for him again, he swatted them away. They reached again, and he hit back. Again. And again, until he leaned over the pulpy, unmoving remains of…something. He was not sure what it was, but after he cleared the red muck from his eyes, he was sure it wasn't Marlee. It never had been.

A frenzy of grief, fear, and rage filled him, as if his blood were on fire and burning his skin from the inside out. He climbed unsteadily to his feet. The forest heaved another ragged breath, the old oak twisting violently in the low evening light. He found the rifle and levered another cartridge into the chamber. At his feet was a fleshy mound made entirely of hands, dozens of them—men and women's hands, black hands, white hands, children's hands, hairy hands, and hands with dirty fingernails. It was something that just days ago would have seemed entirely impossible, a sight that left him feeling as if his eyes were playing a trick on him, or that his mind was teetering on the edge of sanity, threatening to tumble into an abyss. A *thing* made of hands.

He looked at it, probably for too long. A blackened, bloody finger crooked, beckoning him. He aimed the Winchester and pulled the trigger. Levered and fired again. The report from the rifle echoed through the sparse, windswept forest of birch, oak, and witch grass and was answered a moment later by a rolling thunderhead to the east.

He left the monstrosity on its bed of rock and limped out of the hollow to a short ridge that rose over a wide, dusty valley below. The single-street town of Dry Gulch lay far below, the sad, muddy ribbon of the Dunwich River twisting its way through the hills toward it like a worm. The evening light was dimming as the sun dropped into the horizon in the west, while behind him a shadow grew across the land as a storm mounted and pushed its way toward one of the few isolated settlements in the near-deserted high plains of the west.

John Hawes had a decision to make. One path led south where he could put all this behind him, or he could keep going. Maybe he would survive. Maybe he could move on and start a new life away from this place. It was wishful thinking, the kind of thing his grandpa would've called a flight of fancy. Fact was, that's not how things worked out for John. If there was luck in this world, he wasn't the one with it. He had watched his only daughter Marlee die three times this past week. Once from scarlet fever, twice from the *things*. He figured he had suffered enough to call it quits and not feel bad about it, if he wanted. But it did not feel right to turn his back on the town, even if he'd never had much time for the people there. But he figured if he went south something worse would happen than whatever awaited him in Dry Gulch, so he decided it was best to keep on heading in the direction he'd set out on. Maybe he'd get there before *they* did.

He set off down the hill toward Dry Gulch at a limping pace, rifle held loosely at his side. He did not even feel wholly like a man anymore, just a thing that kept putting one foot in front of another. A pissed-off thing that had decided it was time for doing, and that doing involved his Winchester. His legs screamed in agony from where other hands and fingers had clawed and torn at his flesh back at the homestead. He didn't mind so much. The pain reminded him *they* hadn't got him yet.

A storm beat him to Dry Gulch by a mile or so, forcing John to limp through a pounding rain that turned the parched plain into a soupy mess. He had watched a wagon hauling goods heading to town from the southeast since he had gotten down to the flat but didn't catch up to it until long past dark when it was forced to stop as one of its wheels became rutted in a pool of muck. The driver, who wore a heavy slicker and a black open crown hat, was hunched over the wheel swearing and snorting like a charged-up bull when John limped out of the mist, rifle in hand to ask what was the matter.

A thin weathered face swiveled toward him, rain pouring off the brim of the man's hat in thick streams. He fixed John with a look that suggested he was a heartbeat away from pulling his gun.

"This whole goddamn en'erprise, is the matter," the driver said, his voice high-pitched and raw like a mallet run over a steel washboard. He wiped the water from his heavy, gray horseshoe moustache and narrowed his eyes. "You look like hell brought in on a stack of shit, friend."

John could not help but grin at that. It made his face hurt. Everything hurt. He cradled the gun in his arms so the muzzle pointed up and away to show he was no threat, spit, and said, "Could say that, and it'd be an understatement."

The driver nodded. "Help me with this wheel and I'll give you a lift into town, such as it is." He waved derisively at the short stack of clapboard buildings that accounted for Dry Gulch.

John positioned himself behind the wheel, still cradling the rifle in his hands. He guessed the driver was who he said he was, but a man cannot be too careful. The driver ambled onto the wagon and snapped the reins. Horses whinnied, and John pushed. Rain pounded down on him while he threw his full weight into the wheel, waiting for something to happen. Eventually, the muck gave way with a wet slurping sound, and the wagon lurched forward. John fell on his face in the mud, the rifle smacking into the puddle next to him.

The driver hopped down and pulled it out of the puddle. John felt a surge of panic run through him as the stranger stood behind him, rifle in hand. Images of his daughter's dying face flashed through his mind, followed by fingers…hundreds of writhing, fleshy fingers reaching toward him. He spun around. The driver handed him the rifle.

"Might want to unload and dry it out," the man said. "I tried firing one of those wet once and nearly lost my hand."

Hand. Fingers. John shuddered, but nodded quietly and took the rifle.

The driver rubbed the water from his moustache again and motioned for John to climb aboard the wagon with him. He snapped the reins, and the horses resumed their steady canter toward town.

"God awful night, this," the driver said. "What's your name?"

"John Hawes," he answered, staring straight ahead, fingers clutching his weapon.

"Well, John Hawes, I'm Roger Flaherty. Folks call me Rook."

"Nice to meet you, Rook."

"What the hell are you doing out here alone on a night like this?" Rook asked, his deep-set eyes passing over John's wounded legs.

John was never any good at lying. When he was a kid, his momma had told him he was probably smart enough to do just about anything in life, but his penchant for honesty probably meant he shouldn't bother with politics, the law, or selling things. That said, he was not a man of many words either.

"Hunting," he answered, after a minute.

Rook grunted at that. "Not a night I'd pick to be out hunting, but I ain't from around here, neither, so not my place to offer comment. My roadie done and buggered off with some red-haired thing, so I'm filling in on this run. Never been to Dry Gulch before. Anything I should know?"

"It's a town," John said.

Rook let out a belly laugh and slapped his knee, water splashing off his slicker onto John's wounded legs. He winced.

"Not a talker, eh? Fine, I can respect that. Well, judging by the number of buildings, I wouldn't rightly describe this here fine settlement as a burgeoning metropolis. But so long as there's a warm fire and fiery drink, I suppose it'll suffice."

"What're you selling?" John asked, suddenly interested in the man's reasons to come up this far into the high plains.

"Not selling, just delivering," Rook said. "Dry goods, mostly. Though

I suppose there ain't much left back there that's dry. Goddamn weather."

The wagon rattled into town as another thunderclap shattered the sky overhead. John was soaked through and fighting off a chill. The good news was his legs were so cold and tired, he hardly felt any pain at all. Though he worried that as soon as he found a place to sit, he might never get up again.

Dry Gulch was not any more impressive up close than it was from afar. John had actively avoided the place for years on account of the welcome he had received when he first started coming down from the homestead for supplies. The place was insular, as most small towns out west were, but to the point where three families accounted for most of the population. The rest of the folk were drifters, seasonal ranch hands, or men who'd taken a wrong turn on their way somewhere else.

Rook found a stable across from a quiet saloon where a hollow-cheeked boy unharnessed the horses and led them into a shadowy cavern of empty stalls. To John, the barn came alive as the horses were led into its mouth, its loose weathered boards like crooked teeth waiting to chew on the animals. The hay loft's open windows were like hollow black eyes, sucking the night into a fathomless darkness. He shuddered and shook his head, wiping the rain and exhaustion from his eyes. And the barn was just a barn again.

The cold rain beat a steady tattoo against the tired buildings around him.

"You okay?" Rook asked him.

"Let's get a drink," John answered, motioning to the saloon across the way, rifle in hand.

Inside they found half a dozen circular tables and a dull oak bar that stretched along the wall perpendicular to the front door. The bartender leaned over the wood, head resting on one hand, a sleepy look on his face as he scanned an old periodical. There were two other patrons—a cowboy at the bar shovelling food soaked in a thick gravy into his mouth, and an old man in a bowler hat and three-piece suit dozing at a table in front of a half-empty glass of whisky. At the back of the room was a piano, benchless and dusty with disuse. The place smelled musty, like old books and even older wood.

John Hawes decided he had not been missing much by avoiding Dry Gulch these past years.

Rook went to the bar and ordered a couple of drinks while John found a table near the fireplace, which was smoldering enough to begin thawing out his legs. He took off his soaking jacket and hung it over the chair next to him and proceeded to empty each cartridge from the Winchester onto the table.

The old man with the bowler hat perked up at the sound of each brass round tumbling onto the table. He eyed John wearily, considered his glass of whisky, and then sat back and pulled his hat down over his eyes.

Rook fell into the chair across from him, his back to the front door. He slid a short glass with amber liquid toward John. "Bottoms up." He toasted, then knocked the drink back.

John offered a half smile but did not take the drink, instead focusing on wiping the water from the Winchester with the driest bit of clothing he could find, the sleeve of his shirt.

Rook's eyes passed over the dark red stains on his clothing. "I don't mean to pry, but what the hell are you hunting, anyway?"

Truth was, John was not much of a hunter. In fact, he was not really a farmer or a rancher, either. He was a city boy from a poor family with a lot of virtues but few dollars. His prospects were grim before he met his wife, a country girl whose parents had built the homestead out west. She had convinced him to move out there with them and look after it while she tended to her parents' ailing health. Then Marlee had come along. Times were good for a long while, and he learned a thing or two from his father-in-law about homesteading, maintaining a house, and growing food. Enough that when the in-laws died, he could look after his family.

But his in-laws were not welcome in Dry Gulch owing to their pedigree, which John was clueless about as no one ever bothered to define exactly what that pedigree was, small towns and dusty places being what they were. Yet that pedigree seemed to extend to John and Marlee as well. So, they kept to themselves. When his wife grew ill, he found the doctor would not lift a finger, and she passed. He grew bitter over that, but at least he had Marlee. When she got the fever, he tried again, but the doctor said she was beyond help and that even if she had not been, his supplies were low. John distinctly remembered the doctor's shelves were filled with tonics and cure-alls, not that he could read any of the labels. But he kept his opinion to himself and trudged back to the homestead to care for Marlee alone. Three days and nights he spent at her bedside, trying to cool her fever and keep liquids in her. She passed on a Tuesday, just before sunup. He buried her next to the others in a small corner of the yard near a windswept picket fence.

It was another day before they came back. John was inside nursing a bottle, trying to decide whether it was worth carrying on at the homestead when his mother-in-law stumbled through the front door. She looked well, her skin full of colour. She came toward him for a loving embrace.

John Hawes had never been a violent man, but his primal instincts were set ablaze the moment she shambled into the family room. She looked, felt, and sounded normal, but she was dead. And something awoke in John that took control of his body—some ancestral knowledge hidden deep within him that knew what this danger was even though his eyes saw nothing more than an elderly woman.

He killed her first—beat her to death with a mostly empty bottle of whisky that was little more than blood-stained shards by the time he was done. His father-in-law was next. He used his brawn for that, impaling the old man on a picket. Then his wife, with the Winchester, and Marlee too.

Each time their bodies dissolved into fleshy mounds of hands, fingers flicking like hairs on a dog's back billowing in the wind. He burned the hands. But the next day his family came back, and he murdered them again, his heart nearly bursting from grief as he sunk the backside of a claw hammer into his daughter's skull. Again, he burned the mounds, and this time the homestead too—a great tower of black smoke that climbed above the high, wintry plain like some ancient signal.

That evening they didn't come back, but as the prairie sky deepened to a dusky purple, he saw the silhouette of movement flicking away to the western horizon. Whatever *they* were, he had not killed *them* yet. Perhaps *they* couldn't be killed, but John Hawes was just stubborn enough not to care.

"Eh partner?" Rook piped up, "I asked what you was hunting."

John loaded the now-dry cartridges back into the rifle. He reached for one, but his shaky hands caused it to tumble away on the floor, where it rolled beneath the chair of the bowler hat man a table away.

"Hands," was all he said, as he limped toward the wayward round, rifle in hand.

Bowler Hat was fast asleep in his chair, so John tried to reach under the chair without disturbing him. His back and right leg seized up as soon as he bent over, and with a cry of pain, he hit the floor next to the sleeping man like a sack of dirt. The .44 calibre round skittered away as Bowler Hat leapt awake, the hat tumbling off his head and onto John.

"Wha— What is…?" Bowler Hat started.

"Sorry," John said, climbing to his feet.

He went to hand the hat back when something caught his eye—a flash of movement beneath the man's bare scalp, like a vein protruding under pressure. He dropped the hat on the man's lap and tightened his grip on the rifle.

"What the hell are you looking at?" Bowler Hat said, his bald pate red and smooth beneath the flickering kerosene light.

The flesh rippled, and John watched as what looked like a hand floated across the man's skull beneath the skin, vanishing as quickly as it came. He didn't hesitate, levering a cartridge into the chamber and pressing the muzzle against Bowler Hat's scalp in one fluid motion. The trigger snapped, and Bowler Hat's head exploded in a spray of blood and bone that painted the table and wall red as the gunshot rang out through the saloon like a canon. The body slumped over, and the chair went with it.

Rook's chair scraped against the hardwood, but the sound was muffled as John's ears rang from the percussive blast. There was a shout from the bar behind him.

"He's crazy," Rook yelled, getting to his feet and backing against the wall. "You're crazy. Get that gun from him."

John waited for the hands to climb out of Bowler Hat's corpse as it drooled syrupy blood on the floor, but nothing happened. His stomach roiled, and his skin became gooseflesh as panic surged through his body. His vision blurred, and images of murder flashed through his mind. The muscles in his right arm grew tired at the memory of smashing a broken whisky bottle against his mother-in-law's head. He could feel the weight of his father-in-law's body as he impaled it on the weathered picket fence. The claw hammer in Marlee's skull. Her death, again and again. The wheezing sound of her last breath.

A tear down her cheek. *Dad…daddy… How could you?*

And each time he'd done it alone. Seen *them* alone.

His mind teetered on the brink of madness as he waited for Bowler Hat's flesh to ripple, for a sign that he hadn't already tumbled into that fathomless abyss. But the saloon was quiet save the bartender's yell to seize John's gun, and the cowboy's heavy footsteps closing in behind him. But there was nothing more except the ringing in his ears and the deafening realization that he had been wrong.

His chin quivered with emotion, and he could feel the gorge in his stomach rise into his throat. His fingers slackened on the rifle.

Then Rook said, "Oh, good God… What is that?"

John turned toward him and followed his eyes up to the ceiling where dozens of disembodied hands poured out of a hole in the ceiling, skittering across the plaster walls toward the floor as if from a nest. His nose filled with the damp odour of mushrooms.

Bowler Hat's headless corpse began to gyrate, his flesh rippling and splitting at John's feet, revealing a gigantic fleshy mass of hairy fingers bathed in blood, sinew, and bone shard that reached drowsily toward his boots.

Rook pinned himself against the wall, unmoving, his eyes like saucers.

John's stomach settled as a sudden calm washed through him. He was not a madman, he thought with relief, just a dead man. But the time for thinking about it was over.

"Run!" he yelled at Rook. "Run and don't look back."

Rook pushed away from the wall as the first hands dropped onto the ground like spiders. He stumbled through the mess of tables and lurched out the batwing doors into the night as a peel of thunder ripped the sky open and heralded a downpour.

John levered another cartridge into the chamber.

AS LONG AS YOU FEED

by David Niall Wilson

Dim lights split the night sky from the desert. From a distance, it looked wrong, like a wound in the earth. Rookwood was a puppet town held together by rusty nails, bailing wire, and death. Things didn't grow there. Other than some mangy, very hungry coyotes, there was no wildlife. There were a few hungry, skeletal dogs, and there were always cats, bright eyes staring from dark shadows. There were no rats.

The town had once been lively. Wagons moving west for the gold rush had passed through, and Rookwood had provided supplies, entertainment, alcohol, and a hub for commerce. In those days, there had been a market, several saloons, and a livery stable. People had moved in and built houses. There were a few ranches, but they were far out of town because they had to be located where the cattle could graze, and even in its heyday

Rookwood was a small dust bowl.

Then the railroad went in fifty miles to the north. The stagecoaches stopped coming, and the town's heartbeat slowed to a near-death pulse of indifferent despair. Those who remained had nowhere to go and just enough to survive. The ones who left never even glanced over their shoulders.

Some places brood. Visitors to Rookwood sensed they were being watched, no matter how empty the streets. Sounds that wouldn't have any effect on the psyche in a happier place turned heads. Every movement in the shadows drew attention, and then there were the rooks. It made no sense. They had to fly miles to feed, but they nested in Rookwood all year long, coming in black clouds that shifted and spun, drawing dark designs in the sky.

Five strangers rode slowly into town. Four were tall dark men in long coats. The fifth was a woman. They stopped outside the saloon and dismounted. The woman dropped her reins and walked away without a glance. One of the men, after securing his mount, tied hers off to a hitching post. The four waited as the woman pushed through the doors and entered.

The saloon was not busy, but there were some full tables. There was a card game in the corner, and a bored, worn woman with dark, tired eyes leaned on the bar. Across from the card table, seated at an old piano, an even older man sat, pounding at the keys. His eyes were glazed with cataracts, and there was no music on the stand, and the melody was warped and filled with holes. You could make out what song was being played, but something was missing. There were gaps between some notes, and others were missing altogether, but without a break in rhythm.

McGraw had only eight fingers. He swore that he felt ten when he played. If you watched his hands, it seemed as if those missing digits flicked the keys when expected, but there was no sound, so the songs were like picket fences with missing slats. At first it was grating, but the brain is a powerful problem solver. Over time, it was difficult not to accept the sounds as normal. No one paid any attention to McGraw, but when the doors opened, and the woman stepped through, even the piano grew silent. No one breathed for a long moment and then every head turned.

A dark cloak covered her from head to toe, but her eyes flashed so brightly they were clearly visible in that shadow. She tossed the hood back and long black hair curled over her shoulders. No one spoke. It was difficult to say whether they breathed, until she moved. She strode across to the bar.

She leaned forward, suddenly appearing taller than she had before. Though the bar was tall, and wide, her lips easily reached the bartender's ear. She spoke softly, so only he could hear. "There is a woman, Mae Lynne. She has called to me. Where can I find her?"

Silas Boone, the bartender, reached for a glass and his cloth. He tried to lose himself in polishing it. He tried to ignore her scent, and her presence, as sweat leaked down his neck into the collar of his shirt.

He glanced up, met her gaze, and replied. "Upstairs. First room on the left. But she's with a…"

The strange woman pulled back so quickly and so completely she might never have approached the bar at all. She nodded at the four, and they headed for the stairs. No words were spoken.

Before following, she crossed the room to the piano and leaned in to whisper in McGraw's ear. "Play something sad. Play something that will make them weep in their beer and wander home. I need the night."

McGraw did not look at her. His eyes were so glazed, he would have seen an outline, or a shadow.

She pulled back and turned. Her men were driving a skinny cowboy down the stairs, his pants in his hands and his hat askew. He was complaining, almost whining, but for all of that, he was leaving. The tall men cast long shadows. They didn't speak.

McGraw turned, just for a second, and stared at the woman's retreating form. Then he returned his attention to the piano. He knew a lot of sad songs, but one in particular grabbed his attention and he began to play. He leaned in, closed his eyes, and "Für Elise" floated out through the bar. The music was old, and slow, and sad, and McGraw leaned into it, eyes closed.

Everyone else turned, as if their necks were joined by some strange cord that connected them one to the other. All the notes were there. McGraw's playing had not changed, and there was no indication he was doing anything extra to make up for his missing digits. He simply played, and the music flowed. No one had ever heard him play as he might have. No one had understood his loss, so they were silent. He played, and they listened, and the woman and her followers slipped up the stairs and out of sight without notice.

Silas shook it off. He reached out and grabbed Cooter Gillis by the collar. "Get the sheriff." When Cooter didn't move, Boone slapped him lightly. That got the old man's attention.

"Go on now," Silas said. "I'll fill that glass when you get back."

Mae Lynne was enjoying an uncharacteristically quiet night. She'd seen one hand from the Bryce cattle farm earlier in the afternoon. It was a strange time of day, but he had work and little time to spare. Most paydays he rode over to Rookwood to pay his respects and to take his pleasure. He wasn't a bad looking man, and he was gentle—or as gentle as a cowboy was likely to be. Still, she'd been happy to see the south side of his northbound horse heading back to what they very generously called a ranch.

That wasn't what was on her mind. Her thoughts were on another man, a dark man. Mae Lynne sat in front of the cracked mirror on her vanity, running her brush through the long blonde locks of her hair. She didn't stare at her reflection, as had been her habit since she'd been a little girl. Focusing on the surface of the vanity, she fought to erase the memories threatening to overwhelm her. Even with her eyes closed, she sensed his hungry gaze, felt the cold touch of his hand on her shoulder. She remembered the way he'd traced the blade of his knife across her throat, and the words he'd whispered, never silent, threatening her with every conceivable harm, describing things she did not believe a man and a woman could do, but with such precision and detail she was convinced that he did.

He'd paid, but it had not been enough. It might never be enough. And now, every time there was a knock on her door, every time she heard a creak on the stairs, or the sound of a horse pulling up to hitch out front, she shuddered, wondering if he'd returned, if they'd take his money and let him up the stairs, even after all she'd told them. Knowing they would because she was just another commodity, another bottle of whiskey, another plate of grits. The women of Rookwood, those not married, or in some way self-sufficient, were nothing but products, and Mae Lynne was top shelf. No way they were turning away the price she commanded, and she knew that one would pay extra, if necessary.

Mae Lynne stopped brushing and brought a hand to her throat. She clutched a small pendant, the one thing she still had from her family. It was tiny crow on a leather thong. Her grandmother had given it to her, and she'd worn it ever since.

"Remember," the old woman had said. "She will answer if you call. Don't waste her time. Don't take it for granted. It can save you, but you wait, girl. If you can save yourself, you do that. Conjure's not to be taken lightly."

She'd thanked her grandmother, smiling at what sounded like a fantasy, until her fingers gripped the tiny crow. The room had darkened, and she'd felt herself leaning, too far toward her grandmother's bed. Her thighs touched the mattress and she'd stood, watching, as thousands of black specks burst from the depths of her mind and soared, screeching, into an endless sky. It had faded quickly, and she'd caught her breath.

When she opened her eyes, her grandmother was watching her. The old woman nodded in satisfaction. "It has bonded with you. It is good. Remember, only when you truly need her. You will know."

There was no knock on Mae Lynne's door. It opened, and they entered like a flutter of shadows. In the mirror she saw two dark men to either side of her door. She would have turned to study them, but found that the woman, standing very still in the door frame, held her attention with hypnotic ease.

"You called me," the woman said.

The words were like silver bells, or distant chimes. Mae Lynne wasn't even certain they'd been spoken aloud, or that it mattered. She clutched her pendant again, closed her eyes, and nodded.

The woman cocked her head and glanced around the room. There was no judgment in her expression, just curiosity. When she'd taken in the entire scene, she turned back to Mae Lynne. "I smell him. It smells…wrong. He has hurt you?"

"No," Mae Lynne said. "Not yet, but…he will. He spoke to me, said things that…"

"He wants to own you," the woman said. "He wants you to feel as if you only exist for him, and for you to believe that you enjoy it."

"Yes," Mae Lynne whispered.

"Do you?"

Mae Lynne almost hesitated. She thought about his voice, remembered the touch of the blade. A shiver had run through her at that cold contact. Then she shook her head firmly and clutched her pendant tightly. "No. Never. He frightens me, but that is all."

The woman stared at her for a moment, and Mae Lynne was lost in those eyes. Dark hair spilled out from beneath the strange woman's cloak. Her skin was so pale it was nearly translucent, but it shimmered with life.

It's like the moon. She is like the moon.

"It is well, then," the woman said. "We will help you, sister. We will take your burden. But there is a price. There is always a price."

"I have no money," Mae Lynne said. "All that I have of value is myself. My body. My heart."

"Those would suffice," the woman said, "but I will not accept them. You will owe me a debt. When I come to collect, you will not question me."

Mae Lynne nodded. "I am yours, then."

"You already were," the woman said. Then she turned, stepped back into the hall, and the men to either side whirled, their long coats flashing, forming a wall of shadow that sealed off the world. When they passed, the door was closed, and Mae Lynne stood staring, her brush in her one hand and the other clutching the pendant dangling from her throat. She watched the door for a long moment, and then, slowly, she turned back to her vanity and returned to brushing her hair.

Caleb Johnston was a dark man. He lived ten miles from town in a shotgun shack he'd taken ownership of when the previous owner decided to move farther west. That decision had involved the barrel of Caleb's gun, threats to his wife and eldest daughter. But there was more. There was always more. Caleb held a darkness at bay, but barely. He lived among men, had his way with women, pursued the illusion of a normal life…but only at a distance. He'd been playing that part for centuries, moving from place to place, always seeking those where he could remain in the shadows, where there were few eyes, and even fewer of them cared.

He fought the hunger when he was able, but it never lasted. The woman called to him. He felt her across the miles and knew he would take her farther. There was no choice. He would feed, and, if he took too much, he would move on. He wore twin Colts on his hips, and there was a shotgun holstered on the mule, but they were more for show. He wouldn't need them. Not for a shit-splat town like Rookwood, or any other, for that matter. He'd walked dark roads for centuries, one step ahead of the darkness.

Caleb untied the mule and mounted. He'd have preferred a horse, a big one, but they would not suffer his touch. They shied, they bucked and ran. More than one had died, rather than suffer him in the saddle. The mule hated him, but he fed it. It carried him, and he avoided walking too close behind. It was enough.

His hat settled into place so the brim dipped over his eyes, and he turned toward Rookwood, riding into the night. It should have been dark, but the moon was full and the trail was brightly lit. There was no color. He rode through a world of blacks and grays as quickly as he could convince the mule to move. The closer he drew to Rookwood, the deeper the hunger cut. To divert his mind, he thought back to the day it had started: two roads crossing, the candles, and bones he'd purchased from an old woman in a town far away, now ground to dust by time. He had wanted a woman so badly his skin had burned, and he couldn't think straight, but she'd ignored him. Worse, she'd loathed him.

Caleb had gone to the old woman for a charm, or a potion. He'd had a lot of years to realize the selfishness of that, but at the time nothing could have diverted him. She'd given him instructions, sold him the bones, and the candle. In the end, he believed, he could have walked to that crossroad empty-handed with the same result.

When he tossed the bones, and whispered the girl's name. He barely remembered it now—Miranda. With the candles lit, he'd stood in the center of the crossroads, and closed his eyes.

"Is she worth it, boy?" The voice was a whisper, but so loud inside Caleb's mind that it snapped his eyes open.

A man stood before him, hat slouched to one side, a hand in his pocket, eyes as dark as coal. It was hard to make out his features. They melted and shifted, but the eyes were steady.

Caleb started to ask who and stopped. All the conversations of his life had been duels, some truth, some shade, waiting for the other to tip their hand. There was none of that here. This man knew why he was there. The old woman had known, as well.

"She is," he said.

"You want to possess her, to obsess her?"

Caleb's throat was too dry for speech. He nodded.

"There is a price," the man said. "For anything real, there is a price. Do you believe this is real?"

"I do."

The two stared in silence, then the man—Demon?—smiled at him. That smile was filled with sharp white teeth and devoid of mirth. "I believe you may be special, Caleb Johnston. I believe we may strike a different sort of bargain, you, and me. Now and then I see some potential that most lack. You are a hungry man, Caleb."

"I want her." Caleb's voice trembled, but he held steady. He did not want to lose the one thing he'd come for.

"She is yours," the man said, "and many more. The price? When you are hungry…you will feed. When you feed, I will feed. I will make you this promise: it will not end, as long as you feed."

Caleb stood his ground as the man stepped forward and held out a hand to shake. Caleb took it. The pain was instantaneous and bright, like a nail had been hammered through his palm. He tried to pull free, but could not, and the struggle increased the pain.

"Do you give yourself to me, Caleb Johnston?"

He nodded, then more furiously, then screamed, "Yes! Yes, I swear."

The pain ended. Caleb pulled back his hand, stared at the unblemished skin, and glanced up. The crossroad was empty. The candle had burned out, and the bones were covered in road dust. That was the beginning. Before he'd even turned back toward town, he felt the hunger start to burn.

It was burning now. Rookwood was half a mile distant, but he didn't hurry the mule. Something odd was in the air, black and different. He glanced up at the moon and brought the mule to a halt. Rooks had risen from the town in a cloud, skittering across the moon like flecks of dark ash from a fire. Then they were gone.

Very few birds fly at night. Rooks were not among them except he'd seen them fly in Rookwood. Not often, and only when something dark was about to happen. They flew when he entered town, but he was half a mile away, and they were already gone. The hunger sent a deep stab of pain through his chest, and he doubled over, gripping the mule's mane and gritting his teeth. Slowly, he rose in the saddle and straightened his hat. Then he spurred the mule on to Rookwood.

The dark woman stopped by the door, listening to McGraw, just for a second. Then, she nodded in his direction, and the blank notes returned. The old musician never hesitated, but the spell of the moment was broken. She stepped through the doors into the street and the dark men followed.

Sheriff "Stick" Brady was waiting. The sheriff was a man who moved so slowly, it was deceptive. He was tall, rail thin, and stood with one shoulder dropped. In the deep shadows he looked like a tall insect, a praying mantis in a dark hat. He stood, one hand poised over his gun, and watched.

"Evenin'," he said. "Don't believe we've been introduced. Name's Brady. I'm the sheriff in these parts."

The dark men fanned out but made no move. The woman strode to the center of the street and pulled back her hood. She stared at the sheriff, eyes dark and questioning, skin pale as moonlight and so beautiful Brady found it difficult to meet her gaze. Not impossible, however.

"We mean no harm to you, or your town," she said. "There is another we seek, a bad man. He's on his way now. We have come for him."

"I see," Brady said. "Thing is, though, this is my town. Someone needs to be dealt with, I'm your man."

The woman smiled and nodded her head, ever so slightly. "I understand, sheriff, but this is no ordinary man. He will come, and the girl you know as Mae Lynne? She won't exist. He will consume her, and I do not believe there is anything you can do to prevent it."

"We'll have to see about that," Brady said. "But I can't have you standing in the street ready to bushwhack a man. You got a name?"

"My name isn't important," the woman said. "The man we are waiting for goes by Johnston, Caleb Johnston. He's been here before. He's already caused great pain to the girl."

"I know Caleb," Brady said. "Can't say I care for the man. Can't say I think he needs to die, neither."

The woman didn't speak. She cocked her head, like a bird. Boone turned toward the end of the street, and then he heard it too—approaching hoofbeats. Not the smooth gait of a horse, but the determined plodding of a mule. The woman stepped aside and left the way open.

The sheriff didn't glance to the right or left. If he had, he'd have seen those dark men scale the walls of the building so quickly they seemed to float, or glide. The woman had backed beneath the awning of the saloon, and Brady stood alone in the center of the street.

The hoofbeats drew nearer. Caleb Johnston came into sight, and Brady stood his ground. Johnson would have to pass him to reach the hitching posts outside the saloon. He waited.

Caleb slowed as he entered Rookwood. He saw the sheriff standing in the center of the road, but something still felt off. He had nothing to fear from Brady. If he fed, he would survive. He would have to move on, but he was focused on the saloon and Mae Lynne.

"Evenin' sheriff," he said, bringing the mule to a halt in the center of the street. "What brings you out so late?"

Brady remained silent. Caleb saw the man's gaze focusing on his gun hand. He'd subconsciously dropped it to hover near the butt of his pistol.

"Here tell you're here to see Mae Lynne," Brady said. He spoke and moved like he was in slow motion, or out of synch with the world. Most men would have been mesmerized by it. Caleb thought a lot of men had probably been distracted and died trying to track the tall thin lawman. Caleb was not like other men. He only sat, and stared.

"Maybe," Caleb said. "I got some cash, and I aim to spend it. Is that a problem?"

"Well," Brady said, "seems she doesn't much want your company now, or ever. Fact is, I'd be obliged if you'd move on. Always wondered about that cabin, and the family who left. I've never been able to figure what exactly it is you do. I like Mae Lynne. Can't say I care much for you."

Caleb lowered his gaze to the road, then raised it and nodded. "I figured this day might come. Thing is, though, I don't much care what you think. I'll be leaving tonight, you have my promise, but first I aim to spend some time with Mae Lynne."

"Afraid I can't allow that," Brady said. "Best you turn and head on back out of town. Maybe keep goin'."

The shift was almost imperceptible, but Brady's hand strayed closer to his gun. Caleb didn't hesitate. His hand flashed so fast it was hard to believe the gun hadn't already been in his hand. Brady drew, a split second behind. Both fired. Brady's shot caught Caleb in the shoulder and tossed him back in the saddle. Caleb's gun spun wild, flying out of his hand.

A shot from the rooftop to the right had diverted his aim.

Caleb drew a deep breath, shuddered, biting back the pain. He didn't favor the shoulder with the bullet hole through it, and he still had a gun on his opposite hip. As he slipped from the saddle, he drew the shotgun from its holster. The mule stood still, paying no attention.

Brady was ready to fire again, but he hesitated when he heard a shrill cry. He didn't turn his head, but he felt it as the four floated down from the rooftops and flanked him, so quietly they might have been nothing more than the wind. Except, it sounded more like the flutter of wings.

The woman stepped out of the shadows, and in a loud voice, cried, "Caleb Johnston!"

Everything slowed. Brady's gun was raised, but he didn't fire. Caleb had brought the shotgun up level with Brady's chest but held it there. Very suddenly, everything shifted, and the woman stepped between Caleb and the sheriff.

"You will not be visiting Mae Lynne this evening," she said softly. "I know your hunger. I know you need to feed. How long? How many? What did he promise?"

"As long as I feed," Caleb said softly, "It will not end."

"What do you want?" the woman asked.

"To feed. To move on."

"I'm not a fool, Caleb Johnston. Tell me what you want, or I will simply end you."

He tried to smile, as if the threat held no weight, but couldn't quite bring the expression to his lips. "I'm tired. They talk to me, all of them."

"Feed on me," the woman said.

He stared, and then, he stepped forward.

Sheriff Brady raised his gun, but one of the dark men touched his arm, and it floated back to his side. He stood, helpless, as Caleb Johnston approached the woman.

Caleb circled her slowly, as if uncertain how to proceed. Then he closed in. He came up from behind and wrapped an arm around her. With the other drew his knife and held it to her throat. "You want this?" he whispered. "You know what I am?"

"I do," she said. "It is you who doesn't know."

Caleb pulled her closer, pressing the blade tighter, and his head fell back. Even as he acted, he realized the mistake. The two were surrounded in a silver glow. It throbbed, and grew, until nothing was visible in the street but a ball of white-hot light. Two shadows writhed within. Caleb's form grew, pulsed, and grew again. Then he screamed. It was more than he could take in, more than he could transfer. He tried to pull free, but she spun and placed the palms of her hands on his cheeks, ignoring his blade.

Caleb felt fire pour into his veins and tried to pull away. He struggled, but she held him easily, and as he gasped, and his mouth opened, she breathed into him. They left him in a screaming horde, all of those he'd fed on, all of those he'd tortured, and soared into the darkness kicking and jabbing at his throat, his eyes, fighting free. Caleb took that breath in, felt it dislodge the dark contents of his soul, and shuddered. He fell back. Some spark flicked from his eyes to hers and was gone, and he nearly fell.

"I…what have you done?"

"I have taken it from you," she said. "Your hunger. The voices. They are free to move on."

"And…I am free?"

"You made your bargain. When you die, he will take you. I am no part of that bargain. I am here for the others. He has used you, Caleb Johnston. He didn't feed. He used you as a vessel. When you grew too mad to continue, he would have taken you, and they would have been trapped."

Caleb opened his hands and stared at them. He sheathed the knife, but when his gaze returned to hers, it was hard as stone. "You had no right."

He reached for his second gun, not as fast as before, but still too swift for the naked eye. The woman shifted slightly, and the shot caught one of the dark men in the heart. It passed through without damage, and then he shot another. Before he could fire a third time, the dark man pushed his hat back, showing his face for the first time. He couldn't grin… He had no mouth. His eyes were dark, and his face was split by a long, sleek bill. Like a crow. He let out a cry that might have been a caw, amplified a thousand times, and he dove at Caleb's retreating form. The other three followed, their voices rising impossibly, and they were on him.

Sheriff Brady had also backed away. He didn't even reach for his gun, only stared.

The woman wrapped her arm around his shoulder and leaned close. "They will be a while. Perhaps you would buy a lady a drink?"

He turned and met her gaze, lost in it for a moment, then regained his voice. "What…are they?"

"They're hungry, and they're mine," she said. "Some call me the crow woman, but you can call me Lil."

Bits and pieces of what had been Caleb Johnston flew as the odd, slender men fed on his flesh. Just beyond him, the mule stood, nonchalant.

"I think," Brady said, turning away, "that a drink is exactly what I need. In fact, I'm pretty sure it's a full bottle night."

The two walked, side by side, to the tavern as the dark street was stained red.

COSTUMED MOUTH

by Ej Sidle

She walked into the saloon and every head turned her way. I was a little behind the pace, a beat too slow, and by the time I laid eyes on her she was already bristling under the attention. Even wet to the bone, with tendrils of soaked hair covering half her face and water dripping off her dress, she was gorgeous. Fine young thing like her must have been used to folk staring, but there was still something wild and angry about the tilt of her chin, like she was preparing to enact violence upon anyone who dared to stare too long at the delicate line of her throat. The rouge of her cheeks wasn't enough to hide the flush of color working its way up her neck, or the way her shoulders straightened beneath the soaking fabric of her shawl.

Trouble, that's what she was. Trouble blown in from the rainy desert evening, red on her mouth and mud on her shoes and a story caught in the back of her throat. A story I wanted nothing to do with. Maybe the menfolk—the cattle rustlers and fortune seekers I'd been drinking with—had time to lend her a hand and wake up missing their valuables, but I didn't. I wasn't so easily distracted by a pretty face.

Even with the attention, the girl stood her ground. Plenty of grit, with eyes that glittered like a coyote by the firelight, careful and cunning. From across the room, her gaze met mine and held for a moment, her painted mouth curving up into a triumphant smile. Maybe she thought I was a kindred spirit, an oasis of femininity amongst all the men.

There weren't all that many women this far west. The country was still too wild, with gangs of outlaws and beasts and unfriendly locals. Mostly, the little frontier settlements were full of men desperate for work, willing to travel out into the vast emptiness in an effort to line their pockets with coins. The only women were the handful of aging saloon girls, all of them driven west when prettier, perkier models inherited all the city jobs; and me, blown out here on the arm of my late-husband, who had at least had the decency to teach me to shoot before he died.

It wasn't a forgiving sort of place, not even for those of us who belonged out here. For a girl in an expensive dress with gold rings on her fingers? Well. She wasn't a whore, and she wasn't a gunslinger. Just some lost girl caught up in the rain.

She took the spare seat at my little table, artfully rearranging her skirts before focusing back on me. "Miss Sadie Jones?"

I finished my drink in one long swallow. "Mrs."

"Mrs.—"

"Sadie's fine," I said.

"Sadie," she repeated, lightly folding her hands on the table. "Your reputation precedes you."

I sighed. "I don't take jobs from strangers, girl."

She shook her head, eyes beginning to glitter with unshed tears. "Mrs.—"

"Sadie."

"*Sadie*," she said, baring her teeth a little. "My name is Constance Smith. I need your help."

"Why?" I asked.

"Because," she said softly, "my brother has gone missing."

"Miss Smith," I started, shaking my head. "I'm sorry that your brother has wandered off, but—"

"He hasn't *wandered off!*" she snapped, clenched hands shaking. "Our ranch was attacked, and he—" She closed her eyes. "I need your help."

"Talk to the lawmen," I told her. "If some gang has swallowed him up, they're the best bet to find him."

Constance shook her head, eyes hard, mouth a thin, red line. "You misunderstand," she said. "It wasn't a gang, Sadie. It was a monster."

"A monster?"

"Yes," she said, painted lips trembling. "My brother was taken by the Beast of the Storm. I want you to help me kill it."

Well now. The Beast of the Storm was an old story, one I hadn't heard mentioned for years. Sometimes passers-by would ask after it, having heard whispers by firelight out in the wilderness, or thinking they caught sight of it in the shadows of the desert. Some even swore they lost traveling companions to it, saw it emerge from the rain to devour men and horses whole.

The thing about stories—about monsters—was that they weren't real. Or, perhaps that wasn't entirely true. Men could be monsters, could do monstrous things. I'd killed them for it, watched them hang for it. Sometimes, I'd even lost a little sleep over it. But in the end, it was always men driven on by the Devil, not monsters in the night.

"The Beast of the Storm is a story," I said, a little harsher than I intended. "More'n likely, your brother ran afoul of a bear, or a wolf."

"I saw it!" Constance hissed. "I *saw it*, and it wasn't no bear or wild creature! It was a monster, and it took my brother!"

"You sure?" I demanded. "Mind can play tricks on you, girl. 'specially when you're scared."

When I had first arrived in the west, back when my husband and I fancied ourselves ranchers, we'd heard our fair share of horror stories. Bears the size of houses, swamps filled with man-eating lizards, wolves that would prey on unsuspecting caravans. Outlaws and bandits. Hostile tribes. Death, disease, and misfortune. We'd endured each tale with foolishly unflinching cynicism. After all, we thought as long as we had one another, no true harm could befall us.

We'd been wrong, of course. It had been bad luck and worse timing that ended our marriage, though, not a monster from tales of old.

Constance swallowed sharply, mouth an angry line and eyes flashing in the low light. "I know what I saw."

"Then tell me," I snapped. "Tell me all about it, Miss Smith, and I might be convinced to ride out with you."

There had always been stories about things—unexplained, impossible—out in the desert, creatures stalking lone travelers, monsters inching ever closer in the darkness. I'd heard tales of wolves that walked on their hind legs and ate hearts out of chests, of coyotes speaking in the tongues of men, of vicious, carnivorous birds wearing human faces descending on the careless. In the firelight, I'd even heard whispers of men turning into monsters, killing their friends and devouring their flesh.

Me, I'd spent the last decade making a name for myself in places most would fear to tread. I'd seen bears and bull moose and more outlaws than I could ever hope to shoot. Never seen a monster that wasn't just a man making bad choices.

Maybe Constance had, though. She had that look about her, that turn of her chin and that unhappy curve of her lips. Maybe she knew more than she was saying. Maybe she really thought she'd seen something out there in the darkness.

"We have a ranch," Constance said softly. "A few horses, some ranch hands. Nothing fancy, you understand, but we get by. Might even make it rich, if the railway ever gets out this far." She offered me a grim smile, mouth a scarlet bruise. "That's what Jacob used to say, anyway."

"Your brother?" I guessed.

She nodded. "Yesterday evening, a storm rolled in. Jacob and some of the men were fencing, but they rode back in just before it hit. Horses were worked up. I helped put them away before we headed back toward the house."

Her eyes glittered again, and she dashed a shaking hand across them before more tears could fall. "Heard it first. This terrible groaning sound, like the wind getting up under a door and rattling all your bones. One of the men screamed, and Jacob grabbed my arm, and then…I saw it. The Beast."

"What did it look like?" I leaned in across the table.

Constance swallowed sharply, eyes dark. "It came out of the storm. There was nothing, just the rain, and then it was standing there. On two legs like a man but bigger, with teeth like a wolf. It killed one of the men, tore him open and ate him while he was still screaming. W-we made it into the house, the last ranch hand and Jacob and I, but we could hear it outside, eating."

"Then," she said "The horses. It must have gone for the horses, because they were… Have you ever heard horses scream, Sadie?"

I nodded.

Constance shuddered. "Jacob took his guns and went outside. He told the ranch hand, Mateo, to stay with me in the house. We heard shooting, and yelling. And then…nothing. We waited and waited, but no one came back. When the storm cleared, we went out into the yard. No bodies, just empty stables. Mateo stayed to guard the ranch, and I came looking for help."

"You think your brother is alive."

"Maybe," she said softly. "The Beast likes fresh meat, maybe it's keeping him for…for later. In case the weather clears and it can't hunt."

"It only hunts in the rain?" I asked. "In the storm?"

Constance nodded.

I stared at her, wet hair still dripping down her shoulders, painted mouth blurred and ruined by the rain. "You rode through a storm?"

"I did," she said. "And I thought it would be the end of me, but it didn't find me. Maybe it has no need to hunt again so soon."

I sighed. "I don't believe in monsters."

"But I saw—"

"A rabid bear," I suggested.

Constance shuddered. "You won't help me?"

I didn't believe in monsters, not in some Beast of the Storm or any other variant. But something had scared the poor girl enough to send her riding for the nearest town all on her own, a trip that would have been daunting even under perfectly normal circumstances.

I remembered what it was like when it was me riding desperately to find help, knowing that my husband would be long dead despite my haste. I remembered every moment of the bone-jarring race down from the high country, every fork in the road and every wolf I thought I saw in the trees.

"I'll ride out with you," I said slowly, "back to the ranch. I'll have a look around, but I ain't chasing ghost stories, Miss Smith. If there ain't nothin' to find, I'm coming back to town."

"Thank you."

"Don't thank me yet, girl!" I snapped. "You'll be paying me."

She nodded. "Of course."

"Let me get a hot meal into both of us, and then we can head out," I said, already looking for the barkeeper. "You'll need your strength for the ride back."

Constance, with her pretty dark eyes and her bedraggled hair, reached across the table to grab my arm. "No!"

"No?"

She shook her head, eyes imploring me to listen. "It's nearly night. We can't go riding back out in the dark. Not if it keeps raining."

"Longer we delay, more chance your brother has of ending up in the ground."

"Won't do him any good if we die before we get there!" she snapped. "I need to sleep, Sadie. And I need to change out of my wet clothes. We can leave at first light."

I wavered, caught between the thrill of a fresh hunt and Constance's desperate, pleading expression.

"Fine!" I said. "My room's top of the stairs on the left. You can get changed in there."

Constance stood, smoothing her skirts back down. "I'll get my own room, then meet you back here in the morning."

She made her way across to the barkeeper, ignoring the other men as she passed him a few coins. And then, with one blood-red smile back at me, she made her way up the stairs toward the rooms.

"God above," the barkeeper muttered, coming over to me with a fresh drink. "Ain't she somethin'?"

I snorted. "You think anything in a skirt is something."

"Wouldn't hurt you to wear one once in a while," he joked, clearing my empties away. "Listen, Sadie. Ain't my place or nothin', but…the Beast of the Storm…. My sister thought she saw it once, when she was comin' through from the city."

Funny thing about this town was that everyone had a relative who came out from the city. They never said which city, of course, but one of the big ones. Sometimes they'd get waylaid on the road and never make it out to the edge of civilization. Either that or they got one look at the desert and made any excuse to turn their wagons back toward home.

"Which sister?" I asked. "The painted lady or the widow?"

He laughed. "Can't they be the same?"

I toasted him, taking a long sip as he hovered by my table.

"Jus'…be careful, Sadie," he said. "My sister was always the unflappable sort, but whatever she saw on the road that day shook her. She said it came out of the rain, killed all the men, and dragged one of the young girls away. They heard her screaming but couldn't find her, just had to keep heading toward town with her cries all around them, sobbin' and beggin' until she went quiet."

"A bear—"

"Don't know many bears that'll drag a livin' person along beside a wagon," he said. "Not like that."

I sighed. "Reckon you'd have more chance of a human monster drinking at this bar than seeing one in the desert."

"Probably," he agreed. "Especially if them Johnston boys are in town."

"Scarier than anything I'll see out there," I said, shrugging.

"Still, can't hurt to be careful. Jus'…be wary, Sadie. Better folk than you have ridden out into the desert and never come back."

I didn't sleep well. Haven't for years now. Still, by the time dawn rolled around, I could feel the jitter of adrenaline under my skin. I left folded trousers and a shirt by Constance's door, something more comfortable to travel in than the wet remains of her dress.

While waiting for her to appear, I readied the horses. My own reliable mare ignored me, intent on her breakfast. Constance's flashy gelding nudged at my pockets looking for tidbits. The two of them seemed to get along, bumping noses and snuffling at one another.

When Constance emerged, the stable hand gave a low whistle. Half-drowned, she'd been pretty, but in trousers and a loose button-up, she was a knockout. She'd manage to find paint from somewhere, with a hint of rouge on her cheekbones and her mouth a slash of scarlet. Even her hair, neatly braided away, glowed like the mane of a lion. She was a woman ready for battle, even if that battle was just a hard ride back toward her home.

"Let's go," she said, as if I hadn't been waiting for her, as if she hadn't insisted on spending the night.

Leaving town was uneventful. Some of the early traders gave us uncertain looks, and the sheriff raised a hand in greeting as we made our way by the jailhouse. Still, the sky was clear and the horses were in high spirits, so we gave them their heads once we cleared the clutter of the main street.

Constance rode like a woman who had been taught to do so but found no pleasure in it. Her seat was fine, her hands steady, but there was a vacancy to her expression that showed no joy in the endeavor. Maybe she was used to traveling in a wagon, or walking.

I didn't feel the need for chatter, and Constance was a silent companion. She led the way off the main path, deeper into country with which I was unfamiliar. By midmorning the terrain had become rougher, the single-track paths leading through thickets of dense woodland.

Several times I thought I heard something in the woods, movement and noise. Wolves maybe, or something bigger. I kept waiting for outlaws to appear, for an ambush to be sprung, but then the normal woodland sounds returned.

"This ain't a well-traveled road," I said when we stopped to water the horses.

Constance shrugged. "We built the ranch long before any of the towns cropped up. Always seemed like a nice place to find solitude."

"Must have been one of the first to build out here."

"Probably. My family has been here for years, long before Jacob started breeding the horses."

I frowned. "How'd you get supplies?"

"There was a local tribe," Constance said, shrugging again. "They used to trade with us a little, before the settlers kept coming. They've moved on now, so mostly we hunt and make what we need. Sometimes Mateo or one of the others will go into town to trade for supplies. I've been a few times, too."

"Enough to know the path in the dark."

She nodded.

"You were lucky," I added. "It's a rough trail. Could have got into all sorts of trouble, riding it fast in the dark. Plenty of bandits in these parts, too."

"I was so worried about the Beast, I didn't even think about the bandits," Constance said. "I don't remember much of the ride, just the rain and the sounds and how dark it was… Then I was at the saloon."

She shook her head, turning her gelding up away from the water. "Let's keep moving. There's an open stretch up ahead where we can pick up the pace."

Near the middle of the morning, it started to rain. Gently at first, then a downpour. Constance shivered and shuddered in her saddle, looking at me with a grimace.

"Just a storm," I said.

"No such thing out here!" she snapped back, hunching in on herself. "It's coming for us, Sadie."

We rode on, horses sticking close together as the ground began to turn to mud. Then, as suddenly as it had started, the rain eased away to nothing.

"I don't like it," Constance hissed. "Give me a gun."

I hesitated, sitting deep in my saddle and letting my mare slow to a halt before reaching for one of my pistols. "Know how to use one of these?" I asked, handing it across to her when she stopped beside me

"Point at the Beast and pull the trigger," she snapped, clutching the gun to her chest. "It's not going to eat me. I'm not going to let it eat me!"

"It won't," I said, keeping us moving along the trail. "It ain't real, girl. Just your mind getting carried away in the rain."

Constance frowned, those red lips an unhappy line, but whatever she had intended to say died in her mouth as we came out onto a clear stretch of ground. There, a hundred yards ahead of us, the carcass of a ruined wagon lay decimated beside the road.

"Lord above," Constance murmured. "Sadie—"

"Stay behind me!" I ordered, drawing my gun. "Eyes up, girl. Call out anything you see."

We inched forward, horses agitated beneath us, rolling their eyes and tossing their heads.

I could see the bodies of the horses that had pulled the wagon, or what was left of them. They'd been gutted, entrails dragged out of their bodies and left in neat piles. At least one of them had still been alive, if the scrambling scuff of hoof marks through the bloody trail of organs was anything to go by.

"I'm going to dismount," I said. "I need to check for survivors, Constance. You understand?"

She nodded, mouth a blood-red smear against the pallor of her skin.

I slid down from my mare, passing her reins back to Constance before creeping closer to the wagon. All around it was a mess of tracks, human and animal. I tried to make sense of it, but they crossed over one another and vanished into the mud. It was impossible to tell what had happened, only that there had been people here, at least four of them.

The canvas top of the wagon was intact and wet to touch. One of the wheels was cracked and broken; the thing that had sent the wagon lumbering to a halt. Inside, all the supplies were untouched, with weapons still tucked away into the corner.

There were no bodies, other than the horses.

"Probably a bear," I said, glancing back at Constance. "Or a robbery that was interrupted."

"Sadie," Constance whimpered, eyes wide and terrified. "Sadie, look."

The other side of the canvas was covered in bloody handprints. Several of them, frantic and desperate, as if someone had tried to clutch onto the wagon as they were being dragged away. Streaks of blood marked the ground as well, almost lost in the mud.

"What kind of bear does that?" she demanded hoarsely. "What kind of bear guts the horses and leaves all the meat? *What kind of bear—?*"

Above us, there was a clap of thunder. The first drops of rain pattered down around us.

"Sadie!" Constance sobbed, throwing my reins at me. "We have to go. We have to go!"

I vaulted up into my saddle, wheeling my horse around and letting her take off into a ground-eating lope. Constance followed, her terrified sobbing punctuating the rumbles of thunder from above.

I tried to look back over my shoulder, tried to wipe the rain from my eyes to look at the wreckage of the wagon. There was a shadow emerging from beside it, something too tall to be a man, something that seemed to watch us as we fled.

"A bear!" I yelled, looking for Constance, seeing her stricken expression. "Just a bear!"

After all, what else could it be?

We stopped when the rain did, horses exhausted and soaked through. Constance said nothing, trying to wring her shirt out with a grim expression on her face.

"You okay?" I asked.

She shuddered. "What do you think? We're being hunted by a godforsaken monster that's probably already gutted my brother, and you won't even believe that there's anything to be scared of!"

"Oh, there's plenty to be scared of!" I said. "You think a bear attack is something funny, girl? You think I relish riding at breakneck pace through a goddamn storm? There's enough to worry about without making up monsters!"

"Why don't you believe me?"

I shrugged. "So far, ain't seen nothin' that can't be explained by a bit of bad luck and one hell of a nasty bear. I'll believe in some Beast just fine when I can see it with my own two eyes."

Constance glared. "Oh, you'll see it all right, and don't you say I didn't warn you!"

"All right then!" I snarled. "Let's get it over with. Lead on, and let me see this ranch that's been terrorized!"

Constance's ranch was a neat little homestead nestled up against some trees. Even from a distance I could see that the place was well kept, with even fences and uncluttered stables. Still, there was no activity in the yard, and no sign of movement from the house.

"Come on," Constance said, looking up at the sky. "I don't want to get caught in the open when the sun goes down."

By the time we reached the ranch, the shadows had grown long. On the horizon, there was a faint hint of lightning and the distant, threatening roll of thunder.

"Put the horses in the barn! Hurry!" Constance said, sliding down from the saddle and running toward the house. "Jacob! Mateo!"

There weren't any other horses in the barn. No bodies or blood either. I didn't waste time loosening the cinches There would be time to come back and bed them down properly later on, after I'd made sure Constance hadn't found trouble in the house.

I was almost to the back door when the rain started. Nothing gentle about it this time, just a sudden deluge accompanied by a plunge into darkness as the sun vanished into clouds. Thunder rolled directly overhead, low and loud.

Ominous, even by my standards. Still, bad weather didn't make a monster. No, bad weather was just my sort of—

Constance screamed. Loud and sharp, a wailing shriek cutting through the sound of the rain and the groaning of the wind. I drew my one remaining gun, running the last few steps toward the house and crashing in through the back door.

"Constance!" I yelled, stumbling in the dark.

Somewhere ahead, a lantern on the kitchen table gave off a faint glow, just enough for me to find my bearings in an unfamiliar house. There was another crack of lightning, brighter than daylight, and I tripped over something half hidden beneath one of the kitchen chairs.

A body. A man, abdomen torn open, blood pooled all around him in an uneven circle. Half of his skin was missing, flayed off and spread out around him on the floor.

I'd seen death before, even held my own husband as he bled out. And, since then, I'd sent many more men to their graves. None of that prepared me for the body to give a sudden, rattling gasp.

"'ouse," he gurgled, eyes unseeing and mouth a ruined mass of blood.

"It's okay," I lied. "Mateo?"

He shuddered, whimpering something else, a sentence again and again. I leant in closer, ear almost to his mouth. "How…in…in…the…house."

Constance screamed, closer this time.

Mateo shook, eyes wild and bloodied hands scrabbling at me. Then he went still.

I left him on the floor, grabbing the lantern and heading deeper into the house. "Constance!"

"H-here!" she sobbed.

I followed the hitching sound of her breathing, turning out of the hall and into a living area. An open window rattled in the wind, rain pouring into the room as thunder cracked and rattled outside. The lantern guttered and died, but a flash of lightning illuminated the scene.

In the middle of the room stood Constance, and she wasn't alone.

At first, I thought it was a trick of the light, shadows cast by the lightning. But then, as a second bolt lit the sky, I got a proper look. It was too tall to be a man, with dark fur all over its body and impossibly long legs. Its head was shaped like a wolf, with a long, pointed jaw and teeth sharp as blades. And its eyes, with dark pupils surrounded by red, like something looking straight out of the depths of Hell.

I reached out a hand toward Constance, my own feet rooted to the ground. "Con—"

She didn't look scared, or like a woman facing her death. Instead, she laughed, mouth like a bloodstain. "Sadie Jones, I'd like you to meet my brother, Jacob."

The Beast smiled, too, a human expression that distorted its face into something demonic.

I dropped the lantern, gun coming up in one practiced motion. Neither Constance nor Jacob moved, half illuminated by the storm, faces caught in expressions that were impossibly familial despite their different features.

"Why'd you bring me here?" I demanded.

Constance cocked her head to one side, rain plastering her hair to her head. "Do you really want to know?"

"Start talkin' or I'll put you both in the ground!"

"No need for that. See, we've been here a long time," Constance said, absently tapping a hand on her brother's forearm. "Eating is fine. We can manage with most meat, but when it's time to reproduce…well. Beasts of the Storm need to consume the organs of human women. Our younglings take root in the hollow corpse and feast on it until they're born from the flesh. Miracle of life and all that."

My stomach churned. "You killed your workers."

"To get you here," Constance said, smiling. "When Jacob transformed this time, we knew he needed a mate. All of this mess was to lure you in."

I pulled the trigger. As the gun kicked in my hand, Jacob moved. He was across the room like liquid, between Constance and I, a dark flash of motion that ended with my gun skittering across the room and my fingers bent at impossible angles.

The sharp crunch of pain came a moment later. I tried to scream, but the sound caught in my throat.

"It used to be easy," Constance continued, as if I'd never tried to shoot her, as if her brother hadn't walked through my bullets like they were raindrops. "The nearby tribe let us take a man and a woman when we needed them. But then all you *pioneers* drove them away. There aren't many women out here no more, so I had to go looking for one."

I shook my head, cradling my ruined hand against my chest as silent tears began to leak from the corner of my eyes.

"What do you think, Jacob?"

The creature regarded me, still and quiet through each roll of thunder. Then, in a voice like a river rapid, like a storm turned to flood, he said, "She'll do."

Constance clapped. "Perfect! Oh, and Sadie?" She gave me a pitying look. "I am sorry about this. You were so helpful and all that, but this is family."

"You're a monster," I croaked.

She laughed, vicious and unconcerned, mouth red like a massacre. "Come now, what was it you kept saying to me? Oh yes, *monsters don't exist.*"

I felt the words like a physical blow, like claws raking into my chest, like the expression on my husband's face when he realized he was dying. Like lightning, touching against my skin and burning me down to nothing.

In the dark corner of the room, Jacob began to inch closer. His mouth was red with blood, red with death, my own grave rising up to meet me. And behind him, smile on her face, Constance watched.

Bad luck and worse timing. Perhaps I'd get to see my husband again.

Outside, the rain was still falling. I closed my eyes and listened to the storm.

TRADE SECRETS

by Brennan LaFaro

The train screeched to a stop, jostling the passengers around me from their stupors. Murmurs drifted from every direction. At first, I mistook them for the general excitement of having reached our destination, but the wavering tone that accompanies worry grabbed hold of my attention. I jolted forward and leaned toward the window. An ocean of sand flowed toward the horizon, a landscape unlike any seen back east. A thing of beauty, if not for the stunning lack of civilization.

We had arrived early, but not at Buzzard's Edge.

Alarmed mumbling quickly grew to a dull roar, and the engineer made no appearance to assuage his passengers. The panic intensified as men passed outside the windows. One in the lead and two more a few paces back. Despite the knocks and shouts from my fellow travelers, the strangers outside paid no attention, only kept moving toward the front of the train. The crescendo of voices made picking out individual words and phrases difficult, but fear hung heavy in the atmosphere. Likely the masses believed we were being boarded, robbed, but a man such as myself who has worked with lawmen all over this country recognizes authority when he sees it. An air of confidence in their stride and six-shooters at their hip worked in tandem with a gleam at their chest to mark them as officers of the law.

Embracing my opportunity, I plucked my satchel from the floor, then pushed through the stifling crowd to reach the nearest exit. Outside the train, the officers gathered, their faces pale as winter snow. Dear me, but this couldn't bode well. The glass tinked softly as I rapped my knuckles against it. Of the three men gathered, only one turned his head, but that proved sufficient.

As I said, law recognizes its match.

When the officer approached and the passengers realized the door would be opened, the pressure grew at my back, but the man who opened the door drew a massive revolver and held it aloft. "This here's a crime scene," he bellowed. "Get back to your seats and we'll have ya on your way fast as we can." He gave me an inquisitive look as I slipped out the cracked door, dropping to the hard-packed sand below.

"How long's that gonna be, Harden?" shouted a burly man from inside the train. He wore a black Stetson hat and a gaudy red sash tied prominently around his waist.

"Hell of a lot faster if you shut your fuckin' mouth, Fowler!" The officer turned back to me revealing his badge with the word "sheriff" emblazoned across the front. He cocked his head and donned a sheepish grin as if to apologize for the language. "And who might you be?"

"Thaddeus Locke," I said, offering a hand. "Full-time educator, part-time consulting detective."

"Consulting detective?" He raised an eyebrow. "Shit, that's a new one to me, but I s'pose we could use all the help we can get. John Harden, by the way." He didn't raise his hand in return. Nor did he holster the revolver. "Well, Mr. Locke, you don't dress much like an Arizona man. All that black, sun woulda gobbled you up long ago. Where you from, hoss?"

I cleared my throat. "All over, really, but most recently Cambridge. It's right outside of—"

"Boston. I heard of it, though I can't rightly recall where. And what brings you out here from Cambridge?"

"I'm traveling to Buzzard's Edge for, shall we say, a change of scenery. May I ask why you opened the door to me while keeping the rest of the cattle hostage?"

Harden snickered. "Cattle, huh? Maybe you'll fit in here after all. In answer to your question, I guess I just got a good feelin' about you. Dressed real spiffy, too. S'pose you just look like a man who knows his business." He studied me for a moment before continuing. "Detective you may be, but I sincerely doubt you ever seen nothin' like this. Murder, and a real nasty one at that. You sure you want to come along, Mr. Locke?"

"I think you might be surprised at what I've seen, Mr. Harden. If you'd like to point me toward the body, I would be honored to be of service, if I may?"

Harden smirked. "Oh, the guys're gonna love you. Right this way."

Harden and I approached the other two officers. He gestured to a tall gentleman with a salt and pepper beard and a scowl behind it. "This here's Virgil Morgan, and the young fella goes by Billy. Boys, this is Thaddeus Locke. Says he's a consulting detective and wants to lend a hand."

Morgan acknowledged my existence with a series of grunts. Thin as a rail and with a fine coat of peach fuzz about his cheeks, Billy nodded as he fiddled impatiently with a Bowie knife. I shuddered as the steel caught the sunlight. At first, I thought it may have evaded Morgan's notice, but a gruff chuckle escaped the sour frown he wore.

"What's wrong, fancy? Afraid of a blade?" Morgan asked.

Billy laughed so hard he dropped the knife. His cheeks reddened as he bent to recover it.

"I'm not overly fond, if you must know." I made a show of eyeing Harden's revolver. "Should violence be required, I prefer to keep a respectable distance."

Morgan spat in answer. "I'll bet. Tell me, Locke, you a betting man?"

"If the mood strikes."

He glanced at Billy and snickered. "Well, hopefully you're in the mood, 'cause I'm bettin' you ain't ever seen nothin' like this." Having repeated the company line, Morgan gestured for everyone to follow. Harden and I tailed close behind him, while Billy hung back a few steps.

"Don't mind the boy," Harden whispered. "Morgan's still training him. He ain't seen nothin' like this 'til recently. Still wrapping his head around the things that men can do to one another."

I nodded. "Aren't we all?"

Mere feet in front of the halted train lay a brutalized corpse. Blood and barbarity made the human beneath unrecognizable. Though I retained a stoic expression, I must admit this was one of the more ravaged bodies I had ever laid eyes upon.

"I can't imagine they turn up like this in Boston," Harden said, his voice soft and reverent. His trailing eyes seemed more interested in me than the corpse at our feet.

"You are not wrong, Mr. Harden." I crouched for a closer inspection. Dark crimson streaks that bordered on black obscured the identity of the victim and, to the untrained eye, hid the method of their execution.

"Burned, you think?" A curious tone had overtook Harden's voice. Perhaps a test.

"I think not. Dark and unpleasant as the body may appear, smell the air. Have any of you gentlemen ever come in contact with a burned corpse before?"

Morgan and Harden nodded in unison.

"Then you will know it is not an aroma one forgets. And it tends to change your dietary habits."

"So, then what do you make of it?" asked Harden, stroking his chin.

"Hmm, I regret to inform you that this unfortunate person has been flayed."

Two blank stares.

"Skinned. Most likely while alive. I should also add that they have been here for some time, cooking in the midday sun, as it were."

"Mr. Locke," said Harden, glancing sidelong at Morgan. "Who the fuck are you?"

I grinned and opened my mouth to reply when a shout cut me off.

"Goddammit, Harden! You gonna keep us in this sweatbox all day?"

Despite my recent arrival, the boisterous voice rang familiar. Fowler, the bear of a man, once more hung out the train window to make his grievances known. Billy chuckled from his position beside the engine, but Harden ignored the shouts. Morgan rolled his eyes.

"I see you there, Morgan," came the brash voice again. "Don't you need to be gettin' on your way? Find a hooker to suck that pitiful excuse for a pecker?"

"Fuck's sake," growled Morgan, his face taking on the shade of a ripe tomato. He stomped toward the train. "Billy, give me the goddamn knife."

Billy's eyes went wide, but Harden cut the tension with a laugh. "Let it go, Virgil. Don't do anything stupid. Big bastard thinks he's a cowboy. Don't give his shitty little fire any air. Real cowboys don't even wear those red sashes. That's just a story what floated down from Wyoming."

Morgan shook his head. "Got a point, John," he muttered. Although he did not ask for the knife again, Morgan's cheeks retained their furious red hue.

"Gentlemen," I interrupted. "Not to lend too much credence to Mr. Fowler's rumblings, but perhaps it would be best to move the body."

Three nods, and the unconditional acceptance of my services.

Buzzard's Edge's finest dragged the body from the tracks, leaving a rusty red trail of blood behind to paint the sand. The train departed once more, prepared to cover the final five-minute stretch to the center of town. After sharing an obscene gesture, Mr. Fowler took his seat and ceased his complaints as the train rumbled off into the distance. Though Morgan did not protest, he leveled more than a few side-eyed glances at my inclusion. I ignored them in favor of following Harden as he led the way to the town's resident undertaker, cooper and casket maker.

Mr. Meyer, a true jack of all trades, wordlessly directed us to his backroom. He helped us lay the body on a table in the center of the room. With only a nod of his head, he left us to our business.

"Jesus Christ," whispered Billy. He stepped back as his pallor took on a green hue.

Harden leaned over to him. "You can wait outside, Billy. If you want." A comforting gesture, but Billy remained frozen in place, eyes locked on the ghastly image occupying the table.

I cleared my throat and Harden jumped. "Sheriff, you showed little surprise when I first posited the theory of a skinned man, and if you will excuse my saying so, your question of a burn victim lacked conviction." I kept my gaze on the corpse, a man of indeterminate age.

"We suspected as much. The skinning, that is. Haven't been exactly straight with you, Mr. Locke. Wanted to see what you were made of." Harden cleared his throat. "This here's the third such victim to turn up this week missing their outermost layer to shield 'em from the elements."

"All of 'em was left outside of town in the type of unidentifiable state you see here," added Morgan. "Harden might not have showed no surprise, but an outsider who shows up and nails down that method of killin' within a few seconds sure as hell catches my attention."

I turned to meet Morgan's stare. Flames flickered behind his eyes. He had tiptoed to the line of accusation, but he would go no further—not without some kind of proof.

Harden stepped between us. "Cut the shit, Virgil. Thaddeus here was on the fuckin' train when it happened."

"And where exactly were you comin' from?" he snapped.

"Tucson," I replied, "and Tuscaloosa before that, should you need further alibi from a man attempting to help you solve this murder." I took a deep breath as I watched the arrogance drain from Morgan's eyes.

Harden gave a barely perceptible nod and continued. "Morgan's right—'bout the deaths, that is."

"So what can you tell us?" asked Morgan. He nearly succeeded in keeping the edge from his voice, but a trace cut through nonetheless.

I leaned in, squinting my eyes. "This hardly narrows the suspect pool, but this act was not performed by a medical professional." I gestured at a spot at the base of the victim's neck. "The edges are far too frayed. Even with a dull implement, a person with some knowledge of human anatomy would know how to separate skin from muscle without so much…sawing. Tearing."

"Jesus." Harden covered his mouth with one hand.

Without a word, Billy broke from his stupor and stepped out of the room.

Any coloring the Arizona sun had imbued upon Morgan vanished. "What would you say they used?"

"Given the ragged ribbons of flesh, a knife, but something small. More appropriate for paring fingernails than separating flesh from muscle."

"Don't suppose you see anything else that could tell us who or what to look for?" asked Harden, still muffled behind his hand.

I stood to my full height and met each man's eyes before speaking. "Some of this is mere speculation, but…"

"Don't be shy, Locke," said Morgan.

"The clotting suggests the task began when the victim was alive, but concluded after they had expired. As I mentioned, the ragged remains of the flesh speak to the force of the removal. You're looking for a man or woman with the strength of a bull. And with a cruel, vindictive streak to boot. Only a madman could inflict this level of suffering upon a person without personal vengeance in mind. If we can discover a motive for revenge, you'll likely have your killer in tow."

"Shit's sake… Only one glaring problem with that," said Morgan. "We don't even know who this is."

Silence shrouded the air as I studied the victim, my eyes finally landing on his closed fist. "I wonder."

Before either Harden or Morgan could stop me, I grasped the fist and wrestled the fingers open. They remained stiff and fought me through and through, but finally gave way with a terrible crack. A smile crossed my face as I held the small metal disc up to the light. The windows allowed only a pittance of sunshine through, but it was enough to read by.

"What the hell is that?" asked Morgan.

"A soldier's medallion. Are either of you gentlemen familiar with a former Union soldier named Joseph Flanagan?"

I almost grinned as Harden and Morgan stared at me with slack jaws.

When we three had gleaned all possible knowledge from the body, we located Billy and returned to the sheriff's quarters. An uncomfortable silence hung in the air as four internal debates took place.

Morgan spoke first, shaking his head. "I need to go wash up before we do anything else. Feels like I got a dead man stink livin' in my clothes. Won't be able to focus 'til I get rid of it."

Harden nodded absently, and Morgan slipped out the door into the afternoon sun.

After a few moments, Harden spoke. "Joseph Flanagan had a wife—widow now, I suppose. A child, too. Couldn't be older than ten, if memory serves. Billy, you'll come help me inform her. Mr. Locke, you're welcome to tag along."

Billy nodded.

"I'm not sure my presence would be appropriate," I said. "I believe I'll wait here."

Harden nodded. "Soon as you said that name…" A moment passed. "We know Joseph Flanagan well 'round here. Just didn't recognize him in that state."

I narrowed my eyes. "In what capacity do you know him?"

"He didn't care much for the law, I'm afraid. Nor the men who uphold it, like you and me. Nothin' that got him locked up for longer than a day or two, but a string of petty shit longer'n my johnson."

"Johnson?"

Harden turned red. "Well, never mind. I'll see what I can get out of his widow, sweet little lady by the name of Samantha."

I put my hand on his shoulder as he turned to leave. "Any name will do as a place to start. Be merciful, John, but relentless."

"You think?"

"It has always served me well."

Harden nodded, his face impassive. His countenance was that of a man who knew his duty. Western lawmen had earned a reputation in the east for being vicious, if not all that bright. Mr. Harden brought a solemn thoughtfulness to his work, making him a worthy adversary to anyone cold-blooded enough to stand against him.

John Harden and Billy picked up their hats and walked outside. I made myself scarce in the dusty and unkempt station.

Harden burst through the office door just over an hour later. Billy followed close behind.

"Shit in a bucket… I was right," said the sheriff in a sullen tone.

"Do tell, John," I replied.

Billy leaned against the wall and pursed his lips. "Damn, friend. You're sweatier than a jalapeño's armpit. Feelin' all right?"

A peal of laughter escaped my lips. "Quite. Though the Arizona sun will take some getting used to. John was correct in his earlier assessment; I may need some clothes in a shade other than black."

"Got that right." Billy laughed and settled back. "Tell him, Mr. Harden."

Harden nodded. "Samantha's a lovely woman, like I said, but she didn't give two good goddamns about how her late husband made money, so long as he made it."

"Money seemed the only part she was broken up about, truth told," added Billy.

"Interesting," I said, steepling my fingers on top of Harden's desk. "Am I to take it she was privy to Mr. Flanagan's illegal activities?"

He slammed his hat down in front of me and scratched at his balding head. "Certainly seems like he didn't hide no details from her. And now that he's dead, she didn't see no reason to protect him."

"A bold notion," I reasoned. "Has she grounds to fear legal consequences for knowledge of his crimes?"

Harden looked to Billy for a moment. When his gaze returned to me, something twinkled in his eye. "That's the difference between where you come from, Mr. Locke, and where you are now. We follow a code, a set of guidelines, that helps us protect the innocent. Most times that lines up with punishing the wicked, but that ain't always the case."

"So I see." Leaning back in Harden's chair, I let a moment pass. A palette cleanser to return to the more vital subject at hand. "When you said you were right…"

"Ah…" The humble embarrassment dropped from Harden's face, and he replaced his hat upon his head. "That. Yeah, so like I said, Samantha knew the ins and out of Flanagan's business. She said he always worked alone, that he knew he could make a little more scratch taking on bigger operations with a partner, but that he didn't trust nobody."

"Now, we're getting somewhere. Excellent work, Mr. Harden. And why should Mr. Flanagan be so bereft of trust?"

"Don't rightly know. She said he'd always been that way, since long before she met him."

"And how long ago was that?"

"About ten years, when he first moved to town from Texas. He caught her eye, and that was that."

"Hmm, I see no road forward there. So she offered no clue as to any potential enemies the man could have on the wrong side of the law? Think, Mr. Harden. Think very hard."

Harden dropped his gaze, seeming to find his feet very interesting all of the sudden.

Billy cleared his throat. "Like Mr. Harden said, Joseph Flanagan was no friend of the sheriff's office. His wife seemed to think there was one lawman in particular who had it out for him."

Harden raised his head and shot Billy a cold stare. The young man withered under his gaze.

I sat straight up. "Yes?"

Harden opened his mouth to answer, when the door burst open once more.

Morgan filled the doorway. "Come quick, John. There's been another murder."

Harden flew from the room, and without waiting for an invitation, I followed. I did not need to approach the body to know this was the work of the same killer. Tossed unceremoniously in an alley behind Lynch's Tavern, this corpse sang the same tune as the last. All the skin had been peeled from this bear-sized body, leaving them an unrecognizable mass of bloodstained chaos.

"Once again, the ragged edges speak of pain and inexperience on the part of the butcher," I removed a handkerchief from my breast pocket and held it in front of my mouth and nose. Though the cadaver on the tracks reeked of hours spent decaying under the blazing Arizona sun, the freshness of this body troubled my compatriots into silence.

Billy turned that familiar shade of green.

"Go get Meyer," said Harden. "Tell him we could use some more help." He watched Billy turn tail and run. "Kid ain't got no stomach for this," he added as an aside to Morgan.

"They was days apart before. Now, two in a few hours. Shit, boss. This ain't good," said Morgan, his eyes darting side to side. He removed his hat and wiped the sweat from his brow.

"No, Virgil, it surely ain't." Harden's eyes appeared sad, fixed on a detail he did not see fit to talk about yet.

Much of detective work requires instinct and the ability to make an improvised split-second decision. In that moment, I knew what Harden was about to share with me in his office and why he truly sent Billy away.

"Mr. Morgan," I whispered. "There is blood upon your shirt."

Morgan's eyebrows furrowed. "Well, shit. Yeah, of course there is." He gestured to the skinned cadaver. The pace of his breathing increased as he stared back and forth between John and I. His glistening eyes betrayed realization of the off-hand comment as an accusation. "John?" he pleaded.

Harden kept his eyes on the desecrated remains. "That little red sash right there?" He pointed to a patch of scarlet fabric half-tucked under the body. Only a trained eye could have distinguished the small piece of clothing from the gore surrounding it. "That guy on the train you had it out with earlier…Fowler; he wore one just like it. Add that to the size of this here body and I think we got ourselves an identification."

Morgan's eyes ignited. "What the fuck are you trying to say, John?"

Harden shook his head. "Ain't sayin' nothin' just yet. Think we need to get this fella cleaned up and off the street. Then we need to have ourselves a conversation." His next words were careful and measured. "Will you help us, Virgil?"

Morgan took a step back. He licked his lips and stared daggers at me. "What kind of poisonous bullshit has this carpetbagger put in your head, John?"

With a sigh, Harden answered. "Not a lick that wasn't already brewin' in there, I'm afraid. I'll ask again, Virgil; will you help us and come along? If you don't want to answer this time, the question's gonna change."

"Fuck you," spat Morgan.

"Shit," whispered Harden—heartbreak resonated in the single word. A friend and a brother in arms turned killer. He reached for his revolver, but Morgan punched him square in the eye. Harden crashed to the ground in a plume of dust as Morgan turned and bolted from the alley.

Snatching Harden's firearm, I gave chase.

I burst from the alley to see a blur of human being disappear behind the tavern. My late-night detective work usually called for more exercise of the mind than the body, but I took pains to remain in shape for such an occasion as this. Rounding the corner dropped me onto a straight narrow road, Morgan at least one hundred paces ahead of me.

The citizens crowding the streets either took no notice or cared not a whit about the two men barreling through. I barked out repeated "excuse mes" and "pardons," slamming into men and women both in an attempt to close the gap between Morgan and myself. Near the end of the road, he glanced over his shoulder then ducked between two buildings—another alley. With exhaustion setting in, I pushed myself to run harder, faster. If he vanished in that alcove, all was lost with him.

I skidded to a stop just before the opening, a small crevice between a barber shop and a telegraph office. Taking in a deep breath in case it was my last, I darted around the corner. I anticipated two possibilities—either no sign of my quarry or a loaded pistol aimed between my eyes. Yet I came upon neither. Instead, Virgil Morgan sat collapsed in a heap, pitched back against a wall in the abandoned alley. Tears cut trails through the grime caked on his face.

When he caught sight of me, he furiously wiped them away. "Son of a bitch," he whimpered. "Why did I run, Mr. Locke?"

I leveled the sheriff's revolver at Morgan's head and glanced around. Not a soul in sight. "Whatever do you mean, Virgil?"

"I ain't ever killed nobody that didn't have it coming. Not outside the confines of the law, anyway. Got me a temper, but hell, John's always known that. How could he think I'd be capable of…of doin' that to a person?"

The flicker of a grin settled on my face, though I kept the revolver aimed at Morgan. "Because all the evidence points to you. Fowler's sash, your multiple run-ins with Joseph Flanagan. Even the first two victims tie to your name."

Morgan squinted. When he spoke, his voice trembled in a mixture of fear and confusion. "How could you know that?"

"I made sure of it." I glanced around again, but we remained very much alone. "You see, Mr. Morgan, I have a propensity for distributing death. With such an inclination, it is never wise to stay in one area for very long. Even for that short period of time, one must ingratiate themselves within the community. It has worked for me in various small towns in and around

New England, most recently in Cambridge. You see, a teacher arrives in town with a degree of dignity. Respect, if you like. Yet, they remain an outsider, and outsiders are always the first suspects when things go wrong."

Morgan grinded his teeth together, yet he offered not a word. The fury in his eyes from earlier paled in comparison to the blaze that filled them now.

"Bodies are found under mysterious circumstances and, of course, the town will search for someone to blame. The less familiar, the better. But what if that new arrival helped to solve the crime? Furthermore, what if that person could unmask the murderer as a respected member of the community? A priest, a town councilman, a—"

"Sheriff's deputy?" Though fire lit Morgan's eyes, a smirk crept across his face.

I nodded in acquiesce.

"And when you've caught me and the killings don't stop?"

"Oh, they will stop. For a time, at least. Until the itch becomes too much again. Then, I will gracefully bow out and relocate. Mr. Morgan, I think you'd be surprised at my self-discipline. I can hold out for quite some time."

"John'll find you out. He ain't stupid."

"No. No, he is not, but you asked me earlier if I was a betting man? Thus far, Mr. Harden does not realize I have been squatting in town for a week already, listening and learning, moving about only under cover of darkness. He does not suspect that I boarded the train only a few miles outside of town as a stowaway or that I changed from my clothes, soaked in Fowler's blood, while he was interviewing Samantha Flanagan. Shall I go on?"

"You ain't actually scared of knives, are ya?"

With a chuckle, I continued. "If I were a betting man, I'd bet on Mr. Harden being more like those eastern sheriffs than he fancies himself and only seeing what he wants to see."

"Well, then," said Morgan. "Seems you've thought of everything."

"In fact, I pride myself on it."

"Then you already know you can't let me live. I'll sing like a canary."

I cocked my head to the side. "My scapegoats never do make it out alive. Though, I will say, this is the first time I've had to pull the trigger myself."

With his life in imminent danger, Morgan made no move to fight. He inhaled deeply as anger gave way to wonder in his eyes. "Now, how the hell have you managed that?"

"A trade secret for another day, I'm afraid." I smiled as I squeezed the trigger.

The calamitous gunfire drew a crowd so quickly I barely had time to fill Morgan's hand with his own gun and slip the murder weapon into his pocket. Harden, a black and purple bruise already forming around his eye, pushed through the crowd. His jaw dropped and his features sank as he took in the grizzled sight of his former deputy. Ribbons of gore entwined with bits of skull littered the alleyway, all that remained of the murderous mind of Virgil Morgan.

I forced tears to the corner of my eyes and laid a hand upon Harden's shoulder. "I am deeply sorry, John. He left me no choice."

Harden nodded, but said nothing. He studied Morgan's body for a moment or two, then turned his back on it. "Christ almighty, Mr. Locke. Thaddeus. It all right if I call you Thaddeus?"

"Of course."

"I just never thought he had it in him. I trusted Virgil with my life and…shit. To think he was capable of that. Makes my skin crawl, you know?"

"I do not wish to seem indelicate, but who will take care of Mr. Morgan and Mr. Fowler?"

"Anyone but me, for the moment. I need some time to get my head straight before I talk to Billy. I wouldn't hate the company, though. Would you walk with me?"

"I should be honored."

We exited the alleyway and walked slowly down the main stretch of town that led to the sheriff's office.

"You never did tell me what brought you to Buzzard's Edge," said Harden.

"New opportunities, John. Though it seems of such little import right now. I hope you will not think me perverse, but despite today's events, I quite like it here. A nice change of pace from the hustle and bustle of eastern life. Do you happen to know if Buzzard's Edge has need of an educator?"

"I can point you toward someone who'd know, and I wouldn't mind having those investigative skills to call on every so often." Harden widened his eyes as though he'd asked a question.

"Certainly. I am ever at your disposal."

A smile wiped the dour expression from John Harden's face. He clapped a hand on my back as we walked away from the carnage and commotion.

I HAVE SEEN
THE ELEPHANT

by Michael Bailey
[based on a true story]

In eighteen forty-eight a diggin's was settled
        nuggets the size of fists
        plucked from dyin' creek-beds
        panned out seasonal streams
        yeller collected dust

For in this placer-town some men was hanged
        not once, not twice, thrice

In eighteen fifty-love their gilted restless ghosts
haunted the mines by night
drunk on the chilly air
swam splashless 'long long-toms
    nightmare'd the lone sleepless

And in this unestablished place of sin
    Miwok and Maidu wept

In eighteen fifty-two a fourth was strung up high
    same evil oak tree branch
    damn harbinger of death
    both feet all a-dangle
    afore off'rin' to jump

And in this establishment past recurred
    'cause Lynch's law was just

In eighteen fifty-four men gave name to a town
    one perhaps more pleasant
    Placerville was agreed
    a unanimous vote
for fear chased away guests

And in this hang-town 'nother two years passed
    'til the first three returned

In eighteen fifty-six the whole town was burned
    not once, not twice, thrice
each seemed to take its turn
revenge served afire
the fourth waitin' to spoil

For in this ol' dry diggin's there are hells
one for each life 'was took

Hangtown, California – Autumn, 1852

Richard Crone witnessed the original three hangings back in '49 and was convinced no man would ever hang again in the diggings, especially after a near-fourth. Crowds gathered for the lynchings, until realizing what hangings entailed, then dispersed. Once bodies stopped moving, interest fell, like the men. No one wanted to stick around for the sour fragrance of death.

Benjamin Alexander Read, the fourth man they'd tried at the rope that year, once took eleven dollars from him in a game of poker. Richard preferred monte, his sleight-of-hand able to trick the slow eyes of drunkards, yet those in the saloon had talked him into a different game, which he'd lost. And so, he figured Read's horse—two bullets to take her down—would make them square, seeing as the amount he lost could've bought a good horse.

If Read weren't such a seemingly honest man, weren't a *father*, he'd have plunged his knife deep into his gut and not later gone for the horse. The boy's why he hesitated with his blade. He'd seen little Read plenty of times in the El Dorado, before it changed hands to the Elsnters, always trying to un-drunk his father from the tables.

The acting sheriff interviewed Richard then, and again in the summer after getting involved in a game of monte with desperados later arrested for robbing a Frenchman named Prosper Cailloux. Richard had no fewer than three men shake him awake in the early morning. Men asking, "Where's the gold?" After showing them the gold he'd won, fairly, they let him be, for why would he not run if guilty. Plus, his own story matched the barkeep's recounting.

With Benjamin Alexander Read, he'd been approached for reputation. "Bloody Dick," some called him, a stupid *nom de plume*; sometimes simply "The Irishman" on account of his heritage. He hated the nicknames, but he'd poked more than a few who did him wrong. So what if he had a hot temper and a fast hand? Nothing he could do about either. No, with the

Reads, it was Sheriff Rogers out for blood. He'd always had it in for him, even before the new title and badge, for Richard had sliced open the man's cousin's arm for accusing him of using waxed cards. The sheriff had nothing on him, just prodding for information.

"You shoot his horse?" the sheriff asked of the Reads. "A hangin' offense."

"They *say* I shot their horse?"

"Not outright, no, but they've got themselves a dead horse next to their claim, shot twice, and the only person home then was the Read boy, the son, and he sure as hell didn't shoot his father's horse. A man says you was seen there the same night. That true?"

"What man?"

"A man," Sheriff Rogers said, "and I'll leave it at that."

"That so."

"It is so. You shoot their horse?"

"What do the Reads say about the matter?"

"Only that someone came by and shot her dead, though they aren't willing to offer names. I seen the horse. Shot under the ear, again in the neck. The father's not saying anything, not the boy, neither, and the third in their party can't talk at all. But I asked around, and you was seen playing cards with Read, Sr. You pulled a knife on him, I heard."

"I play games with lots of men. I run a table at the El Dorado."

"Everyone knows that. And the knife?"

Richard Crone pulled the blade and showed it to the newly-appointed sheriff, said, "Sure, this one. I was mad for losing a bad hand. Didn't use it on Read, though. Same blade I used on your cousin, if I remember correctly. No one calls me a cheater and doesn't get opened. That why you're here, your cousin?"

"One account says you lost a large sum in a single hand."

"Who hasn't on this hell?"

The conversation went back and forth, but in the end, Sheriff Rogers rode away knowing as much as he'd known riding in: nothing. There *was* nothing. That was months ago, when water still flowed through the cursed town.

September the earth was parched, which meant more miners gambling their gold than digging it out from the ground, or panning piles previously dug, which meant miners would spend it on chance and liquor and women. Good for business and those who ran tables. More men inside than out by the time October rolled through, and that fed business into the winter months. Under the round tents and in the saloons and hotel establishments could be found heat and light, which attracted men as much as what they could expect or want to find inside.

Sporting types from all stretches of land came in from the cold, recognized by their fancy dress shirts, clashing badly with the dirty ever-gambling miners. Fighting fixed boredom, fixed monotony. Shots fired out upon the slightest provocation, yet everyone had the hangings of '49 on the mind, even three years later, and so threats were never much more than slung words or holes put into wood.

There was the Thomas-Young Round Tent, which not long before went by the name Taylor's, as well as Tom Ashton's across the way, the Adams Hotel, James Odle's City Hotel, with Scraton's Eureka Hotel splitting them. The El Dorado Saloon was always booming, though everyone called it the El Dorado, with the "Jackass" or "Hangtree" adjacent to it, formerly the Barkhurst's Placer Hotel, which was now run by the Herricks. Names and ownerships changed as rapidly as townsfolk, yet Elstner owned damn near everything on Main by the end of '50, including the saloon where Richard ran his table, as well as the hanging tree. The Chicago Dining Saloon on Maiden Lane was likewise popular, but nothing like the El Dorado. There, the whole town erupted before dusk and stayed lit—along with its people—through sunup. Stores stayed open past full dark.

Autumn seemed short-lived with winter rushing in early to accommodate the crowds, which is how Richard Crone found himself in the El Dorado slinging cards this chilly October night; Sunday morning, really, for it was approaching two o'clock when trouble met his table.

Whether by intoxication or fatigue, the solid ghost of a dead man approached his table: Manuel, the first of the hanged three of '49—one of the three responsible for Old Dry Diggings in California changing names to Hangtown. The same young man he'd watched hang until dead the previous winter now stood at his table. Rope marks and bruises encircled his neck.

Richard tried to say his name, but his breath caught short in his throat, dry as the creek. He'd watched this man's bowels give out, watched his feet dangle at the edge of a wagon as oxen pulled away. Richard had swung in his own dizziness back then, mesmerized by the slow deaths of all three men, and had stilled only when the last of the hanged men stopped moving. All three had haunted his dreams this last year.

Ace of spades, the first of the money cards.

He signaled the barkeep, who only shook his head, too busy to give much notice. The Irishman wanted a drink more than ever, but that's not why he wanted the barkeep's attention. Surely, he'd recognize the dead fellow walking through the saloon, *smell* him. The barkeep had gone to the hanging, same as everyone else. Yet he ignored Richard and the dead fellow walking by him, turning back to the man he conversed with at the bar—a portly American fellow with fair skin and rosy cheeks. The last of the three hung in '49. Blood seeped out from his shirt as though from a flogging. All three dead men were in the saloon.

Richard Crone shook his head as his hands did so on their own. He blinked hard, twice, one for each of the dead in the room. The morning hours were rushing upon him quickly, was all, the whiskey twisting his sight. When he blinked a third time, the Spaniard in front of him was not Miguel at all, just some tan- or dirty-skinned man of no discernable origin with dark hair draping down to his shoulders. And at the bar, the barkeep filled the glass of a different, white-skinned fellow, clothes untarnished. Spooked, is all. Tired.

"We playing this game or what?" asked the man next to him, a miner.

"Sorry," Richard said.

"*Jouons-nous à monte?*" said another in French.

A familiar face stared back at him with eyes of the dead: neck rotted, tongue swollen and protruded. This third ghost smelled of defecation and piss, which hit him swiftly, though no one else at the table seemed to notice the stench. The last of the three hanged in '49.

Richard Crone blinked again, and the Frenchman was another fellow entirely.

No, this couldn't be happening.

"The hell," he said, the decay lingering.

Each of the three men at his table expected cards, and so Richard asked who was in. The Frenchman's blue hand tossed in a few coins, said something else in his language. After pointing to the jack of diamonds with putrefied fingers—the money card this time around—Richard flipped them over, made them dance, trying not to think of the hanged men, and dropped one of the cards on the floor by mistake.

Not since he was a child had he lost a card, not even in a shuffle.

Intoxicated, no doubt, for his head spun as it had all those years ago. He spilled his drink in reaching down for the fallen soldier and a wave of whiskey flowed across the table, the drink fortunately flowing away from the deck. Righting himself after retrieving the card, he swore, causing all heads in the room to turn. The three ghosts were there amongst the crowd: two at his table, one at the bar. All six dead eyes glowed and burned into him.

"I'll get that, honey," said one of the whores. When not selling herself, she attended the tables, brought drinks, and took away empty tumblers. She didn't seem to mind when a rotted hand brushed her arm. No, she smiled at the dead Frenchman, said maybe later, for she'd just been with a man and still needed to freshen up. She smiled as well at the decomposed Spaniard. And in the time it took for Richard's heart to restart, for air to fill his lungs, she was gone, and so were the three ghosts of Hangtown.

"I seen the elephant," Richard said under his breath, a common phrase heard 'round the diggins' when a soul had experienced far too much of the world at too significant a cost. Over the years, he'd seen many expired men give up the laborious search for gold.

Living men waited for the game to recommence.

"Apologies, fellas," Richard said." Too much of the drink, perhaps."

The three cards were inspected by everyone at the table, the jack tapped, then flipped over, quickly shuffled one over the other, over the other, over the other, and soon even *he* had lost the money card, thought maybe it was the left one, or maybe the middle when they slowed.

"*Millieu,*" said the Frenchman, pointing at the middle card.

Richard flipped it over, not too surprised to see the jack but mostly certain beforehand that the leftmost card was the place he'd intended. Without word, he pushed back the pot.

"*Tu nous as tués,*" the winner said.

"*Nos mataste,*" said the other.

He'd heard enough French to know the difference between formal and informal, knew only that he'd been insulted by the Frenchman's words, and knew just enough Spanish to know the Spaniard had used a word he'd didn't much care for by the way of its inflection, though he knew not what either man meant with their foreign words.

"You killed us!" the man at the bar called out, as if hearing his very thought. Richard knew that whiney voice, which had carried with him since '49: the hanged American.

"No," Richard Crone said. "You're not here."

But they were. His eyes moved from the cards to the bar, where the bloated man raised his glass in a cheer, and then to the dead men sitting across the table.

This can't be happening.

Miguel, Bissi—that was his name—and the American; all three smiled wickedly, smelling of death and putridity that comes just before and long after a person dies, the smell of earth, decomposition, excrement, rot.

The Spaniard spoke next, using words Richard had never heard before. He tossed a handful of coins onto the table and spat a mouthful of black onto the floor, the way blood looks under scant moonlight in the darkness of night. He started to argue as the Irishman stood there, staring down at anything but these rancid men.

No, Richard decided no more cards, no more games. This was all from some fever, he told himself, for the sweat on his brow fell heavily and soaked into his attire as a cold rush swept down his spine, the dizziness overpowering.

"Are we playing or what?" a man said in broken English.

The use of familiar words pulled him out of the trance.

In front of him were men wanting to pass the time with games of monte, not one of them dead. They only resembled those from the past, Richard told himself. Haunted thoughts, is all. And the man talking to the barkeep was just some whiter-than-white fellow in fancy dress drowning in drink.

Get a holda yerself. A few more rounds, then rest.

Three games came and went, and Richard won all three, of course. Then a fourth, and a fifth, his hands as sly as ever, which only made the others at the table anxious. He'd have to let them win a few, he realized, and tried in earnest. But both men were drunker than he, and they each lost two additional games apiece. Frustrated hands pushed both coin and gold as wager.

"Let's call it a night," Richard said, but they wanted nothing of it.

And for the next half-dozen games, he intentionally slowed; any man capable of breathing could have followed the money card, especially since he made it turn up in the middle every damn time. But no, they chose poorly, as if they played with intent to lose.

The core gathering in the El Dorado seemed to watch their game, for he, the dealer, was up maybe a hundred dollars, and the next bet by the Spaniard was considerable.

"This is the last round, fellas," he told them. "Couldn't make it easier for you to win back what you're throwing my way." Richard kept his eyes on the cards, not wanting to look up for fear of death rejoining him at the table. "Last round. After this, *no mas.*"

The Spaniard slid in three ounces of gold as the room hushed. Richard had no plans of taking that gold, for he could read drunkards as easily as cards and understood taking it would bring violence to the table. Three ounces of gold wasn't worth dying for, and this was the last of what this poor man had on him.

"If that's what you wish, you damn fool."

Cards danced a 1-2-3 waltz in front of him, 1-2-3, as a retch of bile worked him, a sour mix of hard spirts and tobacco. He forced it down, cleared his throat. The cards couldn't slow much more than he made them dance initially, 1-2-3, and once again he decided upon the middle in which to place the jack. *Any* man not blinded by kerchief would know where to find the bastard. He even looked at the middle card as he waited for the Spaniard to decide.

The middle, amigo.

The El Dorado erupted in hollers as the young man pointed at the rightmost card, the eight of clubs, Richard knew, for he'd placed it there, as he had likewise placed the five of daggers as the leftmost and the damn horseman between them. The entire saloon knew where to find the jack.

"You're absolutely certain," Richard said, offering an out.

"*Sí,*" the man said.

Everyone in the establishment held a collective breath amid mumbles, perhaps some wondering whether or not they were wrong in their own choosing. There were two dozen standing over the table as Richard let out a sigh and flipped over the middle card.

"*Señor,*" he said, "you couldn't pick the shell with the pea."

"*La triche!*" the Frenchman next to him said.

Richard recognized the same words from long ago, understood the accusation without a need for translation. The Spaniard rattled off a string of Spanish, a few curses he recognized.

"An honest game," he told them, but they wanted none of it.

"He says you cheated," said a man over his shoulder.

"I know what he said, and I did no such thing. I do not cheat, not ever."

"Says you waxed the cards."

"Now why in hell would I do that?"

"*La triche!*" the Frenchman repeated.

"*Engañar! El tramposo!*" said the Spaniard.

"I do not cheat," Richard said again, gritting his teeth. "Say those foreign words once more and I'll carve your heart outta your chest."

"*El tramposo, el tramposo!*"

"Call me a cheater one more time and I'll put my blade—"

"Cheater!" the dead man said, suddenly Manuel from long ago.

In a fluid motion Richard Crone's Bowie knife was set loose from its sheath and plunged into the young man as if on its own accord. And what did it matter? For the boy was already beyond life, hanged prior, and so he pushed until hilt met ribcage. Not blood, but black sludge welled out from the man's chest, straight from his still heart. He thrust it in a second time, twisted the blade as the black bled to red, as if in his second murder the poor Spaniard had been brought back to life only to die again. The expression his face was that of a boy, innocent.

"You will never tell me I lied again," Richard said.

Women screamed.

Chair legs screeched across wood.

A pistol was drawn.

"*Qu'est-ce que se,*" said the Frenchman, which needed no translation.

What is this. Yes, what in hell is all this?!

The young man—perhaps as young as he—fell to the floor, died almost instantly.

"I am not a cheater!" Richard said to the crowd.

He leaned over the fallen and frigidly pulled the Bowie knife from the man's chest with a shaky hand, blood lashing across his face and marking him for murder. He tasted the man's death on his lips and spat it to the floor. Then he wiped the blade with his handkerchief and sheathed his weapon. The only dead man in the room was the young Spaniard before him, toes up.

All three ghosts were nowhere to be found.

Three ounces bet, one for each…

"You've just murdered an innocent man, Richard Crone," someone in the crowd said. "Arrived in the diggings no more than a few days ago, but by no means guilty of any crime other than losing to your sleight-of-hand."

In silence, the Irishman exited the saloon. He staggered home, drunk on both whiskey and what he'd done. Occasionally, he glanced over his shoulder, but no one followed.

Killed the already dead. Already dead.

"Can't kill a man's already gone," he said to the night.

A crescent moon smiled in the speckled sky as lunacy fed into him. He sang an Irish tune aloud, which echoed in the stillness. Once he made it to his cabin, he fell hard onto his bedroll and into a dreamless sleep that swallowed him whole.

Slapped awake, he opened his eyes to the light of morning, the night there and gone in a matter of one long slow blink of confusion.

"You're under arrest," a blurry man said as his hands were tied.

Sheriff Rogers stood pointing a scattergun at his chest.

Two other men did the tying.

"Arrest for what?" Richard said, his dream of the three ghosts a smudge in his mind. "What'd I do? I'm not guilty of nothing. What time is it, I ask?"

The sheriff eyed the sun, said, "Close to eight, I reckon, though I'm not sure that matters at this point. What matters is you killed a man 'bout six hours earlier, unprovoked. Stabbed him, no less. Witnessed by at least ten or more who named you. The kid you killed's the same age as you, maybe younger."

Richard had often been called a kid, a 'mere boy' because of his features.

"I didn't kill no kid," he said, half-remembering.

Only killed what's already dead—a spirit, a spectre.

A fist busted him across the jaw, then, and he fell hard on his side and into the dirt. Boots kicked him in the gut, over and over again, until Richard pissed himself; that, or he'd done so in his sleep for all he could remember. Men smiled over him.

They dragged him all the way to Elstner's hay yard, threw him on the ground right under the hang tree, and then it dawned on him what was about to transpire.

"*No-no-no*, I killed no man," he pleaded. "Honest."

"You killed my brother, you son of a bitch."

A second punch to his face brought blackness and then light. Whoever had hit him then did so a third time, ringing his ears.

Sheriff Rogers spoke through the noise and the blindness, said, "The young man you killed over a damn game'a monte was recognized as this man's brother. I rode out personally to Chili Bar where he was said to be, brought him back to see the man who'd done it. You brought this upon yourself, Richard Crone. You're gonna hang for all you done. Blood's been on your hands for far too long."

"Bloody Irish Dick, he done it," another said. "I saw him."

"Not a hesitation of remorse."

"Stabbed him in the heart."

"Cheated the young man of his gold."

Three ounces, a fool's bet.

The voices came from all directions as his head spun in the dark like it had only hours ago. Then someone turned him toward the rising sun and the black turned to white, then dissolved from red into colors until the world returned properly. A trickle of blood tickled his upper lip from a single nostril and cool-slid down his chin.

"I am not a cheating man," Richard said, defeated. "I'm not a—"

True as that may be, he was held captive for all to see, tied to the trunk of the oak that had killed the three men from '49 who'd haunted him, and where a fourth, Benjamin Alexander Read, had almost died by rope. There, Richard waited for most of the morning, slapped, spat upon, switched by stick, ridiculed in front of a crowd of two hundred angry men, women, and children. Some threw stones. Some threatened with knives—cut him, even.

Less than an hour later, by motion of the sun, that number grew to a thousand, maybe two thousand, everyone armed with something aimed to hurt, anything from pick-handle to rifle to rock to spade. Richard Crone was beaten, bloodied, as his *nom de plume* implied.

"Bloody Irish Dick," said a boy no older than ten, "serves you right."

"What makes any of this right?" Richard called out to the mob.

"What makes you killin' that young man right?"

"Should stab *you* in the heart!"

"Bleed you right here."

He could barely stand by the time they untied him, and he was led to the same building where they'd detained the three desperados before they were sentenced to be hanged. The blood of those men still stained the floorboards brown, and his own blood now mixed in with theirs.

No way will this town hang another. Not me. Not anyone.

"Don't you all remember?" he said. "Can't you see their faces?"

"What faces?"

Within the multitude of miners and townsfolk, Richard searched for the Frenchman— Bissi, that was his name—and for Manuel, as well as the nameless American, but the three ghosts had left him back at the El Dorado, it seemed. No, they were buried long ago north of the diggings, their graves unmarked, bodies fed to the ground.

"I'm only guilty of killing a man already dead."

A farce of a preliminary examination then took place and was allowed to be gone through by a certain Justice of the Peace Humphreys, who Richard had never heard of until this moment, perhaps self-appointed, and a trial of sorts took place in front of the hang tree.

The evidence presented was brief.

"You are hereby ordered into the custody of Sheriff Rogers," the judge said, "with constables Alexander Hunter and John Clark."

"Please don't hang me," Richard Crone pleaded.

"Hang him!" someone called.

"Hang the bloody bastard!"

"String him up!"

"You are to be placed in the county jail at Coloma," the judge said over the noise of those so willing to end his life, and the words offered a glimmer of hope that rushed through him. The mob grew uneasy at those words, but the judge continued. "You are to be placed there until a proper trial can be held and presided over, where a jury of twelve—"

"Hang him!"

"We don't need no jury!"

A lariat then fell over Richard's neck, cutting off his breath as he was pulled to the ground by rope, lifted momentarily off his feet. Men dragged him by the neck, his feet trenching for purchase in the earth, until he came to rest once again beneath the giant oak responsible for the town's own *non de plume*. Oh, how he hated Hangtown. How he hated this godforsaken dried-up worthless hell-hole of a diggings.

If only he'd stuck to riverboat gambling on the Mississippi. If only he'd avoided the temptation to travel out west for something as damning as gold and promised fortune.

Some of the faces he recognized, though most he didn't. Buck Harrigan was there, of course, as well as Wooley Kearny, and a man they both despised who went by nothing more than "Dutch Ben." Even through their hatred of that bear of a man, they must have hated Richard more at this very moment, smiling even as the Dutchman lifted Richard onto his feet only to deal him a blow under the ear, felling him to the earth as if striking him with a sledge.

Hands slapped his face until he woke, body shaken like dirt through a grate.

"You want a fair trial?" someone said. "*This* is yer trial."

The judge had followed the gathering to the tree, as did Sheriff Rogers and the two newly appointed constables, but their voices, if they argued at all, would not be heard over the crowd, for by then hundreds of condemning voices spoke at once.

"Hang him!"

Elstner was there, the man who'd first employed him to run the table at his saloon, once saying, *You got lots of promise in cards, kid.* The man simply stood, arms folded, not saying a word, just shaking his head in disgust, perhaps ready to be rid of him.

A man he recognized approached, threw a deck of cards in his face, which rained down over his boots. One card drew his attention over the others, a man on a horse. If he had the chance to wager his life over a game of three-card monte, he'd choose that particular long-time friend as his money card. No matter who he played, odds would be in his favor 2 to 3. He'd tap the card, make them dance his three-beat waltz, and unless the judge and jury betting against him struck it lucky with their 1-in-3 chance of guessing right, he'd go free.

"You wish me dead?" he asked the crowd. "You want another hung?"

His audience cheered.

Richard Crone thought of the three in '49, how long they'd taken to simply die by the rope. None of their necks snapped, but their bodies lynched and strangled slowly after being pulled by oxen, the largest man for close to two minutes. He thought of the Read boy not long after, lifting his father by the legs, how that near-death had drawn out long until he was eventually saved and brought down. No, if his own death were upon him now, it would be swift.

Swift justice, is that not what these monsters want?

"Have patience, gentlemen," Richard said. "I will give you soon a fair lay out."

The appointed judge tried to hush the crowd, but they wouldn't be hushed, not one person. They continued calling out curses, one riling the next, riling the next, the lot stoked like a raging fire. Richard Crone imagined himself up on the tree's thickest arm, jumping high into the air and then out, falling a good six feet to deal Death's hand.

"If I'm to die today, let me jump from that oak," Richard said, pointing. "You want a fourth hung, then it will be *quick*, lest my neck not snap as it should."

"Then hang yer got-damned self!" exclaimed another.

All this over three ounces of gold.

Richard Crone ran to the tree and eagerly climbed, his fingers raking into its thick skin, unkempt fingernails filling with bark. He managed a foot or so, then slid, and had himself another good attempt when someone yanked hard on the rope tied loose 'round his neck, laying him flat out on his back, thus taking the air from his lungs in a moment of revelation.

Let me die this way.

"*I have seen the elephant!*" he cried, "Oh, I have seen the elephant!"

BONEWEAVER

by Amanda J Spedding

The boneweaver sat, and the boneweaver stitched. Faint moonlight caressed her hands, but her fingers were guided by the bonesong—deep notes that throbbed the sand beneath her creation. A pulse for a pulseless thing.

From the smoldering remnants of the firepit, she beckoned the smoke that spewed from the charred heart in its center and spun it into caliginous thread. Two ribs the bonesong had crooned three nights past then led her here. The young Confederate lay on the other side of the pit, chest split and ribcage snapped, heart wrenched free. The boneweaver took only what was needed. No more.

Coyotes skulked between the yuccas and the saguaros, yipping and whining at the smell of fresh meat so tantalizingly close. But they dared not come near. Not while she was weaving. Not while she was making from the unmade. Dark magic, some called it—foul and wicked. But the desert, which had been here long before things had bones and would be here long after, whispered that it was good.

At the change in the bonesong's tempo, blood hissed across the sand—black-red rivers carving paths in patterns and swirls known only to her. The runic language encircled the bones—a cage from which her creation could not escape, no matter how much it yearned for the light.

The boneweaver sat, and she stitched; forefinger elongated to a needle point, black as a starless night, sharp enough to pierce bone. When the bonesong beat a dirge, the boneweaver complied; one rib to either side of the jaw she took from a frontiersman three towns back, who should have been a better shot. The jaw chattered as she wove, teeth *click-clack-click-clacking* as the heart-smoke tightened beneath her touch, melding bone seamlessly to bone. Two jagged tusks, curved like scythes.

From the bottle at her side, she took a mouthful of rotgut and spat it onto the embers. Flames surged to life in the firepit, rising to lick at the darkness with slathering tongues, casting her shadow long behind her. The jaw chittered and snapped, knowing what was coming but unable to stop it. Ignoring its protestations, the boneweaver took her creation and tucked it into her shadow. Heavier now with its passenger.

How she wanted to rest, but the bonesong was already calling her on.

West. Always west.

From Lottie's prone position on the ridge above Bitterwood, she now understood the old Cajun's warning, though she'd heeded it not one whit. It wasn't just that the buildings were arranged in three concentric circles with no entry point that she could see, nor that each and every building was painted black and shimmered beneath a heat haze that made them appear like they were breathing. When the wind shifted just so, she caught the stench of rot that wafted from the town. Felt it settle in the back of her throat, pungent and wet. Familiar.

"Is a place for the dead, mes amis," the old Cajun had told her, a tremor in his voice as they'd sat around his campfire one night back. "Some dat want to be it, some dat want to deliver it, and some dat want to rule it. You go in, no coming out. Tataille, tataille," he'd said, gripping tight the crucifix around his neck.

Even the people who'd first called this land home refused to go near it, he'd said, "Bad juju. You feel it. In your bones."

And feel it, she did. There was a…*wrongness* to the town that seemed to pulse ever outward. Nothing grew within a surrounding mile of it, the ground not the deep ochre she expected, but the gray of ash. Bitterwood sat like a boil on dead flesh, and every part of her—right down to her bones—urged her to flee and *never* look back. But Lottie Webb hadn't chased Henry "Hatchet" Langford clear across the Territories, hadn't sacrificed two horses and lost two teeth, to give up now.

Her tongue sought the gaps on the upper left of her jaw, still tender from where she'd had to dig out the root of one with her Bowie knife. *Fucking grayback.* Trying to steal her mule and anything else she had. She hoped the knife she'd stuck him with had drawn close the coyotes that stalked her through that godforsaken desert, and those beasts were now gnawing on his fucking bones.

Lottie glanced back to where her mule stood staring at her with contempt. She couldn't rightly say she liked him, but Little Bastard had a nose for sniffing out water. Damn thing was like a coonhound, just more bitey. Still, he'd torn the ear off that Johnny Reb, and had got her through that hellish desert, shaving weeks off her hunt.

Langford was down there. In Bitterwood. Lottie knew it in her bones. Langford had taken more than just her father from her when the outlaw had sunk his hatchet coated with rattler venom into her pa's foot, severing his toes and seizing them as a "war prize."

It had taken two weeks for her pa to die. She'd listened to the sawbones hack into ankle then shin then knee. Heard her father's desperate keening before the ether took him to deep sleep. Bone splintering as they took her pa little by little, trying to outrace the poison. The stink of rot no amount of scrubbing could get out of their home. They had whittled her pa down from the bear of a man who'd faced bandits and gunslingers with a six-shooter on each hip and a shiny star pinned to his chest, to a weeping, gaunt creature begging for death with clawed fingers.

Two weeks it had taken before Lottie put one of her pa's beloved six-shooters under his chin and pulled the trigger.

Langford had stolen her pa from her, tainted her memories of the only parent she knew, and turned her into someone her father would have led to the gallows. But Sheriff Aubrey Webb had taught his daughter everything he knew—how to ride, to track, to fight, to shoot. And Lottie Webb was so very good at the shooting.

She slithered back from the edge of the ridge, decision made. Approaching the town when the sun owned the sky was a fool's errand, and her pa hadn't raised a fool. Keeping low, Lottie made her way back to Little Bastard, who snorted at her approach. She avoided his teeth—just— as she removed his bridle. Then, from the saddlebags, she took the last of her rations, giving the cantankerous mule one of the apples she'd bartered from the Cajun.

"Stay close," she told Little Bastard, though he wasn't one to wander, and headed to the shade of an overhang to get some rest.

She finished the last of her jerky, drank carelessly from her waterskin, then settled her bedroll beneath her head. Lottie closed her eyes, a hand on one of her pistols, visions of vengeance lulling her to sleep.

Three days the boneweaver dragged her shadow across the land. It pulled at her shoulders, kicked at her heels, sometimes sidling so close she could feel its sharp angles and jutting bones. Once, she swore she felt its fetid breath on the back of her neck. That she heard whispers drifting beneath the bonesong, distorting what she had once thought beautiful.

How she wanted to stop, to settle beneath an old tree and listen to the stories in the susurrus of leaves until her gods called her home. But the bonesong pushed her on. Relentless. Desperate, it seemed, to see her work done. Decades it had been since the 'song had called upon her, uprooting her from the mountains she called home, where she had hoped to live out her years in solitude. Peace. Fool, she had been, to think it could be so.

Once a boneweaver, always a boneweaver. The bonesong had been woven into her before she'd ever taken breath. It would be with her when she took her last, guiding her steps in the dance of her ancestors, no matter this new world they had found themselves in. She did not know why the 'song had called on her once more, though she knew it to be her last. Already her steps were slower, not helped by the overlarge boots she had taken from the Confederate. Her dress was ragged at its hem and hung loose on her frame, the color now bleached to the same as the bones she could see through her parchment-thin skin.

The nights granted her some peace, snatching sleep so deep she could not hear the chattering of the bones that snuggled at her back. An hour here, an hour there. Sometimes two if the bonesong allowed it, but never more. She was close; that much she knew. The beast in her shadow thrummed in anticipation. More so, when the 'song turned her sharply left.

She caught the scent of cooking meat long before she spied the campsite. Hare, if memory served. The boneweaver could do with a meal. As could the bonesong.

He had smiled, open and warm, when she had first stepped from behind a Joshua tree. But that smile had fled when his gaze flicked to the shadow at her back. Her creation rose on its hind legs, loomed over her, twice the size of any man. As the creature chattered, the man gibbered in a language she did not understand.

"Tataille, tataille," he said, over and again, scooting backward as a wet patch darkened the front of his pants.

He screamed when her knife sank deep into his gut, and he yanked his necklace free and pressed a dead man nailed to a cross against her skin. But his god held no sway with hers, and she batted his hand away, the creature stretching her shadow to sniff at the dying man's face.

He died slow, begging a dead god for salvation. The boneweaver assured he would get it, just not in the way he believed.

She ate of the hare as the man took a shuddering last breath, then she got to work.

The boneweaver sat, and the boneweaver stitched. Heart-smoke fusing two collarbones to the skull. Horns as sharp as any knife. But the bonesong was not done. Upon its elongated backbone, she wove arm bones and leg—great, long spines that sparkled red in the late afternoon sun.

On all fours, the creature shook itself, a mad glint in its eyeless sockets as it surveyed her work. It took longer to capture it within her shadow, but capture it she did, the bonesong whipping its behind for its disobedience.

Her old bones groaned as she bent to take the old man's hat, threading his dead god on its gold chain between his dead fingers. With her back hunched and her shoulders pressed forward, yoked as she was, the boneweaver followed the bonesong west into the setting sun.

The moon was a cadaverous smirk in the night sky as Lottie made another circuit of the town, its stink thick and weighted. Gray clouds scudded across the heavens, obscuring the starlight, and she sent thanks to her pa for making it so. Knew it was him whose whispers had guided her all the way here.

Pa had said Lottie had her ma's short temper and sharp tongue—a good thing since she'd inherited his shoulders, his height. So, it was his clothes she wore—the same black trousers, black shirt, black derby, and black duster he'd worn that fateful day he'd confronted Langford. She walked in her own boots.

Lottie had added her pa's beloved six-shooters to her own pair, two bandoleers strung across her chest. Her decision to leave her Winchester repeater had been the right one. It was too cumbersome in what would be confined spaces. But what she lacked with that firepower, she made up for in blades.

It was on her third circuit that she found an entrance she was sure hadn't been there on her previous two passes. A narrow aperture she had to traverse sideways to get through. It spat her out into the first ring, and she hugged the stinking wall, pistol in hand as she strained her ears for any sound.

There. Faint. To her left. Music, perhaps. She looked to her right; dark and silent.

Lottie took the left-hand path.

She walked its middle. If entrances could appear at will, whatever distance she had could be the difference between life and death. *Is a place for the dead, mes amis.* Lottie knew it was so, and was glad she'd left Little Bastard unbridled and unsaddled at the top of the ridge.

The music—it was definitely a pianola—grew louder with each step. Had she not paused to gain her bearings, foot held aloft, she'd not have heard the footfall at her back. Lottie dropped, rolling onto her back and firing at the silhouette darker than the darkness.

Her bullets hit home. His did not. He fell to his knees, tried to aim again, but this time her shot took him in the head.

A quick check told her what she already knew. It wasn't Langford.

From her periphery, another pulled itself from the wood like taffy, but Lottie was already firing, striking him in the chest. His shot grazed her arm, burning like fire. He glared up at her, trying to breathe through lungs filling with blood. She shot him between those glaring eyes, then turned and ran, reloading as she went. No way those shots had gone unheard. Her pa's six-shooters in each hand, this time she kept closer to the inner wall, a decision well made when she spotted a breach a little ways ahead. Wider than the last, she still entered sideways. Quicker this time, not wanting to be trapped within.

The second ring was brighter than the first, a flickering light that made no sense. She risked an upward glance. The moon still smirked and the stars still hid. She couldn't explain it, didn't wait around to try. Left or right, it made no difference. Langford, she knew, waited in the middle of this maze.

Again, she followed the music. And the stink. It seeped into her skin, and she tasted it bitter at the back of her throat. One circuit she made. Another. But she couldn't find the entrance she needed.

Her arm still burned, and she stopped to probe it when movement on the wall caught her eye. She must have imagined it. Had to. But she'd not lost anywhere near the amount of blood that would cause hallucinations.

There it was again.

"Fuck off…" she whispered, holstering one of her pa's pistols and quietly drawing her Bowie knife from her boot.

Lottie lunged when she saw the wall blink, driving her blade deep into the wood. But wood didn't have the soft fleshiness that this did. Wood didn't burst white sticky substances and bleed. Wood didn't scream.

She struck again, going for where the throat would be, but this time she hit wood. Proper wood, with its hardness and splinters. A second of indecision, of not wanting to believe what her mind screamed at her to be true, and she drove her blade in again. Another fleshy hit. Another burst of sticky whiteness. More blood. A shriek this time.

Lottie stumbled back, wiping her knife on her duster, shaking her head as a slew of eyes turned her way. Low and high. Middle and ground-level. Matching pairs and not. Brown. Blue. Green. Black. And they followed her progress as she ran, blinking ever rapidly, the light flickering in increasing tempo. Disorienting. Bright. Dark. Bright. Dark. Blinding. Creating specters, making her lash out at shadows.

Vulnerable, when she swore she'd never be again, Lottie roared as she lunged at the wall, stabbing furiously, firing her pa's pistol until it clicked empty. Her screams joined those of the wall as she blinded them. One. Two. Six. A dozen. Stab. Stab. Stab. Stab—

She stumbled into a breach. Cried out in surprise, slashing at hands that shoved her forward to spill into the light. Bright light. Lottie fell to her knees, rolled right until she smashed against something hard, then scuttled, sun-blind, behind what felt like a barrel. It was only through sheer will that she slowed her breathing, settled the pounding of her heart as she waited for her vision to adjust.

Sunlight. Warm on her face, but it couldn't be. It was just past midnight when she'd entered this godforsaken place. When she looked up, it was the night sky that stared back. *No. It can't be. It can't be.* A laugh broke from her—ragged and mad. Why couldn't it be? She'd killed people who'd melted from shadows, seen walls littered with eyes; arms that seeped from passages with no body to command them. Why couldn't the noonday sun blaze in this place while night still ruled the sky?

Lottie looked down at her hands, at her Bowie knife and her pa's six-shooter covered in gelatinous goop and blood-spatter. *Pa.* Pa who had begged her to kill him as he'd pissed himself in sheets that stank of his rot. She returned the knife to her boot, holstered her pa's pistol, and drew both her own, rising fast with her six-shooters in hand.

Empty.

It was a wide circle she found herself in, hemmed in by the only things Bitterwood needed: saloon, whorehouse, butchery, and stables. Three of each. All with the same blood-red signage that dripped to patter against the gray earth. Gallows, too numerous to count, stood at the far opposite arc. There was no graveyard here; the bodies rotted where they fell. Crows picked silently at the remains. There was food aplenty, so they didn't need to fight.

Two bodies still hung from their ropes, one barely holding true—the neck split and stretched, spine showing. It tore a moment later. The carcass dropped with a wet thump, splitting like an over-ripe plum and scattering the crows who squawked at the intrusion before settling once more. But Lottie's gaze followed the head as it bounced down the pile of bodies to roll along the ashen ground…where it was stopped by a brown-booted foot.

Her eyes tracked that boot up its leg and over a chest that held a stolen silver star.

"Nice to see you again, Lottie," Langford said, grinning as he slapped the head of his hatchet against his palm.

The boneweaver didn't need the bonesong to direct her this time. She'd seen the blight from the ridge where she'd found the mule. Bastard of a thing had bit her. Not at all perturbed by the creature pushing at the confines of her shadow. She liked it immediately.

It had followed her across the plain without complaint, quiet for such an animal. The mule hadn't hesitated when they made their way through the first wall that was fortified with the rot of hundreds, thousands. Too many screeching voices to count. But she had gathered those dead to her, tucked them into her shadow for the creature to feast. To grow.

Heavier her shadow grew, and the mule came to her side, let her lean upon him as he guided her into the next wicked ring. A legion of eyes turned her way, but there was carnage here too, spilling down the walls in messy, stinking rivers. The bonesong called, and the boneweaver spread her shadow, casting it along the walls to harvest all that it found.

It was the mule who moved her on, biting at her dress and dragging her along a passage that stank of fear. Blood caked the walls, still wet. Horrors hid within, but nothing could hide from the bonesong. It gathered the dismembered, taking it all as she followed the mule into the light.

Bullets were flying as she stepped into the light of day beneath a night-filled sky. It was here she was meant to be. Felt it in the 'song's aria as it leant strength to her own bones and guided her forward.

Bodies lay strewn across the ground, dead and dying, but the boneweaver ignored them all, her gaze pulled between a tall woman hunkered behind a water trough, and a man using a mountain of the dead as a shield. Both called to her. Both bore traces of the bonesong. This was why she was here. One of them held her blood. A boneweaver in the making.

"Run!"

The tall woman was gesturing madly at the boneweaver with one hand while firing expertly with the other.

"Run! Take Little Bastard and run!"

"Little Bastard," the boneweaver said, her voice brittle from underuse.

The mule kicked her, shoving her out of the path of a bullet.

"Stand still, old woman," the man yelled. "I'll make it quick!"

That one certainly had the temperament of a boneweaver.

Doors slammed open the other side of this wicked circle, and a rush of men—five, all told—stormed out, hollering and hooting. They fired at the tall woman, who didn't duck fast enough. One shot took her in the shoulder before she made herself small, which was quite the feat, given her size.

"Give it back," the woman yelled, firing blind over her head and, impressively, taking out two of her attackers. "You give him back and I'll only bleed you over two days, you fucker!"

"Ain't giving shit back, Lottie! I won him fair and square!"

The boneweaver's gaze flicked between the two. Which was it—

Pain blossomed in her chest, and she looked down to see a prick of red growing wider with each breath. The creature howled at her back as the boneweaver sank to her knees, as the man behind the bodies grinned at her.

"I give you death," he said, sending another bullet to rest beside the last.

The boneweaver looked to the mule. "Move away, Little Bastard." He snorted at her, did as he was told. The boneweaver smiled up at the night sky as a bullet smashed into her forehead.

Her shadow shattered.

Lottie cursed Langford as the oldest woman she had ever seen slumped backward, bone and brain matter painting the wall behind her. The curses died on her lips at what sounded like shattering glass, but fear like none she had ever before felt washed through her when something tore itself from the old woman's shadow.

A nightmare. Made of bones. Human bones.

Twice the size of a horse, it pawed at the ground with what looked like rib bones. Its disproportionately large skull bore devil-like horns and long, curved tusks. Bone spines jutted from its arched back, jagged and sharp. And it was held together by what looked like smoke. But it was the eyes that peppered those bones, darting left and right as they took everything in, that made Lottie piss herself.

Its eyeless sockets honed-in on her, then it swung its mighty head toward Langford. Then back to her. To Langford. To her.

The sound of doors swinging open had Lottie duck once more as a fusillade of gunfire erupted. Bullets pinged off the monster, some hitting those eyes she knew too well. The creature opened its jaws wide, and Lottie dropped her guns to slam her hands over her ears.

It wasn't the roar of any beast she knew, but a shriek of a thousand voices piercing the air like arrows. The beast thundered at the men, the fools who stood their ground firing at a thing from the hells. It gored two, disemboweling them as it charged past, bones click-clacking as it moved. The nightmare creature turned low, swinging behind it a barbed tail she hadn't noticed. It tore one man in half; flung the leg of another over the wall. It bit the head from one, and swallowed another whole.

Lottie watched, mesmerized as the man tumbled down into the cage of bone that made up the beast's torso. She watched him beat against those bones and scream a scream Lottie couldn't hear.

It was over in moments, the remaining men nothing but smears upon the ground.

Lottie snatched up her guns and glanced over the trough, but Langford was—

The cold kiss of steel pressed into the back of her head.

"Tsk, tsk, Lottie," Langford said. "Drop the guns."

She did, and Langford kicked them away and sighed. "I thought you were better than this."

So did she. The crushing weight of disappointment fell upon Lottie. No vengeance would she have, no peace for her pa.

"Turn around, slowly," he said. "I want to look into your eyes when I kill you."

Lottie glanced to where the monster watched on, head tilting left and right like a puppy. A big, ugly puppy made of bones with screaming people in its not-stomach.

"There's a good girl," Langford said.

She glared up at him from where she sat on her heels. "Kill me. But know I'm coming back to fucking haunt you."

His laugh was filled with genuine mirth. "All for this?"

Langford pulled free the leather string around his neck. From it hung her pa's toe bones, flesh removed, and white as snow. He jangled them before her, laughing once more. Lottie snatched her Bowie knife from her boot and lunged. She knocked his gun aside and drove her blade up into his groin. Lottie twisted until she hit bone, then left it lodged there.

She yanked the necklace from Langford's hand and kicked him away. "My pa is not a war prize!" She held the last of her father against her chest.

Langford raised his gun, but before he could fire, the monster pounced. It tore Langford's arm from its socket before driving one of its tusks into the man's chest and heaving him up. Lottie watched Langford scream as he slid slowly down that tusk. Smiled as the beast ate him bit by bit. Feet, knees, hips chest.

When it was done, the beast turned to Lottie. She could die now that the last of her pa was back with her. Lottie closed her eyes as the monster opened its jaws, yet it wasn't the clack of teeth meeting that she heard, but a song.

A voiceless song that guided her hands to tie her pa's bones around her neck.

The song slithered into her flesh to nest in her bones, its name a reverent whisper. "The bonesong."

THE WOUND IS COVERED

by Taylor Rae

"I warned them that if I ever had to come into this country again on a hostile expedition no man should be spared; I would annihilate the whole nation. I have treated these Indians severely, but they justly deserved it. They will remember it."
- General George Wright, in writing to Major W. W. Mackall,
September 30, 1858

Horse Slaughter Camp, September 14, 1858
The horses have been screaming all night. I reckon they know they're next to die.

The soldiers started early in the dawn yesterday. They tore down cottonwood and poplar trees to build a massive corral and funneled our coalition's herd into it. Their campfires burn like devil-fire in the moonlight, and the reek of dead horses lingers in my mouth, even up here. It tastes like a shallow grave.

We watch from the hill until the light fell too low as the white men who call us savages hang sixteen of our friends and warriors—their prisoners. Then they round up 900 Plains Indian horses into that corral, and one sturdy little pony who made the journey from my mother's homeland among the peaks of 'Ekwiiyemak to interior Salish country. One proud, defiant horse who never should have trusted a woman like me.

Jumie.

I can see her down there now, my unmistakable painted pony. Dried gore spatters her hide, staining the white patches of her coat crimson. Jumie tosses her head, over and over, stamping and snorting. I have only seen her do that when a mountain lion stalked our trail. If that's her war-dance, my heart aches to join her. She's my fellow warrior-woman, another piece of my soul, the only real friend I've got in the whole damned awful world.

She isn't just a horse. No Indian horse is *ever* just a horse.

The dead horses are piled both outside and inside the corral, like a sacrifice to the white men's angry god. At first, they were walking the horses out to be shot, until that took too long and the good general ordered they start shooting directly into the corral. The horses now lie slumped in horrific shapes, limbs splayed, noble heads crushed under one another's bodies. Their lips have rolled back over grimacing teeth, their eyes frozen wide with forever-fear. The ground is black with old blood. Foals, hog-tied and lined up for judgment, had their skulls clubbed in, spewing gray and bone. Weren't worth the bullet.

"I still say we go in and get 'em," I mutter. "Break down a wall. Let 'em run out."

The warrior to my right is Ruth, a Schitsu'umsh woman who helped lead the charge. Her Indian name is Chatteqegweł—Blue Bird—but she carries the Christian name like a blunt sword. Her face is war-filthy and regal, the line of her brow as sharp as the knife at her belt. I barely speak Schitsu'umsh or French, even after five months living among her people at the Cataldo Mission and a lifetime of my French daddy's best efforts.

Hell, Ruth can speak every language I know better than me, including English. But we settle on that as our common ground.

"I told you this isn't your fight," she says.

"They killed my friends and stole my horse. They *made* it my fight."

Ruth's stare cuts to mine. One of those Union bastards blew off her left ear in that final battle on the Spokane Plains, nine days ago. It gives her a cock-eared coyote look. She seems so much older and wiser than me, and it fills my stomach with something like shame and admiration.

"You're being foolish and proud. You'll die for nothing," she says. "We'll all die for nothing."

"If we stop now," I hiss, "they did die for nothing."

Ruth's eyes soften with exhaustion. "You should just be glad they only got your horse. This isn't your land. You can still go home."

I am scared to my soul that she's right. I ain't nothin' but a failed half-breed: too Indian for the whites, too white for the Indians. My mother raised me on the road, chasing my daddy's fur-trading business. She taught me songs for a language I couldn't speak and words for mountains I'd never seen. She whispered Kuuchamaa's sacred stories in my ear, and I tried to imagine the kind of mountain the Creator would call home.

I visited, and even if it's the Creator's home, it ain't mine anymore. The only place that felt like my village was the open road and Jumie's broad back, carrying us into the wide wild west. Now she's doomed to die down there alone, afraid, all because I decided to fight for a woman I barely know, who has no idea of the thrum that pulses through my whole body when she looks at me. It's the feeling of your first winter sunrise— impossible hope in a dead world.

"I don't have a home," I tell her. "But if the Union gets its way, none of us will. And that don't sit right with me, either." It's close enough to true, and easier than whispering the rest of it now, with all that death below us.

She just murmurs, "I'm going to go talk with the others. Plan where we go next."

Before I can nod, she lopes off to the few-dozen other warriors gathered on the ridge, just out of sight of the camp. I pull a spyglass from my belt. I bartered it off a French fur trader on the bank of the Coeur d'Alene lake a few months ago, just before I made my way northeast to the Cataldo Mission site and met Ruth. The Schitsu'umsh treat me rightly, and the Jesuits remind me of my father, a Frenchman himself: ain't always right, but aims to be good-hearted.

The glass is a mite foggy, but I can see well enough. The wide rolling eyes of the horses. The swollen faces of our warriors, hanging outside the army camp like a threat. And there, the Devil himself, General George Wright. He sits beside an officer's tent, the canvas walls flapping in the wind. Even all the way out here, he makes his underlings bring him furniture, and he sits like a man already imagining himself back east, in the president's office—recounting his subjugation of the savages, lounging in a wooden chair, propping his bloody boots on a steam trunk, smoking a pipe. His eyes have a sunken, lightless look to them, like the dead eyes of the horses. Other officers stand smoking or drinking around him, glancing out into the dark, as if they think we're foolish enough to attack again now.

The general's eyes only brighten when he lowers the pipe from his mouth to yell at some kid too scrawny for his uniform coat. "Don't be scared, boy. Just shoot the damn thing."

I flick the spyglass to the boy. He's shaking so bad when he raises his rifle that the general and his fellow officers start laughing like vultures. His pale face is crimson and wet. But he aims and fires, and I know by the sound exactly what he's hit. I could pick out Jumie's voice out of any herd. She falls shrieking, and my whole body quivers to leap up and shoot that damned smirk off the general's face.

The good general starts an exaggerated clap. His voice carries even over the cries of the horses, the still-ringing shot. "It's a miracle from God Himself. The boy grew a set."

The officers laugh and laugh. That wicked light gleams in Wright's eye.

Ruth has already gotten deep in an argument I ain't linguistically equipped to follow, but I do know this: Whatever I have to do, I'm going to kill that bastard general myself.

September 15, 1858

We keep our distance as the army men move on down the Spokane River, burning villages and storehouses, choking the sky in smoke. Most of our ragtag coalition are warriors from local nations: Schitsu'umsh, Yakama, Spokane, Palouse. A handful of them resolve to head east, regroup, send word to all villages they can reach.

We all fight or we all die.

Qualchan, Yakama Chief Owhi's son, is one of the fiercest of them all. I don't have to understand him to be convinced by the surety of his speech. He could fill anyone with the blood-beat urge to die fighting, just from the way his brow hardens and he points at the horizon like it owes him a better story than this.

"I'm tired," Ruth tells me. Most of the survivors left with Chief Owhi, Qualchan, and the rest of the coalition, but the two of us stayed behind with a handful of other stragglers headed home or out to spread the message. "I'm tired of watching my brothers and sisters die."

I don't argue with her.

Before we leave, she obliges me, and we descend into Horse Slaughter Camp. I climb through bodies already distended with heat and rot. The reek sends me reeling, but Jumie died here nobly, and dammit, if there is any God or Creator, I'll honor her as she deserves.

When I find her, I do what I can. I can't remember my mother's songs anymore, but I close her eyes and pet her cold forelock and whisper, "I will cover this wound."

It's a Schitsu'umsh saying, and it feels fitting: I will make this right. I will fashion the scar of my heart with General George Wright's blood or die trying. The saddle is wedged under her body, so I slice the cinch on her bloated belly to take the blanket, the only part I can afford the energy to carry. I tuck it into my satchel, alongside the linen dress and sensible shoes I carry.

September 18, 1858

I wait three days to burn Jumie's blanket, the way my mother said all great Kumeyaay tribe members' clothing should be burned. We're camped on the Spokane Plains with our meager fire, the largest we dare. I didn't know the right thing to sing or the right way to dance for my mother's funeral, either. I just sat there cold beside my father and watched her linen dress burn.

Ruth sits beside me and asks, "What else do your people do when someone in your village dies?"

I shrug. "My mother knew. She died before she could tell me."

She leans her uninjured ear against my shoulder. "Then whatever it is you feel is right," she says, softly, "is what your people ought to do."

I bite back a smile, but I can't stop the wet that rolls down my cheek. Ruth doesn't say anything, but she doesn't move either. We sit together and watch the saddle blanket burn down to nothing but spirit and ash.

September 24, 1858

I ain't seen this myself, but I heard it thirdhand, a day or two after. Ruth translates for me from a Yakama scout. The recounting makes her go tawny and bloodless with dread.

Qualchan is dead. General Wright captured his father, Chief Owhi, to lure him out. When Qualchan entered the army camp, they fastened a makeshift gallows shaped like their holy cross, bound him like a coward, then strung him up by his neck and strangled him.

His wife, Whist-alks, survived to tell the story. How the general made her watch. How his eyes lit up, devouring every moment of anguish on her face, like it excited him. And after, how he told her, with his eyes as black as the Devil's, *You will remember my orders now, won't you?*

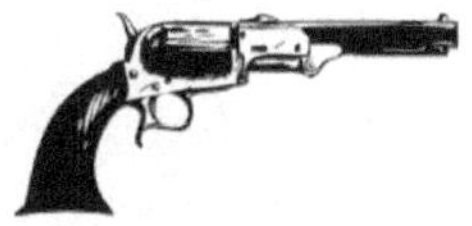

September 25, 1858

We're traveling across the Spokane Plains on foot, moving parallel with Wright's troops to avoid any army scouts, when Ruth asks me that dangerous question. "How would you do it? If you killed him?"

I don't even pretend to think about it. I've rehearsed it a hundred different ways in my mind, and I always imagine that tiny, private sanctuary behind the pulpit. It's candlelit and so dark I reckon he won't question a white-looking woman until the knife is already in his back.

"I'd invite him to seek refuge at the glorious Cataldo Mission." My eyes dart to hers. "Someplace he feels spiritual. Might even feel safe enough to get him alone."

Ruth's face darkens. She shakes her head, coldly. "Did you learn nothing from what just happened? The war is over. We lost. They will punish all of them—the whole village."

"Not if the bastard's dead."

"General George Wright ain't the only white bastard in the Union Army. I'll just be bringing the devil home."

I frown at the clear blue sky. It's too easy to look up and forget about all that death ahead and behind us. "Then we make sure they know it was me."

She reaches for my hand as we walk. The sentence that comes out of her mouth is familiar, but for once, she sounds regretful. "You'll die for nothing."

I squeeze her hand back. "No. I'll die for Jumie."

I don't dare say, *I'll die for you.*

September 30, 1858

My father was a gentle man. He learned to braid my hair, and some nights we would sit beside the fire while he plaited my hair and my mother prepared grits and jerky and a salad of scavenged berries and pine nuts.

You're lucky, he told me. He spoke French, but I can only remember the feeling of it now. *You can pick what world you want to belong to. Not many Indians get the choice to hide.*

When he said that, I was watching my mother peel scales from pinecones, plucking the seeds apart. She caught my eye and winked and smiled, and I had no way to tell my father how much it pained me that no one would think my mother was my mother.

For once, as I walk toward the Union camp, I'm grateful I don't look like my mother. I wear my black hair in a bun, the way a proper pioneer lady would. The boys at the edge of the camp are eager for a good story, and I have the war-wounds to match. The bullet that whistled past my shoulder a few days ago becomes an Indian savage's arrow that nearly killed me.

"Please," I cry. "I need to see General Wright immediately."

Turns out, I reckoned him right. General George Wright ain't a man who can turn down the chance to hunt an Indian for sport. After a few fake tears, I am escorted to the general's private tent with my Indian-bead satchel and nice white lady linen dress. He told me it wasn't right to see an unmarried lady alone like this, but I insisted I was too scared of the savage man who attacked me.

General George Wright's quarters have the get-up-and-move efficiency of any American field camp. There is a folding wood table against one canvas wall, with maps of the Spokane Plains, handwritten notes and marks. His revolver sits beside it.

"I promise you, Ms. Stephens"—the general's voice jolts me to attention, and I snap my stare to his, looking attentive at my fake name—

"not even the smartest Indian is getting past my men. And they don't come that smart."

He winks and smiles. He takes off his army cap and tosses it onto the table, then eases down into the wooden chair beside mine.

I hide my hackle. "The truth is, I think the savage I'm looking for is mighty close."

"The war in this region is won, Ms. Stephens. I've made it clear to every one of those damn rascals that if they impose on any white settler or traveler through these lands, or if they venture off their designated property and start more of that animal fighting they do…" He shook his head, severely. "They need a firm hand. They need to know there are no other options. And I assure you, Ms. Stephens. I have left them no other options."

"I reckon you haven't." My bag rests on my lap, but I figure he hasn't noticed the beadwork yet. Maybe he takes me for a vain, empty-headed woman who bought something pretty.

"You tell me what I need to know, and my men will find the brute who attacked you and bring him to justice."

"It happened actually just a little ways past here. He killed my horse and my traveling companions. I could show you on the map."

General George Wright nods and turns toward the desk. He's easily a head taller than me. If I do this wrong, he can just grab that revolver and end me as quickly as that terrified white boy ended my horse.

"It's a dangerous thing, a woman like you out here in wild lands like this, alone."

"It is dangerous," I say.

I reach into my satchel and pull out a rock. It's a heavy stone, made from this earth. This isn't my home, but it feels fitting to use the land he's desecrated to get my revenge. My arms ache as I lift it over my head and say, "It's dangerous for the wrong man."

The good general turns, and his arm flies up, but I am already moving like the hand of the Creator. I swing that rock down as hard as I can…once, twice. The thud against his skull is hard, and then surprisingly soft, like punching a squash. He crumples with this wet, agonized noise and wails more cowardly than I have ever heard any man or beast cry.

When the soldiers rush in, they don't see a Kumeyaay woman standing there, avenging her horse and her land and her friends she barely got to know. They see a mad white woman, spattered in blood.

That's who they hang, too.

I laugh, and I let them.

SUFFER NO HARM

P.L. McMillan

The Stranger was dusty with the roads he'd travelled, his face grimed with weeks between baths. The bartender of the Loose Skirts Saloon—a thin man named Cecil with a carefully trimmed mustache—watched him lay hands on Sweet Peach, now the youngest lady working, with a flinch. Lady Red, who sat at the honky-tonk piano, dancing out a tune, watched the Stranger as well, her smile easy, gentle, perfect. A graveyard chill ran over Cecil, and he tasted sour copper at the back of his tongue. Clearing his throat, Cecil pulled a bottle of whiskey from a shelf. His hands shook, leaves in strong winds predicting a storm.

The Stranger yanked Sweet Peach between the tables in a rough mockery of a dance, hands clutching at her hip and back. She tried to push away and laughed when she couldn't, as if it were all good fun. But her laugh rang false.

The other five ladies were engaged in their own activities. Tammy Lee dealt cards for Old 'Baccy Joe and his friends. Jester Ann regaled a full table of cattle drivers with raucous tales. Raven-haired Betsy Bee was at the bar matching Dr. Ambridge shot for shot. Up on the second floor, Juliet and Clementine were plying their trade. But despite being busy, Cecil knew the women on the first floor were watching the Stranger. Watching him pull Sweet Peach around. Taking his measure.

Cecil tapped two glasses down on the scarred counter and uncorked the whiskey. "Stranger," he called, and the man glanced across the tables at him. "Wet yer whistle with me."

The Stranger stopped and Sweet Peach pulled out of his arms, slipping through the tables like a snake, to sit by Lady Red's side. The other woman wrapped an arm around Sweet Peach, playing with one hand. In Lady Red's protection, without breaking her smile, Sweet Peach began to sing along to the piano.

The Stranger frowned, watching his quarry escape, then sauntered to the bar, taking no care and knocking into several occupied chairs.

Cecil poured two glasses of the amber liquid, slid one in front of the Stranger. He didn't bother to smile.

"Thanks, boy," the Stranger said and knocked back the alcohol.

Cecil poured him another.

"How much—" The Stranger let out a rancid burp. "How much for that whore?"

Nodding at Sweet Peach, the Stranger held out his glass, and Cecil obliged with more whiskey.

"The women set their own prices and manage their own business." Cecil hadn't touched his own drink. He only watched the Stranger suck up the free alcohol like a horse to water after a long, hard run. "'Round Bitterbend, you'd best be careful of crossing the wrong path."

"Whose path? That whore's?" The Stranger barked out a harsh laugh and pulled back his stained duster. Underneath was a small pistol in bad need of a clean and oil, jammed in a dirty holster.

"You wonder why Bitterbend has no sheriff? Sit a spell." Cecil refilled the Stranger's glass again. Better the bastard be drunk than dead by the end of the night. "I'll tell you."

ON THE FIRST DAY

A blight came to Bitterbend. When the sheriff arrived, it drizzled some. Not enough to be helpful, just enough to be uncomfortable. Jonah Jebediah had the face of a vulture, all sharp angles, a long hooked nose, and cruel black eyes. A hungry look about him. Always.

He came here, to the saloon, after getting settled. He came straight to where you're standing now, Stranger, and he grabbed me by my collar and yanked me near clear over the counter.

"Listen here, boy," he said. I could smell the 'baccy chew on his breath. "Only ways I'll tolerate whores in *my* town is if I get to make sure the product is worth the real estate. Do you get my meaning?"

"I'm not the owner of this saloon, sir," I told him, and he let go of my collar.

I caught myself from falling. I'll tell you, Stranger, that my heart was racing faster than ever I've known.

"Get the owner then, boy," Jebediah said, and spat brown 'baccy juice onto my freshly cleaned floor. "Don't waste my time now."

"The owner isn't in town."

His fist struck, lightning made flesh. I hit the floor, my jaw throbbing, blood on my tongue and a tooth loose. That's the type of man Jonah Jebediah had been.

The sheriff came back that same night. I'd already warned the ladies. Back then there were eight of them. Lady Red stood when Jebediah entered. He was followed by six others, men that we'd known. He'd made short work of finding allies in Bitterbend but then, a rat always multiplies and the West is full of yellow-bellies looking for someone to follow. I won't bother with their names. They're as dead as Jebediah, dust to the wind and all that.

But they came in here as bold as brass, seven men ready for a fight.

"What a pretty bunch of whores," Jebediah said, getting right in her face. "But you're a bit old for my tastes."

He spat 'baccy right onto the hem of Lady Red's dress. His rats snickered. Red, though, she's got nerves of steel, didn't even flinch. I think the sheriff was unnerved by that. Most likely angered, too. A man like Jebediah wasn't used to people standing up to him. He was used to them falling in line.

The sheriff walked around her and looked at the other ladies. They stood just up there, along the railing on the second-floor hallway. Jebediah pointed at Honey; she was the youngest of them, barely eighteen and only six months in town.

"I'll take that one," Jebediah said, and the hungry look on his face grew.

Poor Honey went pale and stepped back, hiding behind Jester Ann.

"You'll not be taking anyone, Sheriff," Red said. "I don't like the look of you, so I think we shall refuse your patronage."

The sheriff's face snarled up, and he bared tombstone teeth stained yellow. "The fuck you talking about, girl?"

"You can leave now. We're closed tonight." Lady Red stared down the rats at the door and I can tell you, Stranger, her stare is not something to dismiss.

In the moment that followed, time crawled. I heard the building creak in the dry wind that growled down from the north and the grind of the sheriff's teeth as he clenched them tight.

Then he smiled. He tipped his hat.

"We'll be back," he promised, and led the way through the saloon's double swinging doors into the night.

"There'll be trouble, Lady Red," I told her.

Red looked up to the second floor, at the other ladies. "We can handle it."

But I seen how her hands were clenched, how pale her face was. Lady

Red—a veteran at the Loose Skirts Saloon, used to dealing with drunks, vagabonds, outlaws, and worse—was worried. And that scared me more than the sheriff's smile.

ON THE SECOND DAY

That trouble came the next night. You see, Honey had a sweetheart. The pastor's son, no less. They thought they were so sneaky, meeting at night, in the church. But we all knew. The pastor was pressuring his son to save the young girl by getting married, starting a family, and rescuing her from sin. The sheriff got her while she was on her way back home. One of the rats must of told him.

I won't go into the details, Stranger. It'd be enough to make any man's stomach turn. I'll say this for Honey, though… She fought him. Honey was a good girl, a brave girl. He beat her bloody, broke her sweet face, and strangled her. Honey ended up dead, but the sheriff wound up with a face clawed to ribbons and none of the prize he was looking for.

That made him mad. It must have.

ON THE THIRD DAY

That's when we found her. He had strung Honey up right out there from the porch roof so's we'd find her in the morning, naked, cold, dead. Her blood painted the planks, her tears dewed her cheeks, and deep bruises calicoed her skin. The women didn't allow anyone to touch Honey. They cut her down and locked up the saloon.

Bitterbend was tense. It was a stand-off, you see. The sheriff made it clear. Give him what he wants or be strung up like poor Honey who'd told him no.

I stayed here, behind the bar all day, with my dead pa's shotgun. Chances were I'd blow my own foot off before getting the sheriff, but I had to try. The women of Loose Skirts have always been good to the Lockner family, y'see.

No one came by. Not the sheriff, not any regulars, not the pastor.

At dusk, Lady Red sent me home. The air was heavy. Churning clouds choked back a black horizon and distant thunder rolled through the ground. Something was coming. I could see it in the look on Lady Red's face. Taste it in the lightning on the air. Hear it in the silence of Bitterbend.

My house—well, it's just behind the saloon. The Lockners have lived there for generations. We've been the caretakers for the Loose Skirts Saloon for as long as I can remember. That's not important to the story, though. What's important is that my front door overlooks the back lot where Tammy Lee grows the vegetables for the saloon.

It was the sound that woke me.

Through the thunder and the dance of rain on the roof, through the growling storm, I heard the whispering. Like snakes hissing. Hundreds…thousands of snakes. It was late and dark as anything, but I was awake.

See this hair on my arms? It had risen like Christ himself on that third day. At first, I fumbled for the candle. But as I found my box of matches, I couldn't bring myself to break the darkness. It all felt different, y'see. Not natural. And to shatter that with light…? Blasphemy of the highest order.

I stumbled down the hall to the front door. The whispers went deep and low. They made the very floorboards shiver, and my heart skipped a beat. Opening the door, rain hit my face like icy buckshot.

They were out there, in the storm.

The Loose Skirts women knelt in a circle, naked as when they were born. Overhead, purple lightning laced through clouds, throbbing like a living thing as the thunder roared. Their hair flowed loose over their backs. Rain crashed over their bodies. And—I'll promise you this on my mother's grave—their skin glowed like moonlight. They were as stars in the storm-darkened night.

Right hands raised, the seven women swayed, twisting their bodies like snakes dancing to a flute. I could see knives in their hands, strange things as thin as splinters and the purest silver. I could hear the beat in my head. It strummed through me, hm-hm-HMM. Something like that. Their other hands pinned large, brilliantly-colored snakes to the mud. The animals writhed and snapped, their fangs as bright as the blades that hovered above them.

Down the knives slashed, slicing the serpents in two, from jaw to tip of tail. The women scooped out the tiny organs and tossed them to the middle of the circle, then stuffed vibrant purple flowers into the serpents. Their hands stained crimson rose, fingertips straining for the boiling clouds above, the chanting grew louder. It became a tempo for the heart of the storm. Their bodies swayed, dropped, slithered in the mud, limbs entwined as their voices ascended and called and called.

My racing heart became the bass, thump-thump thump-thump, and they twisted around the dead snakes, blood in mud in hair on faces, ululating. And somewhere in the distance, even through the thunder, I heard something answer.

I ain't ashamed to admit that I fled. Hid beneath my blankets as a child might.

ON THE FOURTH DAY

Jebediah and his men came in the morning. They found the doors locked, so they broke those two front windows. See this scar above my eye? One of the bricks they threw struck me there, knocked me near senseless.

He sent some of his men around back; they tore up Tammy Lee's garden and broke my windows too. The sheriff didn't come in, though. His goal wasn't to break in. It was to terrorize.

ON THE FIFTH DAY

With midday came Rattlesnake Renee on a horse as black as night. She wore a jacket and pants of snakeskin, a necklace of fangs round her neck, a wide brim hat to ward off the sun. Her left cheek was scarred where she'd been bit and poisoned by a rattler, yet survived.

I see the recognition in your eyes, Stranger. Yes, she is one and the same. *The* Rattlesnake Renee—bounty hunter and, as it happens, the owner of the Loose Skirts Saloon. A woman of towering stature and flaxen hair, skin kissed harshly by the sun.

High noon, she rode into Bitterbend and met Sheriff Jebediah right in front of the saloon. I was here; I watched it all.

"Who the hell are you?" he asked.

Renee swung over, hit the road, sent up puffs of dust, no sign of the rain that had come the night before. She kept one hand on her saddle. Her eyes, green as poison, watched Jebediah like prey. She said nothing.

"I don't 'ppreciate strangers in my town, y'hear, girl?" he continued.

Behind him gathered his six cowardly men, as predictable as shit follows a pig. Renee's jacket caught the sunlight on its scales, glittering like gemstones, and she said nothing, just stayed as still as a snake in grass.

"You deaf, whore?" He took one step, a second step.

Renee's hand—the one that had rested on her saddle—slashed forward. In it, a whip made of snake skin. It lashed Jebediah's face, cut it open like a knife through butter, and his skin curdled away from a scarlet wound. Blood rained down to the ground in crimson drops, and he screamed like a child, clutching his head as he stumbled back.

It took a second, Stranger. I watched it from that window right there. The sheriff howled like a mad beast and looked up at Renee through stained hands. His posse fell on him, pulled him away, down the road in the direction of Doc Ambridge's place by the general store.

I knew he'd be back. And with more hate than ever.

Renee tied off her horse in front of the saloon, pulling her bags from the saddle. "Cecil," she said as she entered, boots hammering on the floor. "Keep an eye on my horse. Keep the saloon locked. We're not to be disturbed."

I stayed up that night, shotgun in hand, behind this very bar. Jebediah didn't come then. Reckon the stitches and sedatives the doc gave him kept him down. I wish I could say it was a quiet night. They sang. For hours. It wasn't English. Wasn't any kind of language I could understand. And they danced. At least, I have to assume that's what the sound was. The sound of flesh sliding around and around on floorboards. Because if it wasn't their bare feet then…well…

ON THE SIXTH DAY

Rattlesnake Renee left. She'd spent the night, then slipped out silently while I slept on the floor behind the bar. A five-dollar bill was left on the counter. Renee always left me gifts when she visited. As a child, it'd been candy. Now it was cash. Not that I'm complaining.

Lady Red came down when I began to sweep. She put seven glasses on the bar.

"Cecil." She turned to me and grabbed my hands. Her eyes caught me like a fly in a web. "See these glasses and heed me. We are opening tonight. When Jebediah and his men come—and they will—you will serve them at no cost. But you will serve them with these glasses and none other. Understand?"

The glasses were delicate, pretty things with nary a crack or chip. Each caught the light streaming through the window and glistened with faint oily colors.

"Allow no other to drink from them, Cecil."

Returning upstairs, Red left me with the glasses. I picked them up, one by one, and placed them on a shelf behind the bar. As I did, I saw that each had a tiny drawing etched on the bottom: a snake biting its own tail, forming a circle. Each smelled faintly of something acidic.

Sheriff Jebediah arrived at dusk with his minions in tow. I was behind the bar. The regulars were at their tables, and the ladies were their usual selves. Lady Red stood from the piano and came to the bar when she saw them enter. She braced a foot against a stool, allowing her dress to shift and show skin.

Calculated, you see. As calculated as a snake's rattle.

The sheriff was in a state. Renee's snakeskin whip had left a diagonal slash through his face, which Doc Ambridge had tried his best to stitch up. Jebediah's skin was blotchy, angry, and the right corner of his mouth was caught up in a sneer from the injury. It suited him, that sneer. It suited just fine.

"Welcome, Sheriff," Lady Red said, as sweet as sugar. "Cecil, pour the sheriff and his men some whiskey. Top shelf, and on the house, of course."

Think what you may, Stranger, but I did it. I took those seven glasses down and filled them each with my best whiskey. I didn't care what happened to Jebediah, but I felt a pang for those spineless men who'd chosen to fall in line with him. I'd grown up with some of them. Been to a couple of their weddings.

"I think we got off on the wrong foot, Sheriff." Lady Red gestured at the glasses I'd laid out. "I'm of a mind to rectify that mistake."

Time stopped—a hiccup in the world. Jebediah's eyes narrowed.

Then the other ladies stood and went to the men behind the sheriff, pressing against them, smiling. The sheriff's eyes crawled up Lady Red's thigh. He licked his lips and the bottom of his cut leaked blood onto his tongue. The sheriff smiled.

"Damn right." Jebediah spat on the floor and strode to the bar, finishing his drink in one gulp. "Look what that bitch did to me!"

I refilled his glass, just as I've been with yours, Stranger.

"I'm sure I can make it up to you, Sheriff," she replied. "In fact, I guarantee it."

His men joined him at my bar, drinking from their glasses. Their eyes roamed over the ladies' bodies, hungry and oblivious. Every time a glass was emptied, I filled it.

The sheriff's hand whipped out, and he grabbed the back of Lady Red's head, dragging her close. A thread of blood ran from his wound over his lips, and dripped from his chin. Whatever he saw in her eyes, he let go in a hurry, but kept his smile and threw back the third glass I poured him. "Let's go then, whore."

Seven glasses on the bar, empty. Seven men and women disappeared upstairs.

I closed up early that night and sent my regulars home. Looking up, I went to my house and sat against the front door, and watched the shadows move behind the curtains on the second floor until I slept an uneasy sleep plagued by the hissing of snakes.

ON THE SEVENTH DAY

The sun rose. I woke up and went to the saloon. There were seven bodies hung from the front of the jail. All seven men were naked, slit from jaw to pelvis. Their bloated faces were contorted in chilling expressions of agony, their eyes stained red with burst vessels, and their tongues—Lord... Their tongues were swollen so large that they stuck out from between each man's lips. And if you looked closely, Stranger, you could see an oiliness to their tongues and a sheen of strange colors.

And that's not all. Their organs were set in delicate piles directly below their heads, a purple flower placed on top of the piles. Each man had a snake jammed into his slit throat, the serpentine tail hanging down like a bizarre tongue.

Three wives and three mothers wept for their husbands and sons, but said nothing. Four children wailed for their dead fathers. But the people of Bitterbend accepted the fallout of the stand-off that had gone on for those seven days. We buried our foolish six in our graveyard and burned the sheriff in the street.

Now look up, Stranger, see those glasses and mind that, in Bitterbend, no harm may come to the ladies of the Loose Skirts Saloon.

Cecil finally picked up his own glass and tossed back the whiskey. Lady Red moved on to a rag-time song, and Sweet Peach got up to dance. But the Stranger didn't move. He stared at the row of seven glasses, set between two bottles of the saloon's finest whiskey, three shelves up.

"So, if you're interested, I am sure the ladies would be happy to accommodate, Stranger," Cecil said. "So long as you're respectful."

The Stranger gulped down the last of his whiskey and slapped a five-dollar bill on the bar. "It's late," he replied, quietly. "I mean to hit the road at dawn, so…"

With that, Cecil watched the Stranger stumble out of the saloon. Betsy Bee waved Cecil down to where she sat next to Dr. Armitage, who was passed out on the bar.

Betsy held out her shot glass, which Cecil faithfully refilled.

"You scared away a customer, Cece!" she said with a theatrical pout. "You should work on your conversation skills."

Cecil just smiled and refilled her glass once more.

GHOST FESTIVAL IN THE DESERT

by Wen Wen Yang

"Would you like another story?" I asked the white workers.

The Chinese men were watching me expectantly as I finished collecting the white men's empty bowls. The air still carried the sweet scent of hoisin sauce and beef. I had given them the meals with chopsticks sticking upright. The white men had laughed because they could not eat Chinese food with chopsticks. They still preferred my food to their white cooks' though.

The white men were varying shades of brown from the relentless dirt and unforgiving sun. Yellow light from the campfire flickered across the men's faces.

Charles killed a moth that ventured too close and wiped his hand against his pants. He picked at his teeth with a wooden splinter. "How about a game of poker?"

The men groaned, tired of losing their money. Charles had Crenshaw's favorite gun, an Army-issue 1860 Colt 44, and a stack of IOUs from Louis.

"Tell the talking pig one," said Patrick, leaning against his pack. The other men around the campfire grunted their agreement.

Crenshaw spat his tobacco, then replaced it with another pinch of chew.

Johnson snorted. "What about that hairy king one?" His eyes always lingered too long on me, as if he could see through my clothes and bindings.

I glanced at the tents where the other Chinese people slept while the white men stayed in the railroad cars. The latter still hung their windchimes while we had taken down anything that made noise. Hell, their railroad car doors were wide open to the night breeze. Idiots.

I took a sip of tea, then started to clean my knives. "I'll tell you a different one. It's a good ghost story."

The Chinese man washing the clothes sucked his teeth. If you were going to run a laundry, a "knight of the washtub" as they called it, you had to work through the night. He was about my height, his cue hanging down his back.

I had shorn my hair short like the white men. I told them it was to keep the lice off. After tonight, I will grow my hair back.

"It's about a man who came to this gilded country in search of his missing brother," I said.

The laundry man's hands slowed. The white men's clothes hung on the clothesline behind him, haunting in the full moon's brilliance.

"It was his older brother," I said. "The Chinese word for it is Gege."

Some men repeated the sound.

"Sounds like burping." Charles yawned and stretched like a cat.

I ignored him. "Gege had sent money home for his grandparents, parents, and younger siblings. Monthly letters."

"Shit," Charles spat. "He would have saved some money if he sent one a year."

"Until one day, his grandmother—we call her Nainai—started wailing. 'He's dead!' she cried. 'They killed him and hung him from the second story.'"

Charles shifted in his seat. "I don't like this one. Can't you tell the one about the wolf in the woods?"

"I'll tell that one after."

Charles draped his arm behind his head and started whistling. I did not tell him to stop. Let the ghosts come.

"Nainai was a wise woman." I rubbed at a stubborn spot on my smallest knife. "She knew how to bundle children up when they had fevers, where to hang mirrors to repel dangerous spirits, but her protection could not stretch across the ocean. So when the monthly letter from Gege didn't come, his younger brother, we call him Didi, came here, to the beautiful country."

"Was he looking for gold?" Patrick asked.

"Pfft, we'd already gotten it," answered Charles.

The men chuckled.

I nodded. "Yes, he couldn't pay the foreign miners' tax. He started working on the railroad like Gege before him. Though he was paid half of the white mens' wages, he started sending money home. Some men may have come to this beautiful country and never sent home a single coin. But Gege and now Didi made sure his family had coal for warm nights and meals to fill their bellies."

"That's some good kids." Johnson rubbed his eyes.

"But what happened to the older brother?" Patrick insisted. "That isn't a full story, Cook. You can't let that be the end."

I set my knives aside and picked up a pair of scissors. I started cutting pages out of a tattered Bible I found a few miles back. "Do you remember what I told you about the Ghost Festival?"

"Yeah," Patrick chuckled. "Your god doesn't provide food, so you gotta feed your ghosts once a year."

"Piss poor god," said Charles.

"We haven't been welcomed to your god." I pointed toward the mountains. "When a minister opened a Sunday School for us up north, they burned down the church." I could feel the men growing tense. "Patrick is right. Good memory, sir. Maybe those men were just sending the church to the dead. For the Ghost Festival, you burn things for the dead to have, like paper houses and fake money."

I tossed the cut-out paper knives and irons, railroad spikes and axes into the fire. They collapsed into black smoke.

"Can't burn gold," Charles pointed out.

"No, no gold for the dead." I cut out a crude handgun from the onion skin pages. "During the first Ghost Festival here, Didi set out the food offering for Gege, trusting Nainai's dream. When the moon rose, Gege came through and told his brother what had happened."

The men leaned closer, their eyes focusing on me. Except Charles. He still stared at the stars.

"His boss had refused to pay him." I shook my head sadly.

The men nodded in sympathy.

"He had counted out how many men had died during the building of his section of the railroad." I held up nine fingers. "The cold, the gnawing hunger. One of his friends had died slowly, crushed under rocks. Gege heard the screaming, then the moaning. Then the silence."

The workers wiped calloused hands across their cheeks. Were the miners remembering the sound of the men's cries in the caves? Did we all cry in the same language: Cantonese, Mandarin, English?

I could have stopped there with this show of emotion. I could have.

I didn't.

"Gege didn't want to die in the desert. Not with his family depending on his wages. So he went to Los Angeles."

The men groaned. "Bad luck, that." Crenshaw spat his chew.

Good. They knew this part—remembered it.

"When the mob stormed the city's Chinese quarter, he was one of the unlucky ones. They strung him up with a clothesline."

The men twisted in their seats.

"Gege heard them before he saw them. The Chinese people had tried to barricade themselves inside. Foolishly, they thought they would be safe behind locked doors. Then he heard the sound of cracking wood, the windows bursting into shards. When the door gave in, they ran upstairs. There was a young boy in front of him. Gege had outran him and left him to the mob.

"When Gege returned during the Ghost Festival, there were nail marks on his neck from where he tried to remove the noose." I had wept and pounded the ground with my fists. Had he cried for Mama, Baba?

"I heard they cut off one of their fingers to get a diamond ring." Patrick sucked his teeth.

"Where would a Chinamen get a diamond ring?" Charles shot Patrick a glare that could have burned paper. "It was probably glass."

"It's what I *heard*," Patrick protested. "They make more on laundry than some miners do."

A silence covered the white men like a heavy blanket of snow.

Did the mutilated Chinese bodies haunt these white men's dreams? Could they hear Gege's screams? Or hell, maybe they just needed to take a piss. I can't read minds.

They yawned, heads nodding against their will.

"What happened to the men who killed him, Cook?" shouted the laundry man. It was the first time I'd heard him raise his voice in front of the white men.

"All eight convictions were overturned." I called back. "Technicalities." The anti-coolie clubs—good old boys saving their men.

"So what did Didi do, Cook?" The laundry man wrung out the shirt. His biceps strained against his sleeves. "Did he go home?"

"Sadly, he had no money to get home. He decided to work in the mining towns. He thought, maybe it would be safer than Los Angeles. Didi did the usual work." I burned paper bullets. "Laundry, herbal medicine, even cooking. He got really good at cooking."

I winked at the laundry man.

When the workers joked that we all knew each other, that we were all related, did they understand the consequences of that truth?

"And today is the Ghost Day, of the Ghost Month. My nainai told me it was dangerous to be outside in the dark."

The men were slow to react. The poison from their meal was starting to take effect. "What? What did you say, Cook?"

"Do you believe in ghosts?" I asked louder. "How many dead Chinese men are there for every mile of track?" I tossed the last bit of the paper weapons into the crackling fire. The embers danced upwards, lighting the faces of the ghosts approaching the campsite.

They had heard Charles' whistles calling them. They had seen the clothes hung up under the full moon's light. The white men had devoured the offerings meant for the ghosts, with upright chopsticks like joss sticks.

"Did you think you could run far enough from Los Angeles?" I shouted, my voice echoing against the rocks.

Legions of Chinese ghosts dotted the horizon with their wide brimmed hairs and cues hanging over one shoulder. The living Chinese men erupted from the tents, swinging their hammers and railroad spikes. I grabbed chopsticks from the empty bowls and snuck up behind wide-eyed Louis, then stabbed two chopsticks into his ears.

They remained there like bicycle handlebars.

I drove another pair of chopsticks up Patrick's nostrils. His blood flowed down my hand, dripping from my elbow.

Swinging his body aside, I ripped apart his nose. The chopsticks gave a *squick* as they left his brain.

I wiped them against my pants, leaving two red streaks. His body twitched.

Johnson came roaring at me, and I plunged the chopsticks into his eyes.

My hand found my cleaver. I danced around the fire and caught Crenshaw across the neck. The first two spurts were the largest sprays, but his hand interrupted the subsequent gushing. He fell to the ground, the blood slipping between his fingers. His gasps sounded wet.

One man tried to run. A ghost caught up with him, holding a newly acquired paper knife. It was strong enough to puncture him, right above the belly button. It smelled of shit.

Charles fired his gun at the approaching ghosts. *Bam, bam, bam.* The sound echoed in the camp. *Bam, bam, bam.* The bullets bounced off rocks and whizzed into sandy dirt.

I longed to trace my cleaver across his throat. He was the one my brother had heard breathing in his ear as the clothesline landed under his jaw. Charles had stood as close as a lover before dropping my brother over the balcony.

There was a chorus of white men's shouts as they emerged from their railcars. I watched the ghosts chase men down mineshafts. Their screams echoed up as they fell to the eighteen hells. The mines were not satisfied with this meager sacrifice. Gray shadows dragged a shrieking man down. He left a brown dust trail.

Charles tried to grab a ghost's long braid, but it was like grabbing clouds. He finally turned to run, then turned his gun on me.

The gun clicked empty just as an iron smashed into the side of his head. Charles's eyes rolled up into his head, and he fell forward. The laundry man behind him didn't even acknowledge me before he spun and crashed the iron into another white man's face.

The paper guns had paper bullets. They tore through the white men's flesh just the same as metal.

"What yellow evil is this?" one man shouted as he hefted his miner's pick against the invading ghosts. Two appeared under him and sunk him straight into the dirt. Sand swirled for long moments before it finally stilled.

The massacre could have lasted minutes or hours. But eventually, we realized that only the Chinese people remained. The desert filled with Mandarin, Cantonese, Hokkien, Shanghainese, and others I could not name.

I finally unclenched my fingers from the knife's handle. The blood had started to dry, and my fingers were sticky.

I searched the gray crowd for a familiar face—one that shared my father's broad nose, my mother's narrow eyes. A young ghostly man separated from the other ghosts and tipped his fedora to me. He looked the way I remembered, without the bruised neck and scratch marks. The offerings must have filled him out, as he no longer looked gaunt.

"Were you the little brother?" asked the laundry man beside me.

"Thank you for your help earlier," I said, ignoring his question.

"Hell, he'd be handsome if he wasn't dead," commented the laundry man.

"Careful. If you were a woman, I would offer you a ghost groom."

I scrutinized his face as it split with a smile, bright with crowded teeth. "I think I could be your sao zi." *Older brother's wife?*

I laughed. "How did I not guess it before?"

She snorted. "With your anger, you were too focused on the white men." The laundry woman held out her calloused hand. Dried blood was embedded in both our hands.

I shook hers, smiling. "Then, you would call me xiao gu zi." *Husband's younger sister.*

She laughed, surprising me with a fearless sound I had not heard in a very long time. We had been keeping the same secret from the men. When she finally released my hand—or I released hers—my cheeks were burning.

I spent the rest of the night telling Gege about my search for his killers in the past year. Each railroad station, miners' town, mile of track brought me closer and closer to this final revenge. Without the red mist clouding my vision, I kept catching the laundry woman's glances.

The ghost grinned at me, eyes crinkling. "Xie xie, mei mei." *Thank you, little sister.*

"There is enough money in these dead mens' pockets for a boat ride home," I told him. "I will tell Nainai that you are at peace, if she doesn't already know."

He looked over his shoulder at the laundress. "What about Old Gold Mountain? Maybe you can make some more money there. Our village always seemed too small for you."

My brother grinned impishly. "Besides, who else will burn offerings for me here?"

We helped the ghosts loot the camp. The clothes and furniture fed the fire. We laughed as we furnished the ghosts' homes in the afterlife. The bonfire was loud in its hunger pangs.

When the sun started to rise, the ghosts stepped back into the darkness. After I cook everyone some breakfast, perhaps I will find enough for the boat fare home. Or enough for a home by the ocean for a cook and a laundress.

THE PATCHWORK MAN

by Ben Monroe

They call him the Patchwork Man because of all the scars. Scars around his wrists, up the side of his face, circling around his neck. Folks figure he's probably got lots more scars than that, but nobody's seen him undressed to know for certain. Leastwise, nobody who'd admit it.

On the rare occasion when he comes into town, kids yell out, "Here comes the Patchwork Man!" and women clutch their skirts and shoo the children indoors. Men make sure their guns are loose on their hips. Most folks in town just feel there's something off about him. Then there's the deep, red scar around his neck that looks like maybe he once got away from a hangman's noose. And that gives folks pause.

Funny thing is, though, as far as folks can remember, he's never hurt anyone. He stays by himself outside of town, only coming in every few months for supplies he can't make or grow on his own. But the fact he hasn't actually hurt anyone doesn't stop the gossip and rumors. Especially not in a place like Deliverance, a town folks only ever go to in order to escape their past and disappear.

So, on a Thursday morning in late summer, the Patchwork Man came into Deliverance to the usual commotion of whispered voices and accusatory looks. The sun was still low in the east, but already the day was hot and dry. As he came in from the west, the wide brim of his faded brown felt Stetson kept his face in shadow, and the sun out of his narrow, mismatched eyes.

He strode along the dusty main street through town on his long, gangly legs, leading a gray and brown pack mule behind him with a simple hemp-rope lead. The mule was well-fed, brushed, and taken care of—a strange contrast to the Patchwork Man's blotchy, sallow skin, and trail-worn attire.

Ignoring the stares and whispers, the Patchwork Man approached the general store where a small blond boy sat on a bench, licking a peppermint stick and watching him cautiously. The Patchwork Man tied his mule up to a hitching post in front of the store, then removed his hat, dipped his hand into a trough of water and sluiced it over his face and through the long black hair that ran over his scalp to the nape of his neck.

"Hey mister!" the kid shouted at him. "That's horse water. It ain't for people."

The Patchwork Man looked at the boy, surprised the kid hadn't run off screaming. "That so?" he said, his voice like gravel, just above a murmur.

"Yeah." The kid licked the candy. "You'll get horse slobber on ya."

The Patchwork Man nodded. "Guess I might." He tugged the rope to make sure it was snug on the hitching post. Satisfied, he removed a few of the empty bags tied down over the mule's back.

A raven swooped from the sky and landed on the edge of the roof over the porch. It cocked its head and stared at the Patchwork Man. In turn, he looked up at the bird. The black bird hopped up the sloping overhang, stabbed its beak at a beetle crawling along the slats., then tossed its head back as it crunched and swallowed the wiggling bug. Then it glared at the Patchwork Man, opened its beak, let out a shrill *caw-caw-caw!* and took flight once again into the bright blue morning sky.

"That bird sure don't like you, mister," the boy said.

The Patchwork Man shrugged. "Guess he don't." Then he stepped up onto the slat board porch, his legs so long that he skipped the two steps up entirely, and walked toward the store's front door.

Through the rippled glass window in the door, he saw a woman approach. She waved to someone inside, turned her head, and a startled look sprang over her face. It was a look the Patchwork Man had seen many times before.

He gripped the doorknob with his long-fingered hand, opened the door, and stepped aside to let the woman exit. He tipped his hat with a quiet "Ma'am," as she came through.

The woman wore a plain gingham dress, buttoned up to the throat. Her golden hair twisted up in a plait and topped with a wide-brimmed hat. She came through the door warily, eyeing the Patchwork Man, and keeping wide of him, then turned to where the boy sat, happily licking sticky peppermint off his hand. "Josiah, are you all right?"

The boy looked up and smiled. "I'm fine, Ma. Can we go now?"

She looked from the boy to the strange man and back. "Yes, let's." She crossed the porch to take the boy's hand. "Oh, ugh. Wash that sticky off your hands."

"Aw, mom…" The boy stretched out the vowels until they almost tore in half.

"Come along, Josiah," his mother said, just above a whisper. She looked back over her shoulder as the Patchwork Man entered the shop.

He had to stoop to enter, but he was used to that as well. Most doorways weren't built for people of his stature. As he rose to his full height, he caught the shopkeeper's eye and nodded. Only the two of them were in the store, and the shopkeeper looked nervous.

"Amos," the Patchwork Man said, a curt greeting.

"Mornin'," Amos replied. "In town long?"

The Patchwork Man shook his head. "Just picking up a few things."

He wandered the aisles of the store, filling his bags with supplies. Dry goods, two pounds of nails, twine and rope, just the bric-à-brac he'd built up a need for. Almost as an afterthought, he grabbed a handful of sugar cubes for the mule. Most things he used on a regular basis, he made or grew himself. The little single-room shack he called home, he'd built with wood scavenged from deadfall and a few boards he'd bought in town. It wasn't much to look at, but it kept cool enough in the summer, and dry enough in the winter. A few folks from town had come out to keep an eye on him while he was building it. Peter Gaines had said the shack was solid, and that the Patchwork Man had real craftsman's hands. The Patchwork Man figured he might be right. No way to tell for certain, anyway.

As he picked from the racks and crates of goods in the store, the shop door opened with a slow, low creak. He looked toward the front of the shop to see Marlon Whateley, the sheriff of Deliverance standing in the doorway. His tin star glinted in the morning light through the shop's windows. Two men followed in Whateley's wake. Both of them had their eyes on the Patchwork Man, their hands resting on the guns at their hips.

"Mornin', Amos," Whateley said as he approached the shopkeeper. "Slow mornin', I see."

The Patchwork Man finished filling his bags and brought his goods to the counter.

Amos sorted the purchases and tallied the costs. "I reckon it is."

"Was that the widow Anderson I just saw leaving?" Whately asked.

Amos nodded. "I believe it was."

Whateley grabbed a glass jar full of penny candies and removed a lemon drop. "She's a pretty one, that's for sure. Might have to pay her a visit later." Whateley popped the sticky yellow candy into his mouth and sucked on it. "Hey, fella," he said to the Patchwork Man, staring at him with cold eyes. "You planning on being in town long?"

The Patchwork Man turned slightly and looked down at Whateley. "Not long. Just needed a few things."

"Well, that's a good thing, I suppose," Whateley said. "This here's a quiet town, mister. Don't need no circus freaks coming along and stirring up trouble."

The Patchwork Man turned toward Whateley. "Have I done something wrong, *sheriff?*" he asked, disdain dripping from his words.

Whateley looked into the Patchwork Man's eyes—one cobalt blue, the other dull gray, like lead—and took a half step back. "Now there, fella. You wouldn't be threatening an officer of the law, would you?"

Two loud clicks echoed in the shop's silence as Whateley's deputies pulled back the hammers on their guns. The Patchwork Man saw their hands were tight on the grips, ready to pull the blue steel weapons from their holsters at a moment's notice.

"That'll be two dollars, mister," Amos said, his voice quavering.

The Patchwork Man turned back to the shopkeeper and paid for his goods with a handful of coins and bills. He lifted his bags and threw them over his massive shoulders. "We done here?" he said to Whateley.

"For now," Whateley replied. "The road out of town goes straight that-away, in case you missed it." He pointed toward the edge of town.

The Patchwork Man adjusted the bags and walked out of the shop, ducking low again as he went through the door. Once outside, the sounds of town surrounded him. Distant conversation, the rickety squeak of buckboard wheels, and the occasional clop of hooves. He slung his bags over the mule's back and fastened them down., then let the mule eat a few sugar cubes out of his cupped hand. As the mule lapped up the sugar, Whateley and his cronies emerged from the store.

He untied the mule as Whateley pointed again at the road running through what served as Deliverance's downtown. "That-aways," Whateley repeated.

The Patchwork Man pulled the brim of his hat down a bit lower, shading his multicolored eyes from the sun, and led the mule out of town. His passing was much like his arrival. Conversation stopped as he walked through the downtown, nervous eyes following him until he disappeared around a bend in the road.

His boots left deep prints in the dusty trail as the Patchwork Man led his mule away from Deliverance. He normally avoided going into the town, and his run-in with Sheriff Whateley was a reminder of why. Other people tended not to like him around. Of course, the feeling was rather mutual.

The Patchwork Man walked fast, his long legs chewing up the miles, and the mule had to stay in a trot to keep pace. About a mile outside of Deliverance, he heard squeaking and rumbling up ahead, and when he came over a low rise in the trail, he saw a buckboard wagon being drawn by a single horse. As he walked closer, he saw the woman and boy sitting on the bench at the wagon's head—the same folks he'd spoken to outside the general store earlier. The boy had the horse's reins gripped tight in his small hands, and he was concentrating hard on his task of keeping the wagon going straight.

He led his mule around the wagon and slowed as he came up level with the drivers. "Ma'am," he said.

The woman turned toward him. "Good morning again, sir."

The Patchwork Man couldn't help noticing her scoot a little closer to her son and put an arm around him.

"You live out this way, too?" she said, making polite conversation despite her nervousness.

"Yes, Ma'am," he replied. "Got me a little place on Sumner's Creek. It's not much, but it keeps my bones warm."

"I know the creek," she said. "It cuts through our farm."

The boy added, "Our cows drink from it, too. Do you have cows, mister?"

The Patchwork Man nodded. "Just one, for milk. And a few chickens for eggs."

"Coyotes got our chickens," the boy said. "We ain't had eggs in weeks."

"That's a shame," the Patchwork Man said. "I'll bring you some next time I have extra."

"You don't have to do that, sir," she replied.

"It's no problem. I hate for 'em to go to waste."

"And you got just one cow?" the boy said. "What do you eat?"

"I make do," the Patchwork Man replied. "Mostly, I plant—corn, beans, whatever'll grow."

"Don't bother the man, Josiah," his mother chided.

"He's no bother," the Patchwork Man said. "Honestly, I find him refreshing."

"He's a little chatterbox," his mother said.

"Children ask questions," the Patchwork Man said. "That's how they learn."

"Do you have children, sir? Or a wife?" she asked.

"No, ma'am," he replied. "I almost took a bride once, I suppose."

"What happened?"

He looked off into the distance, seeing the plains spread out before him, lonely stands of low mesquite and chaparral dotting the otherwise barren landscape. "Just didn't work out, I guess," he replied, solemnly.

"I'm sorry to hear that," she said.

He nodded. "You're Mrs. Anderson, am I right?"

A quizzical look crossed her face for a moment. "Yes, Cassandra Anderson. Why?"

He hitched a thumb over his shoulder back toward town. "The sheriff mentioned you back in town. Seems he's got intentions toward you. I've a bad feeling about him. He said he might want to pay you a visit. Thought you might want to know."

She looked at the Patchwork Man, and he noticed her eyes wandering over his scars. But he was used to that. "Thank you for the warning. I dare say he won't find a warm welcome if he does."

They continued in silence until the trail forked in two different directions. Just beyond the split was Sumner's Creek. Or what there was of it. That late in the summer, it wasn't more than a thin trickle of water in a parched arroyo. She tugged the reins, bringing her horse and the cart to a stop. The Patchwork Man paused beside them.

"I don't want to overstep myself," the Patchwork Man said. "But, if there's trouble, come find me. Just down the creek from your farm, right?"

"You think there'll be trouble, mister?" the boy said.

"Of course there won't be," Cassandra said. "Sheriff Whateley's all talk."

"Still," the Patchwork Man continued. "If there is, you know where I am."

She stared at him for what became an uncomfortably long moment, her eyes on his. But he could tell she was looking him up and down, taking in his towering, unkempt build.

"Thank you," she said. "And I suppose this is where we part ways."

The Patchwork Man nodded. "Yes, ma'am," he said. And then to the boy, "Remember, boy. I'm just straight down that way." He pointed down the trail as it ran south along the creek.

"Okay, mister!" Josiah replied. "I'll remember."

The Patchwork Man led the mule away. Behind him, he heard the rhythmic creaking of buckboard wheels as the Andersons' wagon started up again, and a thin splash as it crossed the trickling creek and trundled up the other side.

Cassandra Anderson was slicing potatoes for dinner when she heard a knock at the door.

Josiah looked up from the book he was reading. "Who's that, mom?"

"I'm sure I don't know, Josiah." She walked through the small house to the front door, cleaning her hands on her red and white gingham apron. She opened the door to find Sheriff Whateley and one of his deputies standing on the porch. *Dalton*, she recalled. *Ellis Dalton.* "Evenin' Sheriff, Ellis. What can I do for you?"

Beyond them, the sun was setting, a riot of red and orange along the distant western horizon. Two horses were tied loosely to the porch rail.

Without waiting for an invitation, Whateley stepped into the small house. Ellis followed on his heels. She winced at the smell of rotgut whiskey drifting in after them.

"Just checking in, Cassandra," Whateley said, scanning the interior of the small farmhouse. "That big fella followed you out of town, and I thought we'd make sure you got home okay."

She straightened her apron and stood a little straighter. "Well, as you can see, we got home just fine." She turned to her son, who was eyeing the conversation intently. "Josiah, why don't you go wash up for dinner?"

"Listen to your mama, boy," Ellis said, a wolfish grin on his stubbled face.

"Okay, Mom." Josiah then went outside.

"Whatever you're making sure smells good." Whateley entered the kitchen. He lifted the lid off the pot on the stove, smelling the heady broth of the simmering stew within.

Cassandra noticed his eyes roaming the entire time he was wandering through her house. Like he was looking for something. Or someone.

"You sure that fella didn't give you no trouble?" he said, turning back to her.

"No, none. We walked together and spoke for a bit, and then he went his own way."

"He said he might bring us some eggs later," Josiah said, bounding back into the room, his face dripping with water from the pump around the side of the house.

"Well, ain't that right neighborly of him?" Ellis shot a look at Whateley.

Whateley nodded. Then he dipped a wooden spoon into the pot of stew, drew it out, and took a taste. "Tastes as good as it smells." He turned to Cassandra, smiling with his mouth, but his eyes remained impassive. "That's good you can rely on the kindness of your neighbors. He's a neighbor, I assume? I've heard he's made camp down the creek a ways."

The conversation had her on edge. Whateley was pressing her for information, and she didn't know why. "I suppose he is. He and his mule went south along the creek. I doubt very much we'll see him again."

Josiah looked disappointed. "What about the eggs, Mama?"

Whateley ruffled the boy's hair. "Don't you worry none about that, boy." He cast his eyes back to Cassandra. "If you need eggs, I'm sure your mama and I can work something out."

Cassandra took a step back toward the kitchen. "Sheriff, I think it'd be best if you and your deputy left now."

"Now why's that?" Whateley asked. "Just being neighborly myself. Ain't I being a good neighbor?" He turned to Ellis with a wide grin on his face.

Ellis nodded. His eyes glinted dully in the lamplight. "Sure, you are, Sheriff. Bein' right neighborly."

Josiah looked nervously from his mother to each of the men, then back to her. "Mama?" he said, weakly.

For a moment, the room was still, quiet. No sound but the somnolent hum of a fly circling the kitchen, and a gurgling from the stew bubbling on the stove.

"Shame about Mr. Anderson," Whateley said, walking toward her. She backed up to the countertop. "Must be hard on you and the boy. Out here. All alone." He stepped forward, and she smelled the whiskey on his breath.

"Sheriff," she said. "Whatever you're looking for, I can assure you that you will not find it here."

He was inches away from her. His hand shot out and landed on her arm, gripped it tight and pulled her forward. "You must get lonely out here."

Then slowly, just to the side of his vision, a long, shining knife appeared. It was slick and cloudy with potato starch, but wickedly sharp all the same. Lamplight glinted on the razor-sharp edge. Whately's eyes narrowed as he stared at Cassandra.

"Sheriff Whateley," she said coolly. "I'm going to ask you and Ellis to leave one last time."

The stew pot gurgled, the lid rattled and banged with releasing steam.

Whateley grabbed for the hand she was holding the knife in. He snatched her wrist just as she pulled the blade back to strike. It slashed along his shoulder, cutting through his linen shirt. Whateley yelped in surprise, then back-hand slapped Cassandra across the side of her face. She fell to the counter, stunned, a smear of red across her pale cheek from his hand. Crimson bloomed in the cotton, and then in thick runnels down his chest to stain trails down his front and running down his arm to drip from his hand in thick red splats on the rough slats of the pinewood flooring. "*Mama!*" Josiah charged toward the kitchen. He'd only taken a few steps when Ellis grabbed him by the collar, then encircled the boy's neck with his arm.

Whateley grabbed her hand, wresting the knife from her grip. "Well, now." He leaned over her, his face right next to hers and pressed the blade against her cheek. "That wasn't exactly a *neighborly* thing to do, now, was it?"

Pain lanced through her face as he sliced the knife downward. A shallow cut, but long and red, and blood flowed down her cheek.

Ellis dragged the boy through the sitting room toward the front door. Josiah was kicking and screaming the whole way. He scratched at Ellis's bony, calloused hands, drawing trickles of blood, but Ellis was too whiskey-numbed to notice.

"Ellis," Whateley yelled across the house. "Get that damn kid out of here."

"Come on, kid," Ellis growled. He dragged the boy toward the door. With his free hand, he scrabbled for the latch and threw it, pulling the door open. He yanked the boy out onto the porch and shoved him down the stairs.

The horses snorted as he landed nearby.

"Josiah!" Cassandra shrieked, and tried to run to the boy, but Whately still had her wrist caught in a crushing grip.

Ellis looked down at the kid lying in the dust and laughed. "Bet you wish your daddy was around, don't you, kid?" He turned to go back into the house, and past him, in the last setting rays of the sun, Cassandra saw the Patchwork Man approaching the house, holding a covered basket in one hand. "Well, look who's come to visit," Ellis said, descending the steps. His hand settled on the grip of the pistol at his side.

The boy looked up at him. "Mister," he said. "Please help…."

"Here, boy," the Patchwork Man said, handing him the basket. "Just like I promised."

The boy took the basket, then wiped tears from his eyes. "Mister…" He pointed at Ellis. "Him and the sherriff… They're tryin' to hurt my mama."

The Patchwork Man looked at the boy. "Where's your mother?"

The boy pointed to the house.

"I think you better just turn your ugly self around the way you came, fella," Ellis said.

The Patchwork Man shoved him aside, sending him sprawling into the dirt. He climbed the stairs and was at the door when a *crack!* split the night air, and he looked down and saw a small hole in his shirt. Thick, yellow slime welled up in the cavity, then oozed from the hole.

He heard a woman's scream inside and charged into the house. Cassandra was struggling with Whateley in the kitchen, where the sheriff held her by the throat with his left hand, blood from her cheek and his own wound mingling together. With his right, he held the sharp knife just an inch from her wide, terrified eyes.

He strode into the kitchen and grabbed the sheriff's right hand with his own massive hand. He squeezed, and a crunch sounded low and dull through the small room. The sheriff yelled out in pain, fingers going slack and dropping the knife.

With one hand, the Patchwork Man lifted the sheriff by the throat and held him two feet above the floor. He turned to Cassandra, who had retrieved the knife and was holding it in front of her defensively. "You all right, ma'am?" he asked.

She pointed the knife at Whateley. "He attacked me, and my boy," she said, her voice shaking with barely controlled rage.

"That so?" The Patchwork Man turned Whateley to face him. The sheriff's face was turning purple.

Then racing footsteps and a gunshot echoed off the walls of the small house. The bullet pounded through the Patchwork Man's chest, burst out and hit the wall just a foot away from Cassandra.

He turned to see Ellis standing just inside the doorway, arm outstretched, revolver in hand. Ellis thumbed the hammer, took another shot, and the gun barked as a bullet flew through the Patchwork Man's left calf. A moment later, yellow ichor spurted from the hole.

With a yell more of rage than pain, the Patchwork Man threw Whateley. The sheriff sailed across the room and landed atop Ellis, knocking the deputy sprawling. Whately took a huge gulp of air and staggered to his feet. Then he and Ellis scrambled to get through the front door and out of the house.

The Patchwork Man followed.

He stepped out onto the porch, and another shot rang out, taking him again in the shoulder. Yellow ooze sprang up around the wound and trickled in clots from his chest.

"He ain't natural!" Ellis shouted and fired again. Three times in a row, two shots hitting the Patchwork Man and sprays of ochre squirted out of the wounds. The last bullet missed, zinging right by his head. Splinters flew when it crashed into the side of the house.

Whateley was untying his horse and climbed up into the saddle as the Patchwork Man strode forward, step by inexorable step.

Ellis drew his other pistol, raised it to fire. But the Patchwork Man grabbed his wrist and squeezed. Ellis got one shot off into the air and then dropped his pistol as the Patchwork Man ground the bones of his wrist to dust with a meaty crunch, and a pain-filled scream erupted from Ellis' throat. The Patchwork Man twisted Ellis' hand until skin split, and when it came loose entirely Ellis released a roar of agony and terror. A spray of red splashed across the Patchwork Man, as Ellis fell to the ground, cradling his stump and shrieking as he watched his life's blood squirt into the dust.

The Patchwork Man looked over to where Whateley sat astride his horse, eyes wide.

"What the hell are you?" Whateley said.

The Patchwork Man heard Ellis yelling out behind him. He turned to see the deputy squeezing his stump under the pit of his arm, and his gun raised in his good hand, preparing to fire. He kicked the deputy in the chest, hard. A loud crack shot through the night, and Ellis went limp, collapsing face first on the sunbaked ground. Scarlet gushed from his mouth, staining the thirsty dust red.

The Patchwork Man turned back to Whateley, but the sheriff was already wheeling his horse away, galloping into the night. As the sound of pounding hooves receded into the distance, the Patchwork Man walked toward the boy.

Cassandra charged out onto the porch, racing down the steps to scoop Josiah up in her arms.

"You okay, boy?" the Patchwork Man rumbled.

Josiah wiped snot from his nose with his sleeve. "Yes sir."

Cassandra was looking at the Patchwork Man with wide, scared eyes. "Who… *What* are you?" she said.

Spots of clotting ichor had splattered his shirt, his denim trousers, and dripped into the dust. He looked down at her. "Just a man." He turned to the boy. "Take care of your mother."

Cassandra hugged the boy tight as they watched the Patchwork Man begin the walk back to town.

The Patchwork Man came to town in the dark of the night, and this time not a soul noticed him nor announced his arrival. It was near midnight as he strode through main street. Sounds of life, of the living, flowed through the street. A piano belted out a tune he didn't recognize in a saloon down the way, something lively and jaunty, and in direct opposition to the rage simmering in his thumping heart. Lights in the saloon window, and a few other nearby buildings, glared down at him like the luminous predatory eyes of owls.

The Patchwork Man stopped in front of the sheriff's office and town jail. Whateley's horse was tied up in front, and the lights were on inside. "WHATELEY!" Windows rattled at his thundering yell. "Whateley! Come out you coward!"

A crowd trickled out of the saloon, making their way toward where he stood, feet wide apart, glaring at the door to the jailhouse. He heard his name muttered on the tongues of the fearful. *Patchwork Man*, wafted repeatedly through the still, summer night. In the days that followed, some would swear they saw the glowing coal-fires of Hell burning behind his mismatched eyes.

Whateley stepped out into the warm, dry night, flanked by his other deputy, and eyeing the crowd. "That's him! That's the fellow who killed Ellis!" He slapped the deputy on his chest with the back of his hand, then pointed to the Patchwork Man. "Arrest him!"

The deputy looked from Whateley to the Patchwork Man with uncertainty. He took a step forward, and the Patchwork Man raised an open hand.

"I've got no quarrel with you, friend. I'm here for him," the Patchwork Man said, pointing at Whateley.

Whateley pulled a pistol from his belt. The moonlight glinted off the blue steel barrel. "Drop your weapons, fella!" Whateley said, his voice quavering.

"I'm unarmed." The Patchwork Man raised his two massive open hands to his sides. "You think you can take me before I get to you, go right ahead." He strode forward, clouds of dust erupting from the ground underfoot as his long legs ate up the distance between him and the sheriff.

Whateley's gun blazed as he fanned the hammer. White muzzle flashes and the staccato roar of bullets tearing into the Patchwork Man to burst in yellow sprays behind him. Then *click-click-click* as Whateley dry-fired, pulling the trigger on spent cartridges. He looked up with wide eyes as the Patchwork Man grabbed him by the throat with one hand.

The Patchwork Man lifted Whateley off the ground and looked into the sheriff's eyes, his purpling face. He squeezed, and with a crunch, Whateley's eyes rolled back into his skull. His limbs went limp, and the Patchwork Man dropped him to the ground with a thud.

The deputy pulled his gun from his holster and pointed it toward the Patchwork Man who just glared at him. The deputy's hand was visibly shaking, the barrel of his gun making small quivering circles. "Mister, I need you to just walk yourself into that jail cell right now, or I'm going to have to unload this here Smith & Wesson on you."

The Patchwork Man reached up to his chest, dug a finger into one of the bullet holes and squirmed it around. Yellow slime oozed out, and a moment later his finger pulled out a flattened lead slug. He flicked it toward the deputy, and it landed on his boot. A moment later, it slid from the leather top, leaving a trail of yellow alchemical slime as it plopped onto the wooden slats on which he stood. "I said I've no quarrel with you." The Patchwork Man turned away. He walked down the stairs and back through town the way he'd come. The crowd parted as he trod past them with tired, heavy steps, eyes fixed on the horizon.

"You sure you have to leave?" Cassandra asked the Patchwork Man in the early morning glow of the sunrise in the east.

"Killed the town sheriff, one of his deputies," he said, and shrugged. "They'll be coming for me soon, if they aren't on their way already."

"If I told them what happened…"

"It won't help. I'm used to people fearing me. It's for the best if I just go my own way." He turned to the boy. "You take care of my cow and chickens for me until I come back, okay?"

Josiah nodded. "I will! You bet!"

The Patchwork Man turned away, tugging on the rope lead tethered to his mule's bit.

"Hey, mister!" Josiah yelled. "What's your name, anyhow?"

The Patchwork Man stopped. He'd been asked that once or twice before and never knew how to answer. Mostly folks called him whatever they wanted to, and he never corrected them. But sometimes he figured he ought to have a name of some sort, even if he'd never been given one.

Most folks at least use the surname of their parents. And while he didn't have parents in the traditional sense, he had come from somewhere. Even if he'd been born of alchemy and logic, instead of biology and emotion, like everyone else. Even if the miserable bastard hadn't so much fathered him as created him. Stitched him together like a crazy quilt from the bodies of murderers and criminals. Jolted him to life with raging thunder and science. And then had tried to kill him in the end.

Nevertheless, don't most fathers and sons quarrel? So as the boy stood there with wide, questioning eyes, the Patchwork Man decided he may as well take his father's name and be done with it. Create his own legacy with that appellation.

He turned and pulled the brim of his hat down to shield his eyes from the rising sun. "Call me Frankenstein."

LAGNIAPPE

During a staff meeting one gloriously stormy night, the idea of having a section titled "Lagniappe" near the end of some of the works published by Brigids Gate Press was discussed. The staff unanimously voted in favor of the idea.

Lagniappe (pronounced LAN-yap) is an old New Orleans tradition where merchants give a little something extra along with every purchase. It's a way of expressing thanks and appreciation to customers.

The Lagniappe section might contain a short story, a small handful of poems, or a non-fiction piece. It might also feature a short novella. It may or may not be connected with the theme of the work.

The extra offering for this anthology is "Voodoo Higgies", a splendidly creepy little tale by Chad Lutzke. Having also created the cover for this book, it seems fitting for Chad's story to end up here. Prepare yourself, for those higgies out there in them woods are real.

VOODOO HIGGIES

by Chad Lutzke

I'd ran a good two miles before stopping for breath. And that's when they caught me—hands on knees, bent over with a line of drool thick as worms running from my mouth. My side felt like I'd been hit by the pissed end of a mule, and my stomach ceased like a fist full of fire at the thought of what might come next.

Not even an hour ago, I'd stolen a potato from Jonathan Garrison. *Mayor* Jonathan Garrison. I was on my way to my brother's house in Chariton—where he'd promised honest work and a comfortable bed—when the hunger pangs kicked in, while standing in the middle of Garrison's land.

I walked through half that field before succumbing, before temptation took me by the hand and led me down a dark road, indeed. But when you're in the middle of enough crops to feed a whole town, picking out a single vegetable don't feel much like thievin'. It feels like a given, like both God and mankind alike would look on with an encouraging nod. Besides, chances anyone but God had seen me pluck the tater were slim. But, as luck would have it, Mr. Garrison's men had the eyes of an eagle and the nose of a hound, because even after those two miles through creek and woods, they had me. And from what they was sayin', the mayor wanted me to pay for that spud with my life.

Now, there were only two of these men, and I suppose had they been without a firearm, I could have taken them. Not because I'm bigger or quicker, but because anyone—man or woman—whose staring death in the face gains super-human strength in that instant. The fear of a shallow grave has a way of turning your fists to hammers and your feet to lightning. But that damn gun. That fucker'll make you stop right quick and get into line, hoping to buy a little time and look for another way out, like waiting for the armed to get distracted. You get a moment like that, it's your only chance. If there was some distance between us, I reckon I'd take my chances and keep on runnin'. But there wasn't but ten feet between my skull and that chamber. The men took me back to Garrison's land. On the way there, I got an understanding that these boys weren't nothin' to make their mommas proud. One of them—the bigger one with the shaved head and two long hairs that poked from a mole on his chin like a daddy longleg hatching from an egg—tripped over his own feet and ate dirt. I choked out a laugh and took knuckles to the eye.

Mole didn't talk much, but the other one did. He went on and on about a whore over in Weslan he thought fancied him. "I can just tell she don't love the others like she does me. I get special treatment."

Apparently, nobody had ever had the heart to tell him that was a whore's job, to make a man feel special. He spoke about these "favors" he'd get, and they lined up with every other whore story I'd ever heard. But the dumb bastard was convinced there was something about him that tickled her just so.

"I'm thinkin' of making an honest woman out of her. She'll have me.

I know she will."

I didn't laugh, as I didn't care for the feel of Mole's knuckles. But I did roll my eyes 'til they hurt.

We got back to Garrison's, gun to my back, and they tied me to an apple tree in the middle of an orchard. By this time the sun was all but set, the sky looked like a bleedin' sea, jagged cuts between clouds lettin' the sun bleed red-orange. It was the most gorgeous sunset I'd ever seen. Most likely because I knew it'd probably be my last.

A fuckin' potato.

Mole ran to get a few horses for some reason while the skinny guy with love for a talented whore stayed behind with the barrel on me.

"You know all's I did was swipe a tater, right?" I said.

"You stole is what you did. Yer a thief."

"Okay, so I'm a thief. Make me work it off. Seems fair to me."

Skinny laughed. "Mr. Garrison wants to send a message. Word don't get out, we'll have thieves stealing all manner of crops."

"You kill me, there ain't nobody to send a message."

"Word'll get out."

"By who? You? It's hearsay, nothing more. You let me go, I'll spread the word. I'll tell them I had to work two day's wages for a single tater, and I was spotted by two hawkeyes who don't mess around. They'll listen to me more than any rumor. People invest in those about as much as pigs do a bath."

"You're a real swindler, ain't ya?" Skinny said.

"Can ya blame me?"

He spit on the ground, wiped his skinny face. "Suppose not."

"Ain't nobody gonna listen to you," I told him. "No lessons learned. They'll take your word with a grain salt, like them rumors 'bout them cursed woods." At this point, I was talkin' shit, making things up. Anything to stop that rope from burnin' my neck.

"What curse?" Skinny's face turned serious. I'd caught his attention.

I looked at the woods, hesitated with my reply, building suspense. "I'd better not go on. Don't wanna speak no truth on it."

"Horseshit. What curse?"

"Well," I said, my head down, like my words held too much weight for them to handle. "Them woods are filled with voodoo-higgies." Not sure anyone in this world or another had ever used such a word. I'd certainly never heard it before.

By this time, Mole was back with two horses, two lengths of rope, and a lantern, which cast a glowing circle around us. New shadows danced on the ground with the flicker of flame.

Skinny held his arm out, making sure Mole kept quiet while I fed the two bullshit. "Voodoo higgies?"

"Spirits, black as…shadow," I said.

"Huh?" Mole said.

"He's lyin'. Don't pay no mind." Skinny's eyes were pretty wide for an unbeliever.

Mole looked around, skittish, like he might just believe every word I said.

I glanced up at the sky. The moon was full. "They come out during full moons, float in through your ears and change your thoughts to do their bidding."

Mole looked up at the moon, brushed at the side of his head where the hair touched his ears. "Where do they come from?"

"They don't come from nowhere, no how, you dumb bastard." Skinny's voice was convincing, but his eyes weren't. They were dartin' about, looking toward the trees, which were now a black, spikey void—a giant centipede belly up.

"Nobody knows," I told Mole. "Some say they can smell death coming and gather to greet it." I thought a moment on whether I should push my luck, but seeing how these two were about as smart as a shithouse hen, I kept at the tale and made it even taller. "I suppose if it's true, we'll find out soon enough, seeing how you mean to kill me and all."

Mole dropped the rope he was carrying, and his eyebrows did a little dance that said he might be shitting his drawers.

Skinny looked at him. "That's enough now. He's just trying to scare us, make us set him free."

"Maybe," Mole said. "But I think I heard of them higgies."

"From who?"

"Momma…maybe. She used to tell us all sorts of—"

"Your momma don't know shit. Now get that rope around his wrist."

I didn't see no gallows, and I sure knew they weren't gonna bring me into town and kill a man in front of everyone for nothing but a potato. This was murder, plain and simple. I told them that, but they had no mind to hear it.

"If it makes you feel any better," Skinny said, "I wouldn't order yer death. But this comes from the boss man, and this here's our job, like it or not. You'd do it just the same if it meant coin in your pocket."

"You're wrong there," I said. "I got myself integrity. Something you two wouldn't know a thing about. You're selling your soul for that coin. And them voodoo-higgies, they're gonna get ya."

A coyote howled somewhere as if to verify the statement, and Skinny dropped the gun. I thought a moment too late to grab it. Mole backhanded me with his fat knuckles again, sent me in the dirt, while his clumsy partner picked up the steel.

With an impatient tone masking his embarrassment for fumbling the gun, Skinny yelled at his companion. "Gimme that!"

Mole handed the gun over, and I kept my seat on the ground.

"I thinks I see them shadows movin'." Mole had a puppy's eyes and a baby's brain. The amount of fear in his eyes was unsettling, spooking even me at my own story.

"Tie his hands, fool!"

With shaky hands, Mole held one end of the rope taut and approached me. I thought his knees might give on the way over.

"Tie one hand to that tree limb there." Skinny held the gun tighter than he needed to and aimed it at my gut.

I played hard to get with Mole until Skinny pulled the trigger, putting a hole in the tree by my head. By the look on his face, I don't think he meant to, because the horses took off running. Mole ran after them, falling not once but twice. Had it been Mole who stayed behind with the gun, I may have had a chance of talking sense into him. But Skinny was a stubborn bastard with a mind to kiss Garrison's ass regardless of it costing the little bit of dignity he might have.

The two of us sat in silence—Skinny with one eye on the forest—while Mole gathered the horses and brought them back.

After I was secured to the tree by my left hand, Mole used another rope to tie around my right wrist, then brought one of the horses over and started tying the other end of the rope to the saddle. And that's when panic finally hit me. I was ready to crawl on my knees to whoever'd listen, begging for forgiveness and vowing to work the rest of my days in those fields to pay for my sin.

"Whoa. Hold on, fellas," I said. "Whatcha got in mind here?"

"Boss man's orders. Gonna split you in two…or four."

If I had any drink in me, I'd have pissed my drawers. I gritted my teeth and spoke through them as quiet as I could, being careful not to startle the horses. If the one so much as went for a stroll, part of me was going with it. "This ain't right, boys. This is damned monstrous."

They didn't seem to be paying no mind. Mole was tying another rope to the saddle, and Skinny stared holes through me in between checking that black void of a tree line with all the paranoia in the world. Then the horse waved its tail and unloaded a geyser of piss that made us all jump when it hit the dirt.

"Ya'll need to calm the fuck down. There ain't no spirits in them woods." I could tell Skinny was talking to himself just as much as anyone else. He looked down, saw the horse piss had splashed on his boots. "Aww, hell." Then he shoved the horse, and the beast took a step forward. But I noticed instead of pulling my arm from its socket, the knot Mole had tied went loose. Not only could the man not walk a straight line without falling, he couldn't knot a rope worth a shit.

As he reached down to tie my foot to the other end of the rope attached to the saddle, I kicked at him, missing. He kicked back, connecting with my manhood. Every bit of breath left me, and my instinct was to grab my junk, but I couldn't with one arm tied to the tree and the other to the saddle, which somehow still held on despite the loose knot. Nausea hit me like a son of a gun, and I spouted a few choice words at the men.

"Yer making it harder on yourself, boy," Skinny said.

Mole reached down for my leg and snatched it, holding tight with a firm grip like you would a hammer. His hand shook more than ever, as he looped the rope around my leg, and I kicked again. But with my arms stretched and my ass on the ground, every attempt was in vain.

I was desperate, and so far the only thing that seemed to grab their attention was the nonsense I'd made up about evil spirits sneakin' in your ears, so I made a whispering sound only Mole could hear, like wind forcing its way through a crack in the wall.

He perked up, looked at the woods, looked at me. Eyes so wide they seemed to glow in the moonlight.

"Their comin' for ya, aren't they?" I said. "Can you hear them?"

"Shut your fuckin' mouth, thief." Skinny pointed the gun at my head.

"I don't know, Francis. Maybe this ain't right. I… I think I can see the higgies. Can hear 'em, too." Mole's chin quivered when he said it.

"I tell you what's not right. That fuckin' knot, you dumbshit. Look at you. Can't even—" Skinny stopped, looked around like he'd heard something. Wasn't but me blowing air through my teeth. "Gimmee that rope."

With one hand still on the gun, pointed in my general direction, he grabbed the rope and tied a slipknot, using his foot to hold the rope down. "First you tie it like this, then—"

That coyote howled again, and again the gun went off, pressed by the white-knuckled finger of a gullible fool scared of shadows he hadn't seen.

One horse kicked out, catching Mole in the head. His forehead flapped back like it was nothing but a funny pink hat he'd been wearin'. He was on the ground before the horse's hooves were, the lantern casting light on a hoof-sized dent in the pale-white skull where his worried eyebrows once sat, eyes still wide as ever.

As the other horse took off, the loose knot slipped off completely, leaving me intact. Then I heard what sounded like a quick belch and saw Skinny's feet go in the air, and the rest of him hit dirt. He'd managed to stick his foot through the slipknot. I watched his head bounce off the ground and his leg bend in ways God never intended, until he was out of the lantern's light and lost to the darkness.

I got myself free from those ropes just as fast as I could and went runnin' straight for that dark patch of trees. Each quick step seemed to create a whisper of its own against the field, trying to give life to my doom-filled words that spoke of evil entities appearing after another's demise. I could still see the look of horror on Mole's face, could still hear his voice declaring he'd heard tale before of something in them woods, where my own bullshit creatures lingered in shadows, hungry for the call of death and open ears

As I ran through Garrison's field, holding my breath and willing my ears closed, I snatched a few taters for the journey ahead. I wasn't sure coyotes ate them, but in case they did, and we happen to cross paths, offering a tater was the least I could do.

AFTERWORD

by Kenneth W. Cain

Whoa. Hold up there, pardner. You didn't think you were getting out of this town without a few words from me, did you? Well, ignore this long gun of mine and take a seat, let me chew your ear a bit more. I promise it won't hurt.

So… It's been a minute. A trying one at that. I prefer to always keep my nose down, working hard. That's how I keep the chronic pain "demons" at bay, and it's also how I deal with all the rest, too. Yes, things get to me. Yes, I lose sleep (I lost quite a bit of it a couple of months back). But I'm a firm believer that positive energy will make me happier and change the world for better, so I try to avoid being negative, if I can. And we humans…we seem to wallow in it, don't we? Not to fault anyone. It's trying times. So I'm sorry if you were expecting more on that subject, but that's what I've got. Well, not *all*, actually…

When the wheels came off the old Stagecoach, I was a bit of a mess. Mentally and physically, actually, since I had two bulging discs at the time the whole SSP thing went down. At that moment, things felt pretty grim, frankly, and not because of anything other than what I was going through personally. So I was working hard not to let myself give up, and I turned my focus to the only thing I *could* do at the moment. And those of you who were paying attention know what business I tended to in order to keep my mind off it all. That's just how I work.

Anyway, we talk about things like imposter syndrome, confidence, ability… We're always our worst enemies when it comes to creativity, it seems. So, not only have I been pretty hard on myself right from the beginning of my career, but, behind the scenes, I've been flogging myself like mad these last two months. In fact, I've been struggling to write much of anything new this entire time. That said, I am, if nothing else, someone who refuses to cave to those negative "voices" in my head. I plodded along a barren trail, a wounded and aging man, when another stagecoach finally stopped. I was guarded, had my six-shooters drawn to defend myself. But that was that ole imposter syndrome rearing its ugly head yet once again. So I holstered my guns and slowed my roll, decided to put on a brave face and see what was what.

That's when Heather and Steve invited me to edit this anthology for Brigids Gate Press. Truth told, many other stagecoaches stopped by my little desolate patch of earth in those days. It got a bit crowded real fast. Sounds exciting, doesn't it? But for someone like me, it's daunting. I felt nervous, anxious, and honestly, it took a lot of soul searching to decide what was right for me at a time when I didn't much feel like doing anything at all but disappear. But they were persistent and kind, so I quickly shrugged off my duster and took up another weapon—this here keyboard.

Tap-tappa-tap-tap. [Blows smoke off the P key]

So you know, I struggle with keeping faith in myself. I woke up each day, had to build momentum right from the start and tell myself that it was okay to accept the kindness people were showing me. To appreciate the confidence they seemed to have in my ability, regardless of where my head was at. I gathered up my belongings, threw my Stetson up on my scraggly old head, and climbed aboard.

And I couldn't be happier.

See, that first stagecoach… That led to some healing. And each subsequent stagecoach that came by…well, that helped me a little more. So I'm appreciative of every last one of you who contacted me, offered some guidance or kind words; you people are great. It took a lot of that to get to where I'm at now, and not all of it came recently. In fact, it's been 52 long years of growth, of me working hard to become a better man, of making mistakes and learning from them, to get to this point. And I just keep trying to look forward, to keep my eyes on the future, on bettering myself and my craft, and being more receptive to every single stagecoach that stops by to say hello along this long, dusty trail.

This particular task, taking what stories we had received during a very short window, all with at least two other anthologies of very similar themes running submissions at the same time, was a difficult one. Not because of the vast number of submissions or the competition created by similar themed anthologies (I'm one of those folks who believes there's room for all of us at the table), but because of the quality of stories we received. This was no easy undertaking. My shortlist changed daily. Same with my acceptance list. It was grueling work whittling down the list to the stories I shortlisted, and then an even harder grind to get it down to the ones I did pick. To their credit, if not for Heather and Steve allowing me to take a few more, it might not have ended up as the book it is now. I owe them both as well as our slush readers my full gratitude. Every step of the way, Heather and Steve have been incredibly supportive and helpful, working with me, always with a singular goal in mind—to create something beautiful. And while not everyone may agree with this assessment, that is what this book is to me—something to be cherished.

These stories…they're not just words. They're little windows into another world. When we read them, we are transported into a different place, a different time, and subjected to otherworldly forces. If I can help make that trip as realistic as possible… Well, dear readers, if I succeed in that, we all get a wonderful mind vacation, right? But know that I absolutely could not have gotten there without Brigids Gate's hard work as well as that of every single author included in this tome. And I would be remiss not to add my wife, Heather, whose support and proofreading have continued to be the backbone of my writing/editing career for many years.

So, now that I've said my piece and thanked everyone, I'll take this moment to jump off your stagecoach. You've been so kind allowing me to ride with you a little ways down the trail, but it's time to get along to the next world. The hard work. Something to keep my mind off the worries of life and creating positive, beautiful things.

I hope to see you there.

Until next time… Pleasant nightmares, dear readers.

Kenneth W. Cain
June 28, 2022

ABOUT THE AUTHORS

Michael Bailey is a recipient of the Bram Stoker Award (and eight-time nominee), Benjamin Franklin Award, and a three-time Shirley Jackson Award nominee. He has authored numerous novels, novellas, novelettes, and fiction & poetry collections. Recent work includes *Agatha's Barn*, a tie-in novella to Josh Malerman's *Carpenter's Farm*, a collaborative novella with Erinn L. Kemper called *The Call of the Void*, and *Sifting the Ashes*, a collaborative and lengthy poetry collection with Marge Simon. He runs the small press Written Backwards and has edited and published twelve anthologies, such as *The Library of the Dead*, the *Chiral Mad* series, and *Miscreations: Gods, Monstrosities & Other Horrors*. He lives in Costa Rica where he is rebuilding his life after surviving one of the most catastrophic wildfires in California history.

Sean Eads has published three novels and a short story collection, and has been a finalist for the Shirley Jackson Award, Lambda Literary Award, and Colorado Book Award. His stories have appeared in numerous anthologies.

Lana Elizabeth Gabris lives in the heart of British Columbia. Her illustrations of flora have been published in several outdoor magazines across North America and her fiction has appeared in The Matador Review, Peacock Journal, The Copperfield Review, and Cowboy Jamboree. She received an honorable mention from the Writers of the Future (Q4 2016) and has been nominated for The Best of Net Anthology & The Shirley Jackson Awards.

Nick Kolakowski is the author of *Absolute Unit* (Crystal Lake Publishing), *Boise Longpig Hunting Club* (Down & Out Books), and other crime and horror novels. His short fiction has appeared in Dark Moon Digest, Mystery Tribune, Shotgun Honey, and various anthologies. He's also the co-editor of *Lockdown* (Polis Books), an anthology of pandemic-themed fiction that was nominated for an Anthony Award in 2021. He lives and writes in New York City.

Jonathan Kemmerer-Scovner lives outside Philadelphia with his family. His work has been published in Killing the Buddha, Horror Tree, and Philadelphia Stories, on whose Fiction Board he currently serves. He has ostensibly eschewed all other forms of writing in order to complete his novel before the eventual heat death of the universe, yet nonetheless, here we are. He believes that every time a bookstore shutters its doors for the final time, a demon gets its wings. Unless it's the cool kind of demon, in which case they no doubt share in his dismay. Follow him @Jonathan_KS.

Brennan LaFaro is a horror writer living in southeastern Massachusetts with his wife, two sons, and his hounds. An avid lifelong reader, Brennan also co-hosts the Dead Headspace podcast. Brennan is the author of *Slattery Falls*, the first entry in a trilogy, as well as *Last Stay*, and the horror western, *Noose*. You can read his short fiction in various anthologies and find him on Twitter at @brennanlafaro or at www.brennanlafaro.com.

Chad has written for Famous Monsters of Filmland, Rue Morgue, Cemetery Dance, and Scream magazine. His short fiction can be found in several dozen magazines and anthologies, and some of his books include: *Of Foster Homes & Flies, Stirring the Sheets, Cannibal Creator, Skullface Boy, The Same Deep Water as You,* and *The Neon Owl* series. Lutzke's work has been praised by authors Jack Ketchum, Richard Chizmar, Joe R. Lansdale, Stephen Graham Jones, Tim Waggoner, and his own mother. He can be found lurking the internet at www.chadlutzke.com

Joel McKay is an award-winning writer and economic development professional. He calls Prince George, B.C. home, where he lives with his wife and two daughters. He has previously published *Wolf at the Door*, an absurdist take on a werewolf crashing a family Thanksgiving dinner and

"Number Hunnerd," a fish tale, published in Tyche Books' anthology *Water: Selkies, Sirens and Sea Monsters.*

P.L. McMillan is a writer whose works have been known to cause rifts in time and space itself… Well, not quite. But writing often makes her feel that powerful. With a passion for cosmic horror and sci-fi horror, P.L. McMillan sees every shadow as an entryway to a deeper look into the black heart of the world, meant to be discovered and explored. Infatuated with the works of Shirley Jackson, H.P. Lovecraft, and Ridley Scott, her dream is to create stories of adventure, of chills, of heartbreak, and thrills. P.L. McMillan lives in Colorado, with her large selection of teas, her husband, and her two chinchillas (Sherlock and Spuds)—all under the supervision of their black cat overlords, Poe and Zerg. Find her on her website: https://www.plmcmillan.com/ or on Twitter: @authorplm

Exposed to the weird worlds of horror, sci-fi and comics as a boy, Damascus Mincemeyer was ruined for life. Now a writer and artist of various strangeness, he's had stories appear in numerous anthologies, including *Fire: Demons, Dragons and Djinn, Earth: Giants, Golems and Gargoyles, Air: Spirits, Slyphs and Swan Maidens, Hear Me Roar, Hell's Empire, Appalachian Horror, Bikers Vs The Undead, Psycho Holiday, Monsters Vs Nazis, Mr. Deadman Made Me Do It, Satan Is Your Friend, Monster Party, Wolfwinter, Crash Code, On Time, Trigger Warning: Hallucinations, The Devil You Know, No Anesthetic, Seven Deadly Sins, A Tree Lighting In Deathlehem,* the *Gallow's Hill* website, and the magazines Aphotic Realm and StoryHack. His short fiction has been collected in *Where The Last Light Dies,* released by Deadman's Tome Publishing in 2020, and his debut novel, By Invitation Only is being queried. He lives near St. Louis, Missouri, U.S.A., and can usually be found lurking about on Twitter @DamascusUndead.

Villimey Mist has always been fascinated by vampires and horror, ever since she watched Bram Stoker's *Dracula* when she was a little, curious girl and when she was traumatized by the chestburster scene in *Aliens.* She loves to read and create stories that pop into her head unannounced. She's had her short stories appear in various anthologies, including *Of Cauldrons and Cottages, Krampus Tales: A Killer Anthology, Campfire Macabre, The One Who Got Away: Women in Horror Vol. 3, Far From Home, Hex-periments, Were-Tales.* She has written *Nocturnal*, a vampire horror series with 3 books already published since 2016. Her short story collection, *As the Night Devours Us*, was published by St Rooster Books in 2022. She lives in Iceland with her husband and two cats, Skuggi and RoboCop, and is often busy drawing, watching the latest shows on Netflix or staying way too long on Twitter @VillimeyS. www.villimeymistauthor.com.

Ben Monroe has spent most of his life in Northern California, where he lives in the East Bay Area with his wife and two children. He is the author of *In the Belly of the Beast and Other Tales of Cthulhu Wars, the Seething* (coming in 2023), the graphic novel *Planet Apocalypse*, and short stories in several anthologies. You can find him on Twitter @_BenMonroe_. Sign up for Ben's author newsletter at https://tinyurl.com/benznews, or look for his publications at tinyurl.com/benz-books.

Taylor Rae is a professional cave troll, hidden away in the mountains of Coeur d'Alene, Idaho. She likes avoiding her neighbors, playing ukulele, and longboarding. Most of her stories involve spaceships and/or magic. She is the winner of the 2021 NYC Midnight Short Story Contest, and her work appears with Flash Fiction Online, PsuedoPod, and *Fit for the Gods* from Vintage Books. More at www.mostlytaylor.com.

Craig E Sawyer is an American writer known for horror, western, sci-fi, and crime, and is a direct descendant of the McCoy family that famously feuded against the Hatfield's over a stolen pig. He has been published by Quill & Crow Publications, Timber Ghost Press, Shotgun Honey, Weirdbook (Wildside Press), Schlock Publications, Crystal Lake Press, Nightmare Press, Monkeys Fighting Robots, Levy-Gardner-Laven Productions, and Skull Dust Press. He is the creator of the horror/adventure comic *The Forbidden Museum*, and the RPG sci-fi board game Escape from Dulce. Craig traveled much of the United States, eventually settling on the West Coast, and he has worked as a bartender, roofer, carpet weaver, bouncer, and actor. Insta & Twitter: @csawyerwriter.

Ej Sidle likes writing stories about magic and monsters, not always at the same time. She currently resides in Scotland, where she has a day job that takes up too many hours, and a canine roommate who doesn't contribute to bills. Ej also enjoys travelling, playing video games, and drinking far too much coffee. Come say hi on twitter @sidle_by.

Amanda J Spedding is a professional editor and award-winning author and graphic novelist. She has twice won the Australian Shadows Award (short fiction; written work in a graphic novel) and was an Aurealis Award finalist (fantasy short story) in 2019. With a love of mythos and horror, she has a penchant for writing beauty into the macabre. She is the owner of Phoenix Editing, editor-in-chief at Cohesion Press, and a pitch-consultant for Blur Studios, where she worked on stories included in the animated series *Love, Death & Robots*. Amanda lives in Australia with her sarcastically-gifted husband and two very cool kids. And cats. She has cats. And two rabbits. We don't talk about the rabbits. Where's her damn coffee? Twitter: @AJSpedding Website: amandajspedding.com.

Joshua Viola is a 2021 Splatterpunk Award nominee, Colorado Book Award winner, and editor of the StokerCon™ 2021 Souvenir Anthology. He is the co-author of the Denver Moon series with Warren Hammond. Their graphic novel, *Denver Moon: Metamorphosis*, was included on the 2018 Bram Stoker Award ™ Preliminary Ballot. Viola edited the *Denver Post #1* bestselling horror anthology *Nightmares Unhinged*, and co-edited *Cyber World*—named one of the best science fiction anthologies of 2016 by Barnes & Noble. His first novel, *The Bane of Yoto*, won the USA Best Book Awards, National Indie Excellence Awards, International Book Awards, and Independent Publishers Book Awards. His short fiction has appeared in numerous anthologies, including *DOA III: Extreme Horror Anthology*, *Doorbells at Dusk*, and *Classic Monsters Unleashed*. He is currently developing novelizations for a new video game franchise from Random Games, led by the creators of the Grand Theft Auto series, and Brent Friedman (*Star Wars: The Clone Wars, Star Wars Rebels, Star Trek: Enterprise, Halo 4,* and *The Twilight Zone*). When he isn't writing and editing, Viola dabbles in art. In 2020, he collaborated with his husband, Aaron Lovett, on AfterShock Comics'*Miskatonic* #1 Cover Alpha Comics variant. As a video game artist, he worked on *Pirates of the Caribbean: Call of the Kraken, Smurfs' Grabber* and *TARGET: Terror.* Viola is the owner and chief editor of Hex Publishers in Denver, Colorado.

Antonia Rachel Ward is an author of horror and speculative fiction, based in Cambridgeshire, UK. Her short stories and poetry have been published by Blackspot Books, Kandisha Press, and Orchid's Lantern, among others. Her gothic horror novella, *Marionette,* will be released by Brigids Gate Press in summer 2022. She is also the founder and editor-in-chief of Ghost Orchid Press.

David Niall Wilson has been writing since the 1980s. He's been nominated five times for the Bram Stoker Award, winning once for short fiction and once for poetry. He's been nominated for the International Horror Guild award in long fiction. David is the author of thirty-five novels, including *This is My Blood, Deep Blue, Gideon's Curse,* and *Hallowed Ground,* a weird western written with Steven Savile. He has over 160 published short stories and has been collected several times, including the award-nominated *Defining Moments.* David is a former president of the HWA and owner over Crossroad Press. He lives in way-out-yonder NC with his wife, editor author Patricia Lee Macomber (Wilson) and a houseful of cats.

Wen Wen Yang is a first generation Chinese American, raised in the Bronx, New York. She graduated from Barnard College, Columbia University with a degree in English, Creative Writing. Her work can be found in Factor Four Magazine, The Arcanist, Fantasy Magazine, Zooscape, and the *Fit for the Gods* anthology. She is working on a dark fantasy novel. Wen Wen lives in Texas with her husband and their dog. She tweets

@muteddragon, and updates wenwenwrites.com. She listens to audiobooks at three times speed and talks just as fast.

ABOUT THE EDITOR

Kenneth W. Cain is an author of horror and dark fiction, and a Splatterpunk Award nominated freelance editor and graphic designer. To date, he has had over one hundred short stories and thirteen novels/novellas, as well as a handful each of nonfiction pieces, books for children, and poems released by many publishers, such as Crystal Lake Publishing and JournalStone. He has also edited seven anthologies. Cain lives in Chester County PA with his family, and suffers from chronic pain. As such, he likes to keep busy and spends more time working than socializing. His full publishing history is available on his website at kennethwcain.com.

As an Active member of the Horror Writers Association, he is chair for the membership committee, heads the Pennsylvania chapter, and was given the 2017 Silver Hammer Award for his service. Currently, Cain helps several publishers with their editing, formatting, book cover, and graphic design needs. Cain resides in Chester County, Pennsylvania with his wife and two children.

At an early age Cain heard a reading of the Baba Yaga folklore and fell in love with dark fiction and horror. That love was nurtured during his formative years in the suburbs of Chicago, listening to his grandfather spin far-fetched tales beside the glow of a barrel fire. Shows like *The Twilight Zone*, *The Outer Limits*, *Alfred Hitchcock Presents*, and *One Step Beyond* furthered his wonder of the unknown, the unexplainable, and he's been writing ever since. In his free time, when he isn't reading or writing, he enjoys the outdoors, fine art, and sports.

ABOUT THE ILLUSTRATOR

Nearly a decade ago, while struggling to find an attractive, yet affordable, cover for his first book, Chad learned to create his own and now offers the same service to those who want striking, yet inexpensive, art to represent their stories. For rates and more examples, including premades, visit www.chadlutzke.com

CONTENT WARNINGS

<u>Crimson Noon</u>
Gore/violence, harm to a child

<u>The Good Doctor</u>
Extreme gore

<u>Sundown Showdown</u>
Implied child death

<u>The Werechrist</u>
Death/dying

<u>Ballad of the Overeager Gun</u>
Death/dying, graphic violence

<u>The Owl Witch of the Comancheria</u>
Torture, death, gore and mutilation, slurs, physical abuse

<u>Ada</u>
Gun violence, derogatory language, inferred assault, suicide

<u>Hands</u>
Violence, blood and gore

<u>As Long as You Feed</u>
Abuse

<u>Costumed Mouth</u>
Injury to animals (offpage)

Trade Secrets

Blood, gore, violence, murder, gun violence, death by flaying (off-page)

I Have Seen the Elephant

None

Boneweaver

Graphic violence. Dismemberment, murder, interfering with a corpse (not necrophilia)

The Wound is Covered

Animal cruelty, racism

Suffer No Harm

Animal death, sexual assault, death and violence

Ghost Festival in the Desert

Lynching/hanging, mutilation of corpses, blood, death of a loved one, racism against Chinese persons

The Patchwork Man

Threat of sexual assault

Voodoo Higgies

None

Paperback ISBN: 978-1-957537=21-4

Welcome to the Weald.
The Five Turns of the Wheel has begun.
With each Turn, blood will be spilled,
and sacrifices will be made.
Pacts will be made...and broken.
Will you join the Dance?

In the Weald, the time has come for the Five Turns of the Wheel. Tommy, Betty and Fiddler, the sons of Hweol, Lord of Umbra, have arrived to oversee the sacred rituals...rituals brimming with sacrifice and dripping with blood.

Megan Wheelborn, daughter of Tom my, hatches a desperate plan to free the people of the Weald from the bloody and cruel grip of Umbra, and put an end to its murderous rituals. But success will require sacrifice and blood as well. Will Megan be able to pay the price?

Paperback ISBN: 978-1-957537-10-8

During the Spring Equinox underneath London, four people enter the caves, but only one will survive. Each trespasser must battle their own demons before facing the White Lady who rises each year to feed on human flesh.

Paperback ISBN: 978-1-957537-31-3

Stewartville. A town living in the shadow of the prisons that drive its economy. Haunted by the ghosts of its past. Cursed by the dark secrets hidden beneath. A town so entwined with the prisons waiting outside the city limits that it's impossible to imagine one without the other, or to ever imagine escaping either.

When a teenage boy digs into the history of the town, he discovers a tunnel system beneath Stewartville, passageways filled with dark secrets. Secrets leading not to freedom, but to unrelenting terror.

Stewartville. Where the convicts aren't the only prisoners.